Praise for Greg Dinallo's previous novels

Red Ink

"Lively, well written, and authoritative . . . *Red Ink* is lovely, and it has a surprise ending that works."
—*The New York Times*

"A powerful and riveting tale, set with stunning accuracy in today's Russia."
—Ronald Kessler
Author of *Inside the CIA*

"Dinallo is well tuned to the ironies of Russia's transition. . . . He puts together the pieces of a complicated plot masterfully."
—*Los Angeles Daily News*

"*Red Ink* is not a book that can be taken lightly; too much of the background and plotting has a resounding, disconcerting ring of truth. For thriller fans who like to be challenged, it is the perfect choice."
—*Orlando Sentinel*

"*Red Ink* is in the black all the way. There is never a dull moment, and the snapshots of life in Russia and Cuba reveal a great deal of the breakdown of communism at the end of the century."
—*Houston Post*

Please turn the page for more reviews. . . .

Final Answers

"Absorbing . . . What keeps *Final Answers* from being just another action novel is its sharp insight into character, its fluid writing, and its careful plotting. . . . Mr. Dinallo makes us believe."
—*The New York Times*

"Adventure fans have a new ace in Greg Dinallo. Now he delivers a knockout punch, a story of the Vietnam aftermath as brutal and vicious as a jungle ambush. Don't miss it."
—STEPHEN COONTS

"A terrific offbeat thriller. The last scene is about as tough as it gets. And Greg Dinallo builds to it with fine confidence and imagination."
—*New York Daily News*

"*Final Answers* is one of too few novels that can be labeled both hard to put down and beautifully written."
—*San Antonio Express-News*

"Dinallo escalates the suspense with each of Morgan's discoveries, and writes about Vietnam's casualties with competence and compassion."
—*Chicago Tribune*

"[A] splendid, wholly credible thriller . . . *Final Answers* is an important story, compellingly told."
—W.E.B. GRIFFIN

"A chilling, haunting thriller."
—ASSOCIATED PRESS

By Greg Dinallo:

ROCKETS' RED GLARE
PURPOSE OF INVASION
FINAL ANSWERS
RED INK
TOUCHED BY FIRE*

*Published by Fawcett Books

Books published by The Ballantine Publishing Group are available at quantity discounts on bulk purchases for premium, educational, fund-raising, and special sales use. For details, please call 1-800-733-3000.

TOUCHED BY FIRE

Greg Dinallo

FAWCETT CREST • NEW YORK

Sale of this book without a front cover may be unauthorized. If this book is coverless, it may have been reported to the publisher as "unsold or destroyed" and neither the author nor the publisher may have received payment for it.

A Fawcett Crest Book
Published by The Ballantine Publishing Group
Copyright © 1998 by Windfall Productions, Inc.

All rights reserved under International and Pan-American Copyright Conventions. Published in the United States by The Ballantine Publishing Group, a division of Random House, Inc., New York, and simultaneously in Canada by Random House of Canada Limited, Toronto.

www.randomhouse.com/BB/

Library of Congress Catalog Card Number: 98-96313

ISBN 0-449-00295-0

Manufactured in the United States of America

First Edition: December 1998

10 9 8 7 6 5 4 3 2 1

For Eric and Priscilla

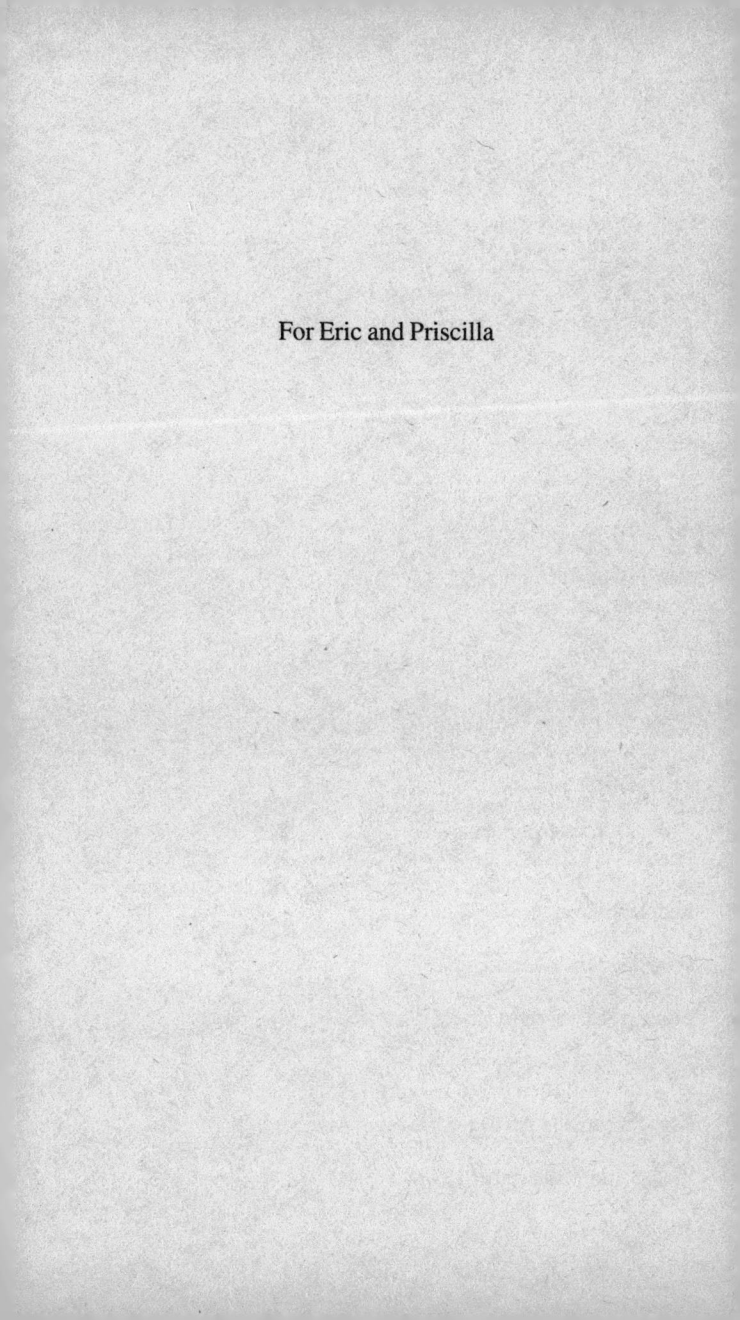

ACKNOWLEDGMENTS

For technical assistance and information I am indebted to: John B. Livingstone, M.D., Professor of Child and Adult Psychiatry, Harvard Medical School; Wayne W. Grody, M.D., Ph.D., Associate Professor of Medical Genetics and Molecular Pathology, UCLA Medical Center; Kathryn E. Kronquist, Technical Director, Molecular Genetics, Specialty Laboratories Inc., Santa Monica, CA; and Judith Wilner, M.D., Department of Human Genetics, Mount Sinai Medical Center, New York. I'd also like to thank Linda Castellano and Melissa Robbins Rutovsky for their individual support; and Lieutenant Robert Duryea of the New York City Fire Department for his technical guidance and enduring friendship.

I am also especially indebted to my agent, Joel Gotler, for his enthusiasm and unending support through five novels; and to my editor at Ballantine, Doug Grad, for bringing this one back to life.

PROLOGUE

The wind was up, mean-spirited and hot as it always was this time of year; and the darkness whistled with unnerving tension, luring the residents of Los Angeles ever closer to its edge. Autumn was when fragile psyches snapped, when the pressure to seek revenge peaked, when safety valves failed, unleashing long-suppressed impulses. The season when L.A.'s freeways buzzed till dawn with suicidal women and homicidal men, and the all-night supermarkets teemed with wild-eyed insomniacs.

"Ninety-nine," the electronic voice said. The checkout clerk swept the next item across the scanner: "Two fifty-nine." And the next, "One sixty-nine." He made quick work of the remaining items, then taxed and totaled them. "Twenty-one eighty-nine," the voice said, printing out the receipt:

```
ROYAL-GLO FIRELOG . . . . . . . . . . . . . . .99
ENOZ MOTH CRYSTALS . . . . . . . . . . 2.59
KNGSFRD CHARCL LTR . . . . . . . . . . 1.69
MRCLE GRO FERTLZER . . . . . . . . . . 2.49
ZIPLOC FRZR BAGS . . . . . . . . . . . . . . 2.39
SCTCH PACKING TAPE. . . . . . . . . . . . 2.29
EVRDY LANTERN BTRY . . . . . . . . . . 4.99
```

GE 60WT 2PK	2.79
SUB TOTAL	20.22
8.25% SALES TAX	1.67
TOTAL	21.89

"Paper or plastic?" the clerk asked without giving the items a second thought. He had no reason to think they were ingredients for a hot new recipe—though they were. Found on the Internet and in anarchist cookbooks on library shelves, it instructed the chef to: saw the fireplace log into slices with a serrated knife. Heat in oven or microwave until they can be crumbled to the texture of kibble. Add the moth crystals, fertilizer, and mix well. Stir in charcoal lighter until a thick sludge forms. Spoon into a quart-size Ziploc bag and seal tightly.

The sawdust in the fireplace log, ammonium nitrate in the fertilizer, and napthalene in the moth crystals made this the most efficient improvised incendiary. It could burn the supermarket that sold them to the ground—but that wasn't its target. No, this fire bomb was being sent on a far more personal mission.

Driven by festering hatred, the gloved hands, which so carefully prepared it, taped the Ziploc bag and the battery to the bottom of a corrugated box, running wires to a detonator and an ignition device made from a lightbulb filament and book of matches. After loosely filling the remaining space with excelsior, they sprinkled it with charcoal lighter and closed the box; then, with obsessive precision, taped the flaps, edges, seams, and corners, burnishing the micro-thin plastic to ensure that the telltale fumes couldn't escape, that their source wouldn't be prematurely revealed, that the explosive secret within would be forever contained. Lastly, they uncapped a black marking pen and addressed the package. The bold, angry printing spelled out the name: LILAH E. GRAHAM

CHAPTER ONE

The sultry gusts swept through the darkness and up the hill into Lilah's bedroom like the quickening sighs of an anxious lover. She shrugged a shoulder, letting her dress fall to the floor, then stepped out of it and began pacing back and forth in her bra and panties, ever present cigarette in one hand, palm-size cellular phone in the other.

The number she'd just dialed rang twice.

"This is Dr. Paul Schaefer," a voice said in soft, reassuring tones. "I'm sorry I'm not available to take your call. Please leave a message after the beep and I'll return it as soon as possible."

"Paul? Paul, you there? It's Liiilahh," she said, drawing out her name in a sexy whisper. She went to the window and squinted into the mercury vapor haze that rose from Westwood's narrow streets. Traffic-clogged and teeming with students, they formed a series of twisting knots that abutted the UCLA campus. An architectural collage spanning seven decades, its eclectic buildings perched on broad plateaus that stepped upward between Wilshire and Sunset—L.A.'s two legendary boulevards. Schaefer's office was in the Neuropsychiatric Institute adjacent to the medical school and research labs. He usually remained after hours dictating notes and reviewing files.

Lilah counted ten floors up and six windows over. Sheets of light came from the horizontal louvers that served as a sunscreen. "Hey, I know you're there," Lilah said, picturing him running a fingertip across his neatly trimmed mustache. "Come on, pick up and talk to me, Paul," she purred, exhaling a stream of smoke into the phone. "Come on, pick up and tell Lilah what you want."

Paul Schaefer sat behind his desk, fighting the temptation. His troubled eyes stared at the answering machine through wire-rim glasses that reflected the glare from a galaxy of designer halogens. Several of the high intensity lamps illuminated an impressive display of Schaefer's diplomas and awards. One was focused on the bust of Freud that peered sternly over his shoulder, another on the blanketed lounger that was positioned to minimize his presence during a session, the remainder on the abstract paintings that his patients often interpreted without prompting from their therapist—as had Lilah, though she wasn't his patient, and it wasn't the depths of her mind that Schaefer had been probing on that lounger.

"It's time to reach out and touch someone, Paul," Lilah went on in her suggestive whisper, running a hand over her breasts sensuously. "Come on, you know you want to. It's the next best thing to being there. . . ."

Schaefer let out a long breath, knowing all too well she was right. He was the one who had initiated the phone sex; who, whenever he couldn't be with her, would lapse into baby talk and parrot the tag lines from phone company commercials. The thought of it, and of what had always followed, made him squirm with embarrassment. He made a notation in a file, then raised his eyes and stole a glance at the photograph of his wife and three children.

"You know what I'm doing now?" Lilah purred. "Sure

you do. Let your fingers do the walking. . . ." She listened to the hiss of the answering machine tape, hoping beyond hope that he'd respond; then, in a more desperate tone, she said, "I miss you, Paul. I really need to be with you tonight. Please, can't we talk about this?"

"No, Lilah, I'm afraid we can't," Schaefer said sharply, as if she were there.

It wasn't her need to talk that troubled him, just her neurotic insistence that it be with him instead of a therapist, as he'd advised. This wasn't the first time she'd called since that afternoon in the Getty's sculpture garden when he told her it was over. And it wasn't the first time he'd been moved by the seductive anguish in her voice, by his longing for the romantic rush of those stolen moments—moments that were suddenly being replayed in the ornately framed mirror opposite the lounger. An impromptu gift from Lilah, the mirror had served them long and well, and now served as a tempting reminder of the soaring passion Paul Schaefer so enjoyed.

"Come on, Paul," Lilah pleaded, "I know you're there. Pick up, will you?"

Schaefer aimed a universal remote at the stereo, filling the room with a pastoral symphony, then removed his glasses and massaged the bridge of his nose. He had made his decision, and neither petulance nor temptation would change it now.

"Why are you doing this?" Lilah asked, her voice rising. "Why are you shutting me out like this? Paul? Paul?"

Schaefer aimed the remote at the answering machine and shut it off.

The line clicked.

Lilah's brows arched expectantly then fell at the sound of a dial tone. She listened to it for a long moment, her mind racing in search of a way to provoke him. She hadn't confronted him face-to-face yet, but she could. She could drive over there right now and make a scene: threaten to tell his wife; threaten to kill herself; threaten to smear him professionally. The impulses rose and fell like the wind. Then, as if at long last accepting the finality, Lilah pressed her palm against the tip of the phone's antenna, slowly telescoped it into the body, and tossed it on the bed.

She was lighting one of the dozens of Virginia Slims she consumed each day when she caught sight of herself in the mirrored doors of her wardrobe—shiny flame-red hair tumbling across her freckled shoulders, firm breasts that could still pass the pencil test, flat stomach, shapely hips, and those long legs that had been turning heads since high school. Not bad, she thought. Damn good, as a matter of fact. She exhaled a stream of smoke, blowing out the match, and looked over her shoulder at the mirror on her dressing table, then glanced at the one perched atop a pedestal next to the window before shifting her eyes to yet another with a carved wooden frame that hung above her desk.

There were mirrors of almost every size and shape in Lilah's bedroom; mirrors with gilded frames, rococo frames, frames of tarnished silver, sleek chrome, colorful plastic, mother-of-pearl, and stained glass; mirrors without frames, hand mirrors, makeup mirrors, and antique mirrors that turned every reflection into a faded tintype.

Lilah pirouetted in front of the long narrow one centered on the bathroom door, then did a little jeté up onto her toes, admiring the curve of her bottom that swelled against the embroidered trim of her panties. Not bad either. And not to be taken for granted. On the contrary, it had taken a lot of workouts to keep that perfectly positioned dimple men found so intriguing from being joined by countless others, to prevent that perfectly smooth bottom from looking like a couple of tired scoops of cottage cheese. Lilah's mother had the same dimple when she was young, but it had since become lost in a moonscape of cellulite. And that worried the hell out of Lilah. Ph.D.s in genetics know the theory of heredity all too well.

CHAPTER TWO

LIKE BEGETS LIKE the sign in Lilah's office declared. "Like begets like," she said to the students in her genetics class. "Reptiles give birth to reptiles; sunflower seeds bear sunflowers." She punctuated it with high-energy body language, billowing her lab smock. The laminated card clipped to the pocket proclaimed: UCLA DEPARTMENT OF HUMAN GENETICS; and displayed her photo, ID number, and name: DR. LILAH E. GRAHAM. "Like begets like," she repeated challengingly. "Anybody know why?"

"Genes," the science majors mumbled, making no effort to conceal their boredom.

"Genetic instructions," Lilah corrected. "Instructions written in a simple four-letter alphabet." She took a piece of chalk and wrote the letters A-G-C-T across the board. "Adenine, guanine, cytosine, and thymine. These four chemicals make up what?"

"DNA," several students replied.

"De-oxy-ribo-nucleic acid," she said, writing it out in her physician's scrawl. "And crazy as it sounds, from broccoli to brontosaurus rex, these four chemicals are the basis for all life-forms. What differentiates them is how the letters are combined in sentences that make up a book called the genome. The data in a single human genome would fill over a hundred L.A. phone books."

Another bored murmur rose from the science nerds.

"Let's talk species," Lilah went on, undaunted. "Mice and men—their genomes vary by less than two percent; chimpanzees and men—less than one; and within a given specie—humans for example—the percentage is infinitesimal; but the impact is vast because these subtle variations account for what? Anybody know?"

"Individuality?" a young woman up front ventured.

"Yes!" Lilah exclaimed. "Whether you're a man or woman, tall or short, have brown eyes or green—"

"Big boobs or small," a gawky student interjected, eliciting a storm of protest from his female classmates.

"Well, ladies," Lilah said, above the uproar, "should any of us, blessed with two X chromosomes, happen to acquire intimate knowledge of Mr. Kauffman's shortcomings, let's remember to blame them on his ancestors, not him."

The lecture hall rocked with laughter.

"These variations," Lilah resumed, "may give an individual an aptitude for law enforcement or medicine. Or determine that he or she will never be an athlete or rock star. When these variations become extreme, we call them defects, diseases, mutants."

"Birth defects," a student called out.

"Frankenstein."

"The Simpsons, Beavis and Butt-head," others chimed in. The responses ran the gamut from Down's syndrome to diabetes to deranged behavior.

The search for a genetic flaw that would account for the latter had long been the focus of Lilah's work; and recently, a team of Dutch researchers, studying genetic linkages within a family—a study prompted by a pattern of sexually abusive behavior among the males—found that they all had the same mutant gene on the X chromosome: a defect in the monoamine oxidase-A enzyme, known as MAOA. This raised an intriguing and highly controversial question: Is such antisocial behavior determined by heredity?

Lilah Elizabeth Graham—B.A. Berkeley, M.D. Harvard, Ph.D. Stanford—designed a research project called the OX-A study, which set out to answer this question by asking two other questions: To what extent is the mutant gene present in the general male population? To what extent in men convicted of sex crimes?

Lilah began by collecting blood samples from volunteers; then, working in the antiseptic glare of her lab at UCLA's MacDonald Medical Research Center, she extracted the raw DNA used in genetic screening. Once isolated, the sticky fibers were cut with enzymes, sized by electric current, and blotted onto a sheet of filter paper. After exposure to a radioactive probe, each "blot" was mated with a sheet of X-ray film in a standard cassette and stored at -70 degrees Celsius. The week-long process produced an autoradiograph. Those with the MAOA defect, or marker, exhibited an obvious shift from the norm in the pattern of lanes and bands.

On this afternoon, Lilah and her staff were gathered around a light table evaluating a fresh batch of X-ray-like "autorads." Her quick, incisive eyes swept across each genetic pattern, detecting the absence or presence of the telltale shift. "Positive," she called out, handing an autorad to Dr. Serena Chen.

The lithe, postdoctoral fellow from Taiwan with the

British accent and obsessive-compulsive demeanor, nodded in confirmation, then ran a light pen across a barcode sticker on the autorad. The corresponding volunteer's data—taken from a consent form completed and signed at the outset—appeared on the monitor.

Serena had just recorded the result with the click of a mouse when one of the work-study undergrads who distributed the mail pushed his cart through the door. He unloaded several bundles of envelopes, professional journals, flyers and the like, along with several boxes and corrugated cartons sealed with packing tape; then he collected the outgoing items and moved on. Serena set the light pen aside and pounced on the mail, ignoring the cartons as she began sorting it into neat stacks.

Lilah knew exactly what she was up to. There was nothing inscrutable about her; nothing stereotypically Asian save the black blunt-cut hair. If anything, she was a typical science nerd: brilliant, driven to excel, ruthlessly competitive; and as the laboratory's ranking junior researcher, she flaunted her ambition and IQ lest her tenure-track position be attributed to affirmative action or minority quotas.

Serena was about halfway through the mail when she held up a large manila envelope and announced, "Bureau of Prisons," getting the attention of the others. She peeled back the flap, removed the contents, and began reading aloud from the cover letter: "Dear Dr. Graham, Enclosed please find signed consent forms and background data on the first group of inmates who have volunteered to take part in your study. We understand that Dr. Serena Chen of your staff will commence work here on Monday the tenth and we look forward to—"

"Well," Lilah interrupted brightly. "It looks like we're going to be sticking violent sex offenders with needles."

"Yeah," one of the lab technicians cracked. "Serena's going one-on-one with the scuzz of the earth."

The group broke into laughter.

Lilah forced a smile. "I wouldn't be so sure of that. Serena, I think it's time we had a little chat." Serena was caught completely off guard. By the time she recovered, Lilah was striding toward her office, the staffers had dutifully resumed their work, and Cardenas, the wisecracking lab tech, had taken over sorting the mail. When finished, he grasped a mat knife in one hand, the largest corrugated box in the other, and began slitting the plastic packing tape that sealed it.

Lilah slipped into her office, leaving the door ajar. The clinical architecture was offset by pastel fabrics and daylight streaming through windows that overlooked the Medical Plaza. She settled at her desk and, in flagrant violation of university policy, lit a cigarette, then began reviewing the data sheets that had come with the letter. Each contained an inmate's criminal record, mug shot, and short biography.

Serena knocked and entered without waiting to be acknowledged. "I don't mean to be peevish," she began in a deferential tone, "but I rather assumed I'd be doing the field work on this phase of OX-A?"

"Well, you know what they say about assumptions, Doctor," Lilah said with a little smile. She was thinking J.R.s were all a little too full of themselves, when it struck her that she'd been no different. She wouldn't hire one who didn't radiate a mild aura of conceit—you have to believe you can do the impossible to have a chance of pulling it off, she often lectured. "Sorry, that was uncalled for," Lilah said, sounding as if she meant it. "I applaud your initiative, Serena, but—"

"I *initiated* this protocol," Serena interrupted, purposely making a play on Lilah's word. "I wrote the grants, generated the correspondence—"

"Under my guidance and signature," Lilah countered gently. She sent a plume of smoke toward the electronic air cleaner perched on her desk. "And the pressure to analyze the data and get that paper written in time for GRASP is on me too, isn't it?" The acronym stood for Genetics and its Relevance to the Anti-Social Personality, and referred to an upcoming conference. Hosted by the Aspen Institute in Maryland, the controversial forum was barely a month away, and time—to process enough samples and produce meaningful statistics—was running out. "I think you're a first-class scientist, Serena," Lilah concluded with evident sincerity. "The best investigator I've ever had, but this prison study requires something more."

"Something more?"

"Yes, the ability to look these inmates in the eye, gain their trust, and get them to spill their guts."

"Why? We're screening their genes, not their minds. They either have the bloody marker or they don't."

"It's not that simple. The Dutch study is taking heat for being light on behavioral data. We have the resources to get into it, and we're going to use them."

"If you mean collaborating with that head-shrinker over in Neuro-psy—"

"You have your opinion of Dr. Schaefer and I mine."

"So I've heard."

"That was uncalled for, Doctor."

"Rather makes us even, doesn't it?"

Lilah filled her lungs with smoke and smiled in concession. "Yeah, but this one's different. We're not after a marker that might presage hemophilia or breast cancer.

We're talking deplorable human behavior. The implications are massive. We must know who these people are. Now—" She paused and brushed the waves of flame-red hair back over her shoulder. "Your interpersonal skills have come a long way, Serena, but you don't need me to tell you they're still way behind your feel for science."

So what? Serena thought. She was a scientist, not a politician! It seemed every time she was about to break out, Lilah found a way to contain her; she'd become convinced her boss was threatened by her brilliance. She was about to argue the point when Lilah handed her one of the data sheets. The photo of a fierce-eyed black man stopped Serena cold.

"Raped his ten-year-old daughter," Lilah said, handing her another. A cherubic Caucasian fellow with a warm smile peered from the photo. "Serial rapist. Thirty-nine victims."

Serena shuddered in stunned silence.

Lilah watched the last wisps of smoke vanish into the air cleaner. "I've got this feeling in my gut that getting to know these"—She paused briefly and decided against using a pejorative—"these *men* is important, and I've got to go with it. Hope you understand."

"I still say, they have the marker or they don't."

"Well, I guess when you get down to it, that's why I'm going and you're not."

Lilah dismissed her protégée, then called Schaefer's office. He'd be with a patient at this hour, which meant she'd get his answering machine, and this time, that's what she wanted. "Hi, it's Lilah," she said smartly after the beep. "Just got word that the first group of prisoners is a go. Need to coordinate our schedules when you have a minute. Thanks." She hung up and hurried from the office.

It was still painful, but this was business, and she had little choice but to resume the strictly professional relationship that had brought them together.

"Mail call," Cardenas chirped, holding up a bundle of envelopes and journals as Lilah approached.

"Thanks. On my desk, okay?" she said, without breaking stride.

"Oh, and those supplies came in," he added, referring to the boxes he'd opened. One contained the sheets of X-ray-like film from which autorads were made; the other, vacutainers used to take blood samples.

Lilah responded with a preoccupied nod, continued to the light table and spent the rest of the day in the bluish glow of the autorads. Then, as dusk fell and thermal winds rose, she went cruising. Campus cruising. Not for blood samples—though there was always a chance she might come up with one—but for a lover. She didn't manhunt often. Mostly when a relationship soured. Sometimes in the sports bars that dotted the village, sometimes in the twisting streets, most often in the gym, the choice dependent on the level of risk she could tolerate; but whenever she did, she usually targeted the soft-eyed ones, the ones with wistful smiles who weren't full of themselves, who had a certain withdrawn quality or vulnerability. They made her feel confident and secure, and quite literally on top of things, which—once she'd brought them back to her condo—they'd quickly discover was the case.

CHAPTER THREE

The workout rooms in UCLA's Wooden Center—the vast complex named after the legendary basketball coach who led the Bruins to ten national titles—were packed with panting, red-faced students. Fueled by designer water four times more costly per gallon than gasoline, their bodies struggled with clanking chrome-plated torture racks while their minds came to grips with the downsizing of corporate America.

It was always a student when Lilah really needed to be in control. She spotted this one at the far end of a row of exercycles, and smiled at the irony when she recognized him. The insecure ones often made the most outrageous comments in class. Faded undergrad T-shirt hanging from his bony frame, thatch of hair plastered to his forehead, eyes riveted to a textbook that was bending the rack affixed to the handle bars, big-boobs-or-small Kauffman was pedaling for all he was worth. Lilah jogged on an adjacent treadmill until he was finished, then orchestrated an impromptu meeting.

"Sorry," he said as she brushed past him, their sweat-slick bodies making brief contact.

Lilah pirouetted, her flame-red ponytail sweeping the

air, and smiled flirtatiously. "Hey, I don't know about you, but that was the best sex I've had in months."

He laughed and pawed clumsily at the floor with his Reeboks. "You know, you look kind of familiar."

"So do you."

"Joel Kauffman," he said, trying to place her.

"Lilah. Lilah Graham," she said, adjusting the straps of her halter. Translucent with sweat, the taut spandex covered her breasts with the same attention to detail as a coat of spray paint.

Kauffman couldn't help but stare; then he grinned nervously, head tilting this way and that. "Graham?" he wondered with a glimmer of recognition. "Lilah Graham . . . We have a class together or something?"

"We sure do, Kauffman," she replied in her most professorial tone.

"Oh God, I'm so lame," the kid prattled, his face burning with embarrassment. "Dr. Graham. Genetics."

"That's me."

"You got me pretty good there this afternoon."

"I got you pretty good now," she said, her face alive with that combination of childlike vulnerability and mature sexuality that men found attractive.

"Yeah, well, you look . . . I don't know . . . younger, I guess. Y-y-your—" he stammered, searching for a word, any word but the one his cupped hands unwittingly described. "Your *leotards* are really cool," he finally blurted. "I mean, like, like you look so different without your smock and glasses."

"Like, you should see me without the leotards . . ." Lilah's eyes—a soft dark blue with the soulful depth of sapphires, which sparkled with intelligence—left no doubt she meant it.

Kauffman forced an uncomfortable smile, his mind racing to find a way to disengage. "Yeah, well, hey, I've got to hit the shower and get back to this," he said, indicating the textbook as he backed away.

Lilah grabbed the ends of the towel draped around his neck, stopping him. "Where you from, Kauffman?"

"Skagit Bay. It's a little town about fifty miles north of Seattle. Why?"

"Rains a lot up there, doesn't it?"

"Yeah, I guess . . ."

"Well, L.A.'s working on a five-year drought, and you can do something about it." Lilah pulled on the towel to bring his face down closer to hers; so close he could see the microfine beads of perspiration on her bosom; then she put her lips to his ear and, in a breathy whisper, said, "Conserve water. Shower with a friend."

Kauffman's Adam's apple bobbed like a channel marker. How to handle a horny genetics professor wasn't one of the case studies in medical ethics class. "Well, Lilah," he said, deciding this was one of those moments when valor wins hands down over discretion, "I knew there was a reason I didn't go to NYU."

Minutes later, still in workout gear, they were hurrying across a pedestrian bridge toward the precast concrete parking structure adjacent to Mac-Med. Darkness had fallen, but the wind was still blistering hot, and their faces were smarting and taut by the time they reached her car. The green Jaguar sedan was a 3.8 model from the mid-sixties, with wires and a sunroof.

"Nice set of wheels," Kauffman said as Lilah swung out of the parking structure, heading toward Le Conte.

"Extravagant set of wheels," she cracked. "I always wanted an old Jag. Something civilized and classy about them. And one day, there it was, waiting for me. I couldn't afford it, but I did it anyway."

"Pure impulse, huh?"

"Nothing pure about it, nothing whatso—oh shit."

"What?"

She reached for her briefcase—a leather tour de force of pockets, pouches, and compartments that served as purse, doctor's bag, and document case—slipped the cellular phone from its assigned sleeve and pushed one of the autodial buttons. "Hi, it's me . . . No, that's why I'm calling. Something's come up. I can't . . . Uh-huh. In the morning. First thing." She listened indulgently, nodding, grunting, as she made the turn into Gayley. "Uh-huh, uh-huh, uh-huh. Mom? Mom, can I . . . *Mom*, can I get a word in here, please? I just said, I'd be there in the morning . . . Yes, I know. I'm sorry about dinner. Tell him I'll be there, okay? . . . Yes, I promise . . . Love you too." Lilah hung up, then sensed Kauffman's curiosity. "She's worried about my father. He's old, he's sick, and he has a daughter who's a doctor." A daughter who cares for him deeply, she thought; a daughter who is terribly frustrated by the fact that—despite all her training, knowledge, and connections in the medical community—there isn't a thing she can do to save him.

"Something serious?"

Lilah slipped the phone back into her briefcase and nodded. "Waldenstrom's disease."

"What's that?"

"An abnormal proliferation of lymphocytes and plasma cells."

He looked off thoughtfully. "That'd thicken the blood and effect immune response, wouldn't it?"

"Very good," Lilah said, shifting into lecture-hall mode,

which provided some emotional distance. "So once a month we do a CBC to check his . . . what?"

"White cells, no?"

"White cells, yes. And plasma count." She punched the gas. The Jaguar responded with a throaty growl and accelerated up the hill toward the glittering lights of Spanish-style condominiums. The tightly clustered units were roofed in tiles of burnt orange clay, and sheathed in soft-edged stucco the color of adobe. Like many such complexes in Southern California, each unit had a subterranean garage directly beneath it, with automatic door opener and staircase within that led up into the living area. But Lilah drove past the ramp that led down to the garages and parked at the curb.

Kauffman's brow furrowed with uncertainty. "You leave this thing on the street?"

Lilah splayed her hands. "I could say it's easier to pick up my mail this way, which it is; but actually I'm an incurable pack rat and my garage is loaded with junk." She got out of the car, set the alarm, and sauntered toward the security gate, her ponytail beckoning Kauffman to follow with its rhythmic bob.

Lilah had already picked up something far more interesting than mail; but as they passed the bank of mailboxes in the courtyard, something caught her eye. The slip of yellow paper taped to her box indicated she had a package in the receiving room where oversized mail and deliveries were held. She considered fetching it, but her curiosity was no match for the sexual current that had been surging through her since she had left the gym. The package would keep till tomorrow, she thought; till next week, if Kauffman's appetite for her matched the hunger in his eyes; indeed, till eternity, if she knew what it contained.

Lilah took his hand and made a beeline for her condo. "Buckle your seat belt," she purred in a sexy whisper as she unlocked the door and pulled him into the darkened entry. "You're in for the ride of your life."

The door had barely latched when she buried her hands in his hair and kissed him passionately. The next thing Kauffman knew, their clothes were strewn across the floor in a haphazard trail that led to the bathroom, and they were caressing beneath a tingling shower. Lilah soaped his lean body until he was lost in the ecstasy, then turned the water to full cold. He yelped, trying to avoid the icy blast, as Lilah slipped from the enclosure, her naughty laughter echoing off the hard surfaces.

"You bastard," Kauffman gurgled good-naturedly, stumbling into the bedroom after her, where they lunged into each other's arms, their glistening bodies sliding sensuously against one another. "Oh, wow," he exclaimed, fascinated by the synchronized movement in the mirrors. "Like we're everywhere at once."

"Make love to me, Joel," Lilah whispered through trembling lips. "Make love to me everywhere." Kauffman soared with passion and began backing her toward the bed. "No. No, wait, wait," Lilah said, kissing him as she spun him around in the opposite direction. She guided him into a chair in front of the mirrored wardrobe and straddled his thighs. "This way. It's always better for me this way."

In truth, she'd never been with a lover and been beneath him. Never. The mere thought of it filled her with claustrophobic terror which she could neither fathom nor tolerate. But it had never been a problem. On the contrary, men always seemed relieved at her taking control. Even her first time, the eager high school wrestling champion with the rock hard body and short fuse had happily spent the entire time pinned to the shaggy carpet in the rear of his van. Maybe it was some sort of primal resonance that made them submit, she thought. Some pleasurable memory of their mothers hovering over them with a fresh diaper and a can of baby powder that made them so trusting.

Joel Kauffman was no different. His eyes widened in brief protest, then glazed in watery abandon as Lilah eased back slowly, capturing him in her tight wetness. "I take it back," she moaned, noticing she was literally face-to-face with her reflection, which, thanks to their position and proximity to the mirror, made Kauffman appear to be salaciously sandwiched between Lilah and her identical twin. "What I said about your shortcomings, I mean." She emitted a naughty giggle, then dipped a shoulder, letting one of her nipples graze his lips. He turned his head this way and that, chasing after it like a hungry infant. His eager mouth soon found its target, sending waves of erotic sensations rippling across Lilah's flesh. She savored the rush and quickened her pace, her flame-red mane snapping wildly from side to side, the soft blue cast of her eyes burning with unbridled passion.

Kauffman arched his back, raising his hips to meet her, then shuddered as the sensation intensified. At these moments, he always thought of a sex education book his parents had given him as a child that likened an orgasm to a sneeze.

For Lilah it was more like an incendiary whoosh. Like an entire book of matches igniting at once, and then igniting again, and again, and again.

CHAPTER FOUR

An entire book of matches igniting at once—a perfect analogy for Los Angeles at this time of year: no dazzling foliage, no crisp arctic air, no frost on the pumpkin here. No, while much of the country reveled in autumnal bliss, Angelenos sizzled in stifling desert heat.

They had a quirk of nature to thank for it.

In mid-October the jet stream, which blew west to east the other eleven months, reversed direction over Utah and backtracked across the steaming Mojave. The superheated air rose over the mountains, emerging as the Santa Ana winds, and raced at freeway speeds down the hundreds of canyons that slashed across Southern California from desert to sea. The humidity plunged to five percent, the temperature soared to ninety-plus degrees, and hundreds of thousands of acres of vegetation turned into brittle tinder. Like ill-fated lovers, the hot winds and dry terrain needed only a spark to unite them in a passionate, self-destructive frenzy until only smoke and ash remained; and every fall, there was always some nut itching to play matchmaker and set their lonely hearts aflame.

Tonight, the nut wore sunglasses and a baseball cap with a ponytail pulled through the back, and drove a dusty Econoline van. It turned into Las Flores Canyon south of

Malibu and began the twisting climb past fine homes set on the lush hillsides above the Pacific. The driver had the serene demeanor and hyperactive eyes of someone who'd been living on the edge of reality and had just fallen off.

At about the same time, Dan Merrick was in his Chevy Blazer on a jammed freeway, popping Tums like peanuts. Someone up ahead flicked a cigarette into the darkness, sending up an explosion of orange sparks. Merrick cursed the thoughtless stupidity and took the Rosecrans exit to Manhattan Beach. Like most oceanfront towns, its clean air, fine schools, quaint shops and restaurants made it a great place to raise a family.

Pyromaniacs and gridlock weren't the only things burning a hole in Merrick's stomach as he parked in front of the stucco-and-tile bungalow that used to be his house; the house he was still paying for; the house he was still paying for while his ex-wife, Joyce, lived in it with another man. He stared into the darkness, wondering how all the happiness and hope had turned to such bitterness and pain. The sound of the Blazer's door opening pulled him out of it.

Jason Merrick's round face looked up at him from beneath a backward cap that proclaimed KINGS. Large block letters across the back of his oversized jersey spelled out THE ENFORCER.

"Hey, how's it going, Dad?" Jason chirped as he clambered into the seat next to him.

"Great," Merrick replied, tugging Jason's cap down over his eyes playfully. "How about you?"

"I'm hanging in there."

"Hanging in there?" Merrick echoed with concern as he

pulled away from the curb. "That clown your mother's living with giving you a hard time?"

"Naw, Steve's okay."

Merrick took a thoughtful drag of his cigarette and exhaled. "Then what?"

Jason waved at the pungent haze. "Mom says I shouldn't be around people who smoke."

"She's right. It's a filthy habit."

"So why do you do it?"

"Because it pisses her off."

"Come on, Dad. She said secondhand smoke is—"

"Hey, it's no longer open for discussion. Am I coming through?"

"Yeah," Jason muttered dejectedly.

Merrick stopped in front of another house and tapped the horn, then sighed with remorse. "Sorry I snapped. You know how I get when fire season rolls around."

Jason nodded. "Mom thinks you're a nutcase." He noticed his two friends hurrying toward the Blazer, and quickly added, "I told her it takes one to know one."

"Hey!" Merrick said, trying to conceal the fact that he was pleased. "I don't want you talking to your mother that way . . . unless she calls me a nutcase."

Jason studied him curiously for a moment, then they both began to laugh.

Twenty miles north in Las Flores Canyon the Econoline van was snaking along a dirt road that ran behind the secluded houses. It turned into the brush just below the windblown crest and creaked to a stop. The driver lit a cigarette and inhaled deeply. Then, eyes aglow with complex emotions that ranged from shame to anger and culminated in a sense of awesome power, placed the unlighted end inside a matchbook, closed the cover, and tossed it out the window.

The tip of the cigarette traced a spiraling path through the darkness to a clump of mesquite. The glowing embers burned from one shred of tobacco to the next until the first match ignited, turning the matchbook into a miniature blowtorch. The intense flash lasted just long enough to set the parched brush ablaze. The tiny circle of flame quickly grew to a diameter of several feet; then, like a lost hiker, it paused in the darkness until a gust of wind gave it direction and force. Half an hour later it had grown into a raging firestorm that sent particles of flaming debris through the air like wind-driven rain, igniting million dollar houses, mobile homes, and makeshift shanties with equal ardor.

While the flames ravaged Las Flores Canyon, the van climbed to a ridge that gave the driver a panoramic view of the inferno. Few fire starters were motivated by festering hatred, few carried out personal vendettas, few used sophisticated ignition devices to keep their distance. Most were driven by more basic urges. This one was no exception. Stimulated by the dazzling pyrotechnics that lit the sky, by the thrill of creation, by feverish hands slipped inside unzipped jeans, the driver writhed in ecstasy and emitted a chilling scream.

Dan Merrick was screaming too, and jumping out of his seat with excitement. While Las Flores burned, and Los Angeles sizzled, he was in the coolest spot in town.

Ringed by Romanesque columns that stood stark white against a crumbling inner city neighborhood, the L.A. Forum housed a half acre of ice on which violent young millionaires were fighting over a disk of rock-hard rubber. Merrick and the boys cheered as a group of players slammed into the boards in front of them, their fierce eyes, clenched jaws, and flailing sticks just beyond the shatter-proof glass.

The Kings center came up with the puck. In an electrifying display of stick-handling, he split the Toronto defense and beat the goalie with a stinging backhander. Lights were flashing, sirens screaming, bells ringing, and thousands of Kings fans were going wild when Merrick's phone began chirping—which was why he didn't hear it.

The cellular hung on Merrick's belt inches from his son's ear. Jason knew what it meant and wrestled with his conscience before tugging on his father's sleeve. "Dad? Hey, Dad! Your phone!"

Merrick groaned, then slipped it from its sheath and thumbed receive. "Merrick."

The L.A. County Arson Squad was housed in an art deco building in Chinatown near the Convention Center. Duty officer Mike Gonzales sat at his console, squinting at the flashing indicators on the wall-sized status map. "Hey, Lieutenant, I got a gig for you."

"Chrissakes, Gonzo," Merrick admonished, turning the phone toward the arena. "You hear that?"

"Kings game. You got the box tonight."

"You're a genius. Get somebody else, will you?"

"No can do. Decker specifically asked for you. Said he wants it done right."

"Bullshit. Decker hates my guts. He said that because I'm at the game. Where's the gig?"

"Malibu. Nasty wildfire. He's set up on PCH and Las Flores Canyon. Says he has a witness."

"Somebody spotted the pyro?" Merrick exclaimed.

"What he said."

"Tell him I'm rolling."

While Merrick was dropping off the boys, the blistering Santa Anas were driving the wildfire in an ever widening triangle, consuming thousands of acres of vegetation and hundreds of homes. Despite the efforts of firefighters, the flames had reached the coast and were threatening the multimillion-dollar estates in Malibu Colony—the beachfront enclave where Hollywood's power elite resided—and the area was being evacuated.

It was about a forty-minute run from Manhattan Beach at this hour; but the wildfires had the freeway backed up, and five lanes of stoplights greeted the Blazer as it came down the curving 405/10 interchange. Merrick hit the brakes and bounced a fist off the steering wheel in disgust.

He had spent the first ten years of his career fighting fires, and the next ten catching the nuts who started them. Part cop, part psychologist, part scientist, he used dogged gumshoe work and painstaking forensic analysis to assemble the charred pieces of the puzzle, and hoped the picture identified the arsonist. Catching one was like the Kings making the playoffs, convicting one like winning the Stanley Cup. The arrest rate was the lowest of any felony. And only one in ten of those went to jail. Identify, arrest, convict—they were Merrick's special skills. The irony was he needed a tragedy to put them to use.

His impatience had gradually turned to gut-burning anger as the Blazer inched forward. He was reaching for the bottle of Tums when something dawned on him. A relaxed smile broke across Merrick's face as he settled back in the seat, savoring it. A witness, he thought; son of a bitch, I got me a witness.

CHAPTER FIVE

On this night the gusts that swept into Lilah's bedroom had taken on an acrid bite that went unnoticed by its occupants. Several hours had passed since they'd burrowed beneath the covers. Now, while Kauffman lay beside her, Lilah tossed and turned, tormented by a familiar litany: The Lord giveth and the Lord taketh away. The Lord giveth and the Lord taketh away. The Lord giveth and ... over and over, the words rang in Lilah's head.

It was her mother's favorite saying, and Lilah always thought of it after having sex. Not that her mother ever said it to her in that regard. They never talked about making love, as Marge Graham's generation called it. No, the saying came to mind because the euphoria and the blissful sleep that followed inevitably gave way to harrowing nightmares.

It was always the same. A spiraling descent into a netherworld where, emotionally spent and physically naked—her flame-red hair, tumbling in sweeping waves across her breasts and pelvis, cloaking her demurely like a modern-day Botticelli—she soared through suede-black darkness to the pinnacle of emotion, then spun out of control and crashed headlong into an explosion of colored lights. The intense bursts were always violet, yellow, and white, and were always ringed by neon-green tentacles that tried to ensnare her.

Lilah fought ferociously, terrified of being caught and of the eerie silence that she tried desperately to shatter, only to find herself unable to whimper, let alone scream. It was like a virtual-reality encounter with no sound track, an encounter she'd had hundreds of times without once getting to the end. This wasn't because she would suddenly awaken in sweat-soaked terror, but because the nightmare would suddenly stop as if someone had pulled the plug, leaving her with a nagging feeling of uncertainty when she finally awakened hours later.

This time it was intensified by a flickering glow that came from the far side of the room. Lilah pushed up onto an elbow, squinting into the glare; then she recoiled at the sight of a raging blaze. Everywhere she looked she saw fire. She frantically rubbed the sleep from her eyes, to discover that the sheets of flame were marching across her television screen, not through her condo; and, having been multiplied by the collection of mirrors, were merely illuminating, not incinerating, the figure in jeans and T-shirt at her desk. "Kauffman?" she muttered sleepily.

His lanky body sagged like a hammock between the chair and a file cabinet where his bare heels rested. He grunted in reply, keeping one eye on the televised inferno, the other on the textbook in his lap.

"What's going on?"

"Wildfires," he explained, getting to his feet. "This town's going up in flames."

Lilah nodded knowingly and sighed with relief. "That time of year . . ." She found the remote next to the pack of Virginia Slims on the nightstand and shut off the television. "Happens every October."

Kauffman was about to protest but sensed she was unsettled and let it go. "You okay?"

"Yeah, thanks, I'm fine. Why?"

"You were really rocking and rolling there for a while. Kinda like you locked horns with things that go bump in the night."

Lilah nodded vulnerably. "Always do after I've been with someone." She sat up against the headboard, the flame-red waves swirling about her shoulders and across her breasts, then reached to the nape of her neck and ran both hands up into her hair several times, her slender fingers gathering it into a flaming column that she began weaving into a chignon with practiced grace. She'd been doing it for decades; ever since her mother denounced her waist-long tresses as unruly and threatened to cut them; and, over the years, it had evolved into a sensuously choreographed ballet—which Kauffman found wholly intriguing. He was still savoring the performance when Lilah pulled a cigarette from the pack with her lips and struck a match to light it. It burst into flame with a sharp pop, revealing the fascination in her eyes. "Something about matches . . ." Lilah said in that seductive whisper, holding it up to him. "The way they sound, the way they smell, the way the tongues of flame start licking at each other and become one . . ."

"You see everything relative to getting your rocks off, don't you?" he prompted with a little smile.

She lit the cigarette, then blew him a kiss, exhaling a stream of smoke that extinguished the flame. "Well now that you mention it . . ."

Kauffman's eyes rolled. "Women are weird. This art major I used to go with said her orgasms were like diving headfirst into a de Kooning."

"I'll have to try that sometime," Lilah said with a mischievous grin. "But I need to dive headfirst into a cup of coffee first. You make any?"

"No. I've been studying."

"Sans caffeine?" she teased incredulously. "You sure you're from Seattle?" She stood up stark naked, took a drag of the cigarette, and headed for the bathroom, pulling a thin layer of smoke after her. Kauffman sat there watching, fascinated by the dimple that winked at him with each step.

Lilah emerged shortly, wearing a clingy robe and a few dabs of her favorite perfume. She had experimented with many over the years, initially favoring the more potent ones that could strike the target from afar; then, on finishing her residency, whether as a symbol of her maturity or an admission that she was an old-fashioned girl at heart, she settled on Chanel's legendary No. 5, the subtle, alluring scent that sophisticated women had been using for decades as a clincher in intimate moments.

Lilah tossed some beans in the grinder, cranked up the cappuccino machine, and soon they were sitting at the counter, sipping industrial strength espresso from cups the size of soup bowls. "My turn," Lilah said, sensing the kid's distance. "You okay?"

"Uh-huh. It's nothing. Really."

"That wasn't very convincing, Joel," she said with gentle concern.

Kauffman took a thoughtful sip of coffee, then made his decision, and gestured to a framed snapshot at the end of the counter. "That's you and Professor Schaefer, isn't it?"

Lilah nodded.

"I think I have him for psych next semester."

"Heard the rumors, huh?"

"Looks like they're true."

"*Were* true," Lilah corrected with a little sigh. She circled the counter and pushed the picture with the tip of her forefinger until it toppled facedown. "Why?"

"Feels a little weird, that's all."

"You mean a student making it with a professor who's been having an affair with another professor who happens to be a shrink with a wife and three kids? What's weird about that?"

Kauffman laughed and loosened up.

Lilah suddenly scooted off as if she'd remembered something, and returned with her briefcase. "Right arm or left?"

Kauffman looked baffled.

"I need a blood sample."

"Blood sample?" he echoed defensively. "Hey, you're not worried that"—he paused awkwardly—"I mean that I'm—"

"HIV positive?"

He nodded. "I'm not. Really, I'm not."

"I know," she said, opening one of the vacutainer kits she used to take blood samples. "Your hemo report. Nice job by the way." In her class, the students ran batteries of tests on their own blood, and on occasion their professor graded more than their lab skills. "Besides, it's a little late to be worried about an exchange of bodily fluids, don't you think?"

"A little," Kauffman replied with a sheepish grin, aching to exchange them again as a tingling sensation spread from the pit of his stomach down the inside of his thighs. The fantasy ended with the glint of steel, the cool swab of alcohol, and the pinch of a needle.

"Come on, make a fist," Lilah said, slipping the vacutainer—a test-tube-like vial with color-coded stopper—into the plastic holder to which the needle was attached.

Kauffman watched it filling, then felt a little queasy and looked away as she released the tourniquet. "What *are* you testing for?"

"A genetic mutation."

"Very funny."

"Seriously—and by the way, the word is probing. I need all the random samples I can get."

"I have to sign something?"

"I think we passed that stage last night." Lilah chuckled lasciviously and ran her free hand through his sleep-tousled curls. "Yeah, everyone does. I mean, I don't care who has the mute and who doesn't. I'm just into the statistics; but informed consent is a hot-button issue these days."

"What mutation you looking for?"

"An MAOA defect." Lilah removed the vacutainer and slipped the needle from his arm. "It's an X-linked phenotype found at the XP11 locus between DXS14C and OTC." She saw his blank expression and added, "Monoamine oxidase A. Number 309850 in Mendelian, if you want to look it up. It's an enzyme that processes serotonin."

Kauffman's brow knitted in thought as Lilah fetched a consent form, peeled off one of the bar-code stickers—there were a half dozen with the same number and code in a row across the top—and affixed it to the specimen tube. "Serotonin . . . It's a neurotransmitter or something, isn't it?"

Lilah nodded and slid the form across the counter. "A stress modulator—controls impulses—unless the gene is a mute and your brain's in sero withdrawal. Couple of studies have linked it to antisocial behavior. Which, if you're into cause and effect theories . . ." She let it trail off suggesting he supply it.

Kauffman's pen paused over the consent form as he thought it out. "A defective MAOA gene—retards the processing of serotonin by the brain—resulting in antisocial behavior."

"Uh-huh. And if we dispense with scientific procedure and cut to the chase, we might conclude that—what?"

The kid saw it immediately and hissed, stunned by the import of what he was about to say. "That some people are genetically programmed to be violent."

Lilah nodded, then grinned seductively. "Maybe even sexually violent." The words were still coming in that sexy whisper when she lunged toward him, burying her hands in his hair, and drove him back against the counter, her hungry mouth devouring his until his lower lip was captured between her teeth. He winced and recoiled, pulling the flesh taut but not free. Lilah held it for a long moment, then smiled slyly and released it. His entire body began trembling in anticipation as she worked his jeans to his thighs, then undid her robe and pressed her body against his. They were clinging to each other in frenzied passion when he cupped her bare bottom in his hands and lifted her onto the counter.

CHAPTER SIX

The previous evening, after being caught on the traffic-packed freeway, Merrick finally reached the Pacific Coast Highway. He raced north on the twisting road that paralleled picturesque beaches, passing long convoys of fire trucks and rescue vehicles.

Multicolored flashers strobed in the darkness. The wail of sirens mixed with the crackle of radios. Iridescent stripes on fire coats streaked the night as frantic crews worked in a blizzard of eye-stinging ash. Overhead, low flying tankers spewed pink flame-retardant foam in the path of the fire, which was roaring across the terrain at twenty-five miles an hour.

Merrick turned into the parking lot of an oceanfront restaurant where a command post had been set up. A group of firemen hovered over maps, plotting strategy and deploying fire-fighting units. "Merrick!" the one in the white helmet growled as he approached pulling on an ARSON SQUAD raid jacket. "Where the hell you been?"

"Making it with your daughter."

"Fuck you, Merrick."

"That's what she was doing."

"Fuck you, anyway."

Battalion Chief Roscoe Decker had black skin, intelligent eyes, and the bone-weary posture of someone being pummeled by a relentless adversary. He turned into the gusting wind and pointed to a man reading a newspaper. His clothes had the ragged edges and oily sheen of constant wear. A long ponytail hung across one shoulder. "Walked out of there without getting his butt barbecued and said he saw who started it."

"He say who?"

"Nope. He said he wants to make a deal first."

Merrick nodded and studied the man for a moment. Most arsonists watched their handiwork from afar like a pornographic movie. Some derived a sense of power from seeing the human chaos firsthand. Others took insidious pleasure in helping fight the fire. A few, driven to be lauded as heroes, claimed to have seen the arsonist at work; and Merrick wouldn't put it past one to stride boldly into the command post and do so.

He palmed his ID case, letting the badge shimmer in the light. "Lieutenant Merrick, Arson Squad. I hear you want to make a deal."

The man looked up from his newspaper and nodded.

"Okay, I get the pyro. You get the film rights."

"I wish," the man said with a wistful smile. "Here's my problem: When I tell you what I saw, you're going to want to know what I was doing there."

"Something illegal," Merrick said matter-of-factly.

"Just being homeless seems to be illegal around here, you know?"

Merrick nodded and lit a cigarette.

"Look, I wouldn't hurt anyone, but I do what I have to, to survive; and I don't want to be fucked over for helping you out. We have a deal or not?"

Merrick dragged on the cigarette and studied his eyes. Rather than the manic glint of someone enjoying the chaos, they had a forthrightness confirmed by steady hands, the fingernails clipped and clean. "Deal."

"Okay," the man began hesitantly. "There's this house up near the crest. I use the pool sometimes when they're out. To freshen up, you know? Anyway, they left a patio door open. I was . . . I was inside raiding the fridge when I saw headlights in the brush. I thought they were coming back, but the driver chucked something out the window and took off. Couple of minutes later—fire everywhere."

Merrick nodded pensively. "You happen to get the plate number?"

"Naw, way too dark."

"Can you describe the vehicle?"

"Yeah, it was a van. Dark one—black, green—it looked real beat up. The driver was wearing sunglasses and a baseball cap . . . and he had a ponytail—long, like mine—pulled through the back. He lit a cigarette. That's when I got a look at him."

Merrick nodded thoughtfully. "You're sure it was a man, not a woman?"

The man cocked his head to one side, then winced. "I couldn't swear either way."

"You just said *he*, several times."

"Power of suggestion, I guess," the man explained, holding up his newspaper. This was the third wildfire in a month, and the front page was covered with stories. "Says eight out of ten arsonists are men."

"They are." Merrick ground out his cigarette with frustration. "And most don't get caught."

The man nodded, then began laughing softly.

"You think that's funny?"

"No, that." He gestured to the inferno, then slipped a wallet from his jeans and removed a driver's license. It had a local address and a photo of an executive in a shirt and tie. The man's face was thinner now, and ruddy from exposure, but the crisp blue eyes hadn't changed. "I used to live here. I would've ended up homeless anyway."

Merrick jotted down his name and D.L. number on a note pad. "Sounds like you've got an ax to grind."

"With the bank that foreclosed on me, not my neighbors. I worked here too." He took an ID card from his wallet. It had a similar photo and proclaimed HUGHES AIRCRAFT.

"Engineer?"

"Missiles," the man replied with obvious pride.

Merrick nodded knowingly. "Yeah, Reagan really screwed it up." He took the man to Decker's map table and had him locate the house from where he saw the van, then peeled a twenty from a billfold. "Stay out of other people's kitchens."

The man smiled thinly and walked into the darkness.

Merrick put out a bulletin for a battered van, dark color, ponytailed driver, then assembled an investigation team: Bill Fletcher, boyish, quiet and new to A.I.; and Pete Logan, a crusty forensic expert with the Bureau of Alcohol, Tobacco, and Firearms based in L.A.'s World Trade Center. He and Merrick had worked dozens of cases over the years.

It was about an hour before dawn when they headed up the canyon to start their manhunt. They heard the hundred-decibel roar and felt the two-thousand-degree heat well before reaching the fire line. The fifty-foot-high wall of flame had just come into view when the Blazer's headlights cut through thick smoke to find a fire truck blocking its way. The crew had been trying to keep the blaze from jumping the road, but a sudden wind shift sent the firestorm racing in the opposite direction, trapping them in a field of dry grass. Within seconds the entire expanse of scrub ignited with an oxygen-sucking whoosh that knocked them to the ground and tore the hoses from their hands.

Merrick, Fletcher, and Logan left the Blazer to help them, but the flames and lung-searing heat drove them back. Merrick buckled his fireman's coat, pulled an air tank from the back of the four-by and began following a length of hose through the blinding smoke in search of the nozzle. It brought him face-to-face with the towering wall of flame.

"Hey! Hey, Dan!" Fletcher shouted, aghast. "What the hell are you doing? Dan? Dan?"

"Nothing you can do, dammit!" Logan protested.

Merrick secured his helmet, hooked the hose over his arm, and strode into the heart of the inferno.

CHAPTER SEVEN

Thick burnt-umber smoke stretched to the horizon like miles of dusty drapery drawn across the morning sky. The winds were still hot and still gusting, and the slip of yellow paper was fluttering wildly against the mailbox labeled L. E. GRAHAM.

Lilah captured it and peeled the tape free. "Go get this for me, will you?" she asked, handing the slip of paper to Kauffman. "Little room around the side there. Should be open."

Kauffman left his backpack and loped off, his eyes already smarting from the microscopic cinders in the air. Lilah removed the rest of yesterday's mail from the box and was giving it a quick once-over when he returned with the package—a corrugated carton about the size of the one the lab supplies came in.

Her head tilted curiously at the bold black printing that spelled out her name and address. It wasn't familiar, nor was the post office box that served as a return. Lilah was about to cross the courtyard and have Kauffman put the package in the condo, but thanks to their lusty encounter, the day had barely started and she was already running late. With luck, she could drive to Santa Monica, give her father his checkup, and make it back to campus in time to

42

teach class—if traffic wasn't snarled, if she made the lights, and if her patient was cooperative. "Better put that in the car," she said, heading for the gate.

The green Jaguar looked as if it was covered with a thin layer of dirty snow. They raced down the hill toward the village, sending trails of soot spiraling from the car's graceful curves. The package with the bold, angry printing—the package that could burn a block-square market to the ground—rode in the backseat along with her briefcase, his backpack, and their gym bags. Lilah ran the light at Le Conte and pulled to the curb opposite the Chevron station.

Kauffman removed his gear, then crouched in the open door and grinned at what he was about to say. "Thanks for the ride, Dr. Graham."

"It was a selfish act," Lilah said with a chuckle. "See you at the gym tonight?"

"Can't," Kauffman grunted. "Histology study group."

"Come by my place when it's over."

Kauffman winced, his head lolling sheepishly. "We usually go for pizza."

"So bring me a couple of slices," Lilah said in her sassy way. She kissed her fingertips, then reached across and touched them to his lips. "Gotta go."

Kauffman stepped back as the Jaguar's exhausts added their noxious fumes to the eye-stinging air; but it was the delicate scent of Lilah's perfume that filled his head now. He inhaled deeply, savoring it, and watched until she made the turn into Wilshire, heading west toward Santa Monica.

Over the years, the sleepy seaside community where Lilah Graham grew up had become a politically polarized battleground where property owners and rent control activists squared off regularly. It had been going on for over two decades now. Ever since the spring of '74—the spring Lilah came home on break from Berkeley and got into a discussion with her father over it.

"Shelter is a basic right," she declared with the self-righteous indignation favored by college students and clergymen. "It shouldn't be exploited for profit."

"Tell that to Thomas Jefferson," her father retorted, unable to reconcile his daughter's views with her upbringing. "I don't know what they're teaching you up there, young lady, but this is America."

"Yeah . . . land of the brie, home of the slaves," she quipped with a smile. "Spare me the national anthem, okay?"

Doug Graham dragged hard on an unfiltered Camel, and suggested they take a walk. "There's this guy I know," he began as they strolled along the golf course that bordered their neighborhood. "Hardworking, nice family . . . wife works too."

"Wow, a liberated woman," Lilah teased. "I thought they were outlawed in Santa Monica."

"Let me finish," her father said evenly, exhaling through his nose and mouth as he spoke. "This couple . . . they scrimped and saved and bought a little house. A few years later they scraped up enough to invest in a building with rental units. Now, thanks to this rent control nonsense, it's damn near worthless."

"Hey, what goes around comes around," Lilah replied in the flippant tone of a rebellious eighteen-year-old.

"Talk English, will you?" Doug Graham pleaded.

"Well, they were sticking it to their tenants all those years. Now, the tenants get to stick it to them."

"I've known them a long time," her father said calmly. "Rents were reasonable. The place was kept up. Did it themselves too: leaky faucets, clogged toilets, paint jobs, the whole nine yards—"

"Hey, life isn't fair, you know?"

"Well, that's one thing we agree on," her father said with a thoughtful exhale. "Now, what if they'd been planning to sell the building and use the money for something special?"

"Like what?"

"Oh, like . . ." he replied, mimicking her, "to take that dream honeymoon they never had."

"Hey, you're really breaking my heart, Dad. Next you'll be telling me their kid needs open-heart surgery."

"What if the kid did?" he asked, setting the hook he'd so patiently baited. "Is it okay to 'exploit shelter for profit' to pay for some things, but not others?"

"Well . . . yeah, I guess," Lilah replied, sensing he'd trapped her.

"Okay, now that we're communicating, what if they had a bright—no, make that a brilliant—daughter?" He paused and his eyes locked on to Lilah's. "And they were planning to use the money to send her to medical school?"

That was the moment Lilah Graham grew up. She'd known her parents owned that building and had spent untold hours working on it. Yet, she'd been so intent on spouting her sophomoric platitudes, she'd blocked the truth from her mind.

Lilah often reflected on that moment, especially when she wrote the monthly check repaying her med-school loans; but today she was more focused on her father's failing health and the intricacies of screening imprisoned sex offenders. The latter prompted her to dig out her cellular and check with Cardenas for messages. "Ruben? . . . Yeah, it's me. Anything going on?"

"Nada," he replied, his attention on one of the many medical school applications he was filling out. "Things are real quiet, boss."

"Dr. Schaefer didn't call?"

"Not on my watch." He sorted through a rack of message slips. "Not on anybody else's either."

"Okay, have him try my cellular if he does." She hung up and angled south toward Santa Monica's Sunset Park section. The rambling enclave of Spanish bungalows and English cottages was home to public servants, blue-collar workers, and young families getting a foothold in the pricey real estate market. The Jaguar cruised past the municipal airport and started down the steep hill toward the golf course. It was just a few blocks to the house where Lilah grew up, to the bungalow with the sunny den where, in the shadow of the exercise equipment he once used regularly, Doug Graham spent his waking hours chain-smoking and channel surfing with the remote that seemed grafted to his hand. That's how Lilah pictured him now, slouched in his slipcovered recliner—the piping frayed, the arms and headrest burnished with grime, the fabric dotted with pinhole-sized burns—encircled by snack tables that held his can of Coors, Marlboros, ashtray, and cordless phone. He'd lost so much weight that the nylon warm-up suits he once favored for their macho style made him look frail and diminutive, like a child in a grown-up's chair.

There was a time when Lilah's image of him was more manly, more heroic, more befitting a man who'd spent thirty years on the Santa Monica Fire Department; a man who had a dozen community service awards and four citations for bravery hanging on the wall behind him, along with the golf trophies and softball plaques.

Lilah turned into the driveway and parked behind her mother's station wagon. She'd been doing it since the day she started driving, and it still topped her mother's list of pet peeves. Lilah had no idea why she did it then, or why she was still doing it now. Probably some Oedipal thing, she thought, one of those petty adolescent rebellions that went unresolved. She ground out her cigarette and popped the Jag's door, stepping into what felt like a blast furnace. Slipping her briefcase from between the gym bag and package on the backseat, she hurried toward the house.

Like most older homes near the coast, it wasn't air-conditioned; and the small oscillating fan in the den strained to keep perspiration from forming on Doug Graham's brow as he squinted at the television where a huge helicopter was taking off from a beachfront parking lot. One of the reporters covering the wildfires was shouting over the deafening clatter. "That's right, Trisha. We still don't know the fate of those five firemen trapped by the inferno. There *are* reports an arson investigator, working in the area, went in after them. A search-and-rescue chopper has just been dispatched and paramedics are standing by to care for survivors—if and when they're found . . . ."

Doug Graham was shaking his head in dismay when he heard the jangle of keys outside and brightened.

"It's me," Lilah announced, letting herself in.

"Marge? Marge, Lilah's here," Doug called out in his dry rasp, thrusting his arms from within the haze of tobacco smoke. "Give us a hug, princess."

"Hugs are on special today," Lilah said, concealing her reaction to his wasted pallor. His stubble pinched when she kissed him, and his breath carried the sour odor of bile. "Sorry I didn't make it last night."

"Hey, I know how busy you are, sweetheart." Doug Graham's watery eyes glistened with sincerity. "I know you're doing important things."

Lilah squirmed with guilt and set her briefcase on one of the snack tables. "So, how's my favorite patient?"

"Lousy."

"Rather be out there hauling hose, huh?" she said, gesturing to the inferno raging on the television.

"Would be too, if I had me a decent doctor." His deadpan delivery gave way to a mischievous twinkle.

A little grin—that was pure Doug Graham—turned the corners of Lilah's mouth as she plucked the Marlboro from his yellow-stained fingers. "Okay, smarty pants, let's have a listen." Doug eagerly unzipped his warm-up suit, revealing an expanse of waxen skin. Lilah's ivory-smooth hands with their long fingers and manicured nails placed the stethoscope on his chest and moved it through a graceful arc that grazed his upper abdomen and ended well below his left armpit; then, gently bending him forward, they slipped beneath the warm-up suit and moved across his back with the same grace and precision.

As always, Doug Graham remained silent and still. He lived for these moments, for the sense of well-being that came from being cared for by the daughter of whom he was so proud; moments that were far more beneficial than anything she or his doctor could prescribe. His illness-glazed eyes, closed in sublime reflection, were brighter and more alive when they opened. "How am I doing?" he finally asked.

"What did Dr. Koppel say?" Lilah asked, draping the stethoscope around her neck.

"I don't care what he says," Doug scoffed. "You're the genius. I care what you say."

"He's your doctor, Daddy."

"He says I should stop smoking."

"He's been telling you that for thirty years." Indeed, the thoughtful internist had been caring for the Graham family for as long as Lilah could remember; and despite her reluctance, as a matter of medical ethics, to become involved in her father's care, the two physicians agreed that if it made Doug Graham happy to have his daughter come by once a month and run a stethoscope over his chest and take a vial of blood, so be it. "Now, let's see if there's any red stuff in those veins," Lilah said with a wink. She took a vacutainer kit from her briefcase, swabbed the site with an alcohol prep, and uncapped the needle.

Doug Graham stiffened apprehensively. "I'm tired of being turned into a human pincushion every month."

Lilah steadied his arm and found the vein on the first try. "How's that?"

"I think you're getting the hang of it."

She laughed and inserted the vial. "Different needle, a butterfly. We use them on babies."

"Babies?" he echoed with an offended whine.

"Uh-huh. Our veins get thinner as we get older. Makes them hard to find. Brittle too. That's why you get those black-and-blues."

"He gets them because he doesn't drink his orange juice," her mother said, delivering a frosty glass to one of the snack tables. A slim, nervous woman with busy hands and anxious eyes, Marge Graham wore her SMFD T-shirt bloused over neat cotton slacks that brushed the tops of her tennis shoes. Her dismissive tone and rapid-fire delivery gave everything she said the sound of frivolous chatter. "Vitamin C prevents bruises. I keep telling your father that, but he won't listen."

"It's too pulpy," Doug Graham said with a scowl.

"Because it's fresh. Fresh has more vitamin C. You tell him, Lilah. Maybe it'll mean something coming from you." Her eyes darted about while she spoke, and settled on the television, where yet another house was engulfed in flames. "Horrible, isn't it? Those people losing everything like that . . . horrible. But as I always say—" Her voice rose with the promise of profound wisdom.

Lilah caught her father's eye, and added another knowing smile to the many they'd shared over the years.

"—the Lord giveth and the Lord taketh away," Marge chirped, not disappointing them. Then, without missing a beat, she turned to Lilah and asked, "By the way, did you park behind me again?"

Lilah nodded contritely, and went about removing the blood-filled vacutainer from its holder and then the needle from her father's arm.

"Lilah, I have to go," Marge whined impatiently. She was an energetic woman who enjoyed being busy; and along with church work and community service, Marge worked part-time at the city's credit union, a fifties-modern-style building on Fourteenth Street opposite Woodlawn Cemetery. "I have to be at work by noon, and before that I have to pick up some flowers at the market and take them to your sister. You must have a mental block when it comes to this, Lilah. I mean, you'd think by now you'd remember not to park there."

"I'll just be a few minutes," she said calmly, packing up her briefcase. "We'll leave together, okay? Soon as I make a pit stop."

Marge groaned and followed her to the bathroom. "So, anything going on?" she asked coyly.

"No, really, he's holding his own."

"I meant you, Lilah. You know. Dating. Maybe a boyfriend or something?"

"I'm afraid 'or something' is where it's at, Mom," Lilah replied, forcing a laugh.

"I'm serious, Lilah. I mean, it'd be nice to have a grandchild before your father . . ." She paused and used her eyes to finish the thought. "You're his only chance, Lilah. How much time does he have?"

"Not enough, Mom," Lilah replied sadly, her soft blue eyes reflecting her frustration. She slipped into the bathroom, closed the door, and sighed, taking refuge in the silence; then she scrubbed her hands and threw some cold water on her face, running her wet fingers through her flame-colored hair. Her lips were chapped from the hot winds, and she was applying moisturizer when she paused and tilted her head curiously, studying her face in the stained mirror.

How many hours had she spent in front of it? she wondered. How many fleeting moments had it captured? How many different Lilahs had it reflected and reassured over the years? The hormone-charged teenager aglow with the euphoria of her first sexual experience one minute—beset by nagging uncertainty the next; the cocky junior high schooler smoking her first cigarette; the awkward adolescent watching herself bud and blossom into a young woman; the precocious six-year-old playing with her mother's makeup, piling her hair on top of her head, her innocent, but knowing eyes now staring back at Lilah from the mirror, triggering waves of anxiety that washed over her in a numbing rush and struck a disturbing chord—a chord whose resonance eluded her.

Lilah pondered it for a moment, to no avail; then, without thought or hesitation, she took a vacutainer kit from her briefcase and began carefully aligning the components on the counter next to the sink. When finished, she methodically tore open the alcohol prep and swabbed the bend in her arm, then picked up the vacutainer holder, uncapped the needle, and made a fist.

CHAPTER EIGHT

Marge Graham was waiting outside the bathroom when Lilah emerged. "I'm saying it for your own good," she said, picking up where she'd left off.

Lilah sighed indulgently and went into the den to say good-bye to her father.

"A family is important, Lilah," her mother persisted.

"I want a husband, I want kids," Lilah said defensively, the sincerity in her voice leaving no doubt she meant it. "When I meet the right guy and have the time to work at a relationship."

"Work? It's supposed to be fun. Whatever happened to falling in love?"

"Marge?" Doug Graham growled over the TV. *"Marge?* Lilah's right. She has important work to do first."

"So do I," Marge lamented. "I'm going to be late."

"Give us a hug, princess," her father said.

Lilah stepped behind the recliner and wrapped her arms around his shoulders. She'd done it often recently. Each time, the hard-packed muscles she'd hugged as a child were what she expected; and each time, the bag of bones she embraced came as a troubling surprise.

"You're my girl, Lilah," her father said softly,

"I know I am, Daddy."

Doug Graham beamed with pride. He always felt energized after his checkup, after Lilah's gentle hands had spent those quiet moments gliding across his skin, bringing his drug-deadened senses back to life. He was sitting more forward in the recliner now, his attention, along with Lilah's, drawn to the rising sound of a helicopter that came from the television.

They watched intently as the chopper circled over the ocean and landed in the parking lot where Chief Decker had set up field headquarters. It was still settling down when exhausted firemen began stumbling out the door into the arms of paramedics. Merrick was the last to emerge. He was fatigued but wasn't injured, and unlike the others, walked without assistance. The media closed in, shoving microphones and video cams in his soot-blackened face.

"Lieutenant! Lieutenant Merrick!" one reporter called out over the whomp of rotors. "We understand you risked your life to save those firefighters!"

Merrick shrugged wearily.

"What happened up there?" another shouted.

"They were trapped. I went in with a hose and brought them out."

"Just like that?"

"Come on, Lieutenant, you're a hero!"

"People want to know what you did to—"

"I did my job." Merrick pushed on, making no effort to hide his discomfort, which was swiftly turning to disdain.

Doug Graham nodded in approval. "My kind of guy."

"Knew you were going to say that," Lilah said. She hugged him again and headed for the door.

"Drink your juice, Doug," Marge commanded as she fetched her purse and followed, checking that she had her beeper. "Beep me if you need anything." Doug aimed his remote control at her in reply and began frantically thumbing one of the buttons as if trying to shut her off. Lilah backed the Jaguar out of the driveway, then waved to her mother in the station wagon and drove off. She was halfway up the hill when she caught a whiff of something. Alcohol? From her arm? No, it was more pungent than that. Nail polish remover? Gasoline? Old Jags were notorious for emitting vapors. Whatever the source, the faint odor was quickly expelled by the air conditioner; and just as quickly forgotten by Lilah, who was preoccupied with more pressing matters. Indeed, she had neither time nor reason to suspect it came from the package in the backseat; no way of knowing what it contained, no way of knowing that the charcoal lighter had vaporized and—despite the obsessive burnishing—acted as a solvent for the adhesive, loosening a strip of plastic packing tape, allowing some fumes to escape.

CHAPTER NINE

Merrick fought his way past the media and headed for the barricade that cordoned off field headquarters.

"Is there an official reason why you're not being more cooperative?" one of the reporters asked.

"Yeah, I'm starving, I haven't slept in two days, and I need a shower."

"Any chance those men shouldn't have been sent in there in the first place?" another needled.

"Were safety procedures disregarded?"

"Should they have had backup?"

Merrick quickened his pace and slipped through the barricade that kept them from following.

"Merrick?" Chief Decker called out, waving him over. "Merrick, you okay?"

"Hey, they didn't get into my divorce, sex habits, or tax returns—it's your ass they're after, Roscoe."

"Well, we know *you're* not covering it, don't we?"

Merrick smiled smugly. "Something on your mind?"

"I hear you took a chance up there. A dumb one. You've always been a pain in the ass, but you've never been stupid."

"Thanks. It's kinda the opposite with you."

"Fuck you, Merrick."

"That's what she was doing," Merrick replied with a little smile.

He grabbed a couple of hours' sleep, then collected Fletcher and Logan, who had returned in the Blazer, and headed back into the canyon. Free-standing brick fireplaces and chimneys dotted the scorched terrain, which had the look of a nuclear desert. Like every other house in the area, the one the witness had located on the map had burned to the foundation. Merrick stuck a cigarette in his mouth, left it unlit, and began walking through smoldering rubble that had once been a gourmet kitchen.

"What're we looking for?" Fletcher asked.

"The kitchen sink," Merrick replied. "Any ideas how to find it?"

"Plumbing," the rookie A.I. replied.

Merrick and Logan exchanged looks and nodded.

"Okay . . . Why the sink?" Fletcher asked, wishing he'd figured it out for himself.

"Witness was looking out the window when he saw the van. Be nice to know where it was parked." Merrick crossed to a thicket of twisted pipes that came from the charred remains of an exterior wall.

This narrowed the search area to Merrick's field of vision. The three men left the burned-out kitchen and walked slowly up the hill, their eyes sweeping the ground for clues; but there were no tire impressions in the rock-hard soil, nor crushed areas of ground cover to be found. Burn pattern and wind direction finally led Merrick to a patch of scorched earth about 150 feet uphill from the house—the point from where the wind-driven inferno had started. "Looks like we got us a flash point here."

Logan donned a pressed-fiber mask and surgical gloves;

then, using a device that resembled a window screen, he began sifting the ashes for the remains of the igniter. Road flares, Molotov cocktails, butane lighters, matchbooks and cigarettes were the most common; and they often contained fingerprints or traces of saliva from which an arsonist's DNA and then blood could be typed.

Fletcher went about cordoning off the area with crime scene tape. Strung between charred stumps, the yellow streamers crisscrossed the blackened hillside, fluttering in the wind like bands of flashing neon.

Merrick knew the vortex of a rapidly expanding fire could transport the igniter vast distances from the flash point, and he drifted off in search of it. He stepped gingerly between charred boulders and blackened trees to avoid destroying or further burying anything concealed by the ash that covered the ground like gray snow. The desert-dry surface eagerly absorbed the drops of sweat that rolled from his face each time he bent to examine a piece of debris. His eyes were methodically sweeping across the terrain when they suddenly locked on to something.

The small rectangular shape was barely visible, but its right angles and sharp edges were clearly out of place amid the coal-like chunks of wood, cinders, blackened roots, and stones. He got down on all fours, pursed his lips as if kissing the ground, and gently blew a thin layer of ash aside, revealing a matchbook. The charred cover seemed on the verge of disintegrating. No advertisement for bar, bowling alley, or restaurant was visible.

Merrick's pulse quickened as he picked it up with a pair of tweezers and turned the edge to the light. Captured between the burned match heads and charred cover, he saw what he thought were a few shards of tobacco, powerfully suggesting this was the igniter.

TOUCHED BY FIRE

Though darkened by intense heat, the back cover was intact; and, as with most safety matches, that's where the friction strip was located. This meant that the matchbook had to be turned over before a match could be struck; and there, bonded to the varnish used to give the cover its slick shiny finish, there, where the arsonist held it while striking a match, Merrick's weary eyes detected the pale ghost of a thumbprint.

CHAPTER TEN

The Jaguar accelerated into the parking garage and began circling up to the next level. Midway down the aisle, it swerved into a space, almost clipping Cardenas, who was leaning against the concrete lattice in his lab coat. The car was still settling when Lilah popped the door and leaped from behind the wheel. "Sorry about that, Ruben."

"Hey, no problem, I work for a doctor."

Lilah smiled at him and opened the back door. "Thanks for coming down."

"Anytime, boss. What do you need?"

"A thirty-hour day." Lilah took her briefcase from the backseat, set it on the roof, and removed three blood specimen tubes from one of the pockets. "This one goes to the medical lab. . . ."

Cardenas squinted at the label. "What's that say?"

"Douglas C. Graham."

"It does?" Cardenas groaned, pulling a sleeve across his face that glistened with perspiration. "I'll never get into med school, my handwriting's too legible."

"Give it time."

"The usual? CBC and plasma? Reports to you and Dr. Koppel?"

"Uh-huh."

"How's your dad doing by the way?"

"Holding his own," Lilah replied, handing Cardenas the other specimen tubes. "I scored these for OX-A."

Cardenas brightened, then raised a curious brow. One tube had a consent form rubber-banded around it. The other didn't. "We're missing a C.F. here, Doc."

"I ran out."

"Okay. I'll hold it till you have a chance to—"

"I don't know," Lilah interrupted. "This conference is breathing down my neck. Better get it in the works."

"Without a number?"

"I really need you to do this for me, Ruben," she pleaded, asking for a favor instead of pulling rank. "Get a blank C.F. from the file, put a bar-code sticker on the specimen, have Serena log it in, and leave the form on my desk. I'll take care of it soon as I can."

Cardenas nodded and slipped the three tubes into the pocket of his lab coat.

"Thanks a bunch. Oh, and put this in my office, will you?" She took the package addressed to Lilah E. Graham from the car and handed it to him, then hurried to the medical school.

Lilah spent the afternoon teaching class. Darkness had fallen by the time she finished. She hurried to the gym and threw herself into a series of exercises designed to defy gravity and the onslaught of genetic coding that she feared was turning her into her mother.

About an hour later she'd showered and was toweling off in front of her locker when her cellular twittered. She draped the towel around her neck, then took the phone from her briefcase. "Hello?"

"Lilah? Lilah, it's Paul."

"Paul?" she wondered, pretending she didn't recognize the name. "Paul? Gee, I don't think I—"

"I know, I know," Schaefer groaned contritely. "I should've gotten back to you sooner, but I've been up to my ass and—" A chorus of female voices screeched through the phone from her end, interrupting him. "Lilah? Lilah, where are you?"

"I'm in the buff," she replied with a giggle, as a group of towel-snapping students sauntered past. "I just got out of the shower and—"

"Lilah," Schaefer admonished. He sat up straighter and set his glasses on the desk. "Don't start, Lilah."

"I'm not starting," she purred in a sexy whisper. "I'm standing in front of my locker . . . massaging my breasts with your favorite moisturizer. You know . . . the smooth, silky stuff that really gets me going whenever you—"

"No, and I don't recall dialing a nine-hundred number, either."

"This *is* the guy who said I could always turn to phone sex if my career went south, isn't it?"

"Look, Lilah," Schaefer said sharply, sensing a clinical reply had the best chance of neutralizing her. "You left me a very businesslike message, and I was very pleased by it. The emotional detachment and strength in your voice indicated you'd made some progress; but what I'm hearing now suggests otherwise. If you can't keep this on a professional plane, I'm afraid we'll have to forget it."

"Of course I can," Lilah said, forcing a laugh. She pulled the towel around her torso, disappointed in herself, disappointed that after being detached and strong, she'd blown it the first chance she got.

"Good," he said, glad she couldn't see the relief in his eyes. "You mentioned the prison study is a go . . ."

"Uh-huh. We're due up there at ten on Monday."

Schaefer's brows arched with concern. "You're right, we'd better make sure we're on the same page."

A half hour later they were in a booth at Mario's, a pasta palace on the corner of Broxton that had treated the neighborhood to the heady odor of garlic for more than twenty-five years. The waiters were so surly and the decor so offensive that the food had to be cheap and good, which was why the place was always packed.

"Monday . . ." Schaefer mused, twirling a forkful of angel hair with one hand and accessing an organizer with the other. It had a calendar, phone directory, memo pad, calculator, fax modem, and interface for exchanging data with computers. "My weekend's jammed. We're taking the kids to Sea World. No time to prepare. Maybe if you—"

"Don't back out of this, Paul," Lilah interrupted, assuming the worst, her soft blue eyes pleading from beneath perfectly arched brows. "Don't do this to me."

"Let me finish," Schaefer intoned reassuringly. "I was going to say, if you go up there alone on Monday and knock off all the blood specimens, it'd buy me until the next session to get up to speed."

Lilah vehemently shook her head no, sending her damp ponytail snapping from side to side. "Bad idea. We have to do each prisoner from beginning to end, and we have to do them together."

Schaefer's fork paused in mid-twirl. "Why? I just told you I'm up to my ass."

"Let *me* finish, okay? These guys," Lilah resumed, lowering her voice, "these fucking rapists and child abusers, they signed up for this study but they don't have a clue what's coming next, right?"

Schaefer dabbed at his mustache with a napkin, then nodded impatiently. "I'm fully able to empathize."

Lilah smiled good-naturedly. "The point is, each one of these—these degenerates who's taken a child's innocence or a woman's dignity, maybe their sanity, is going to be a little anxious when he enters a room and finds a woman there. A woman who's going to take something from *him*."

Schaefer frowned and cocked his head skeptically.

Lilah pressed on, undaunted. "A woman who orders him to roll up his sleeve, ties a tourniquet around his arm, and stabs him with a needle."

"Jeezus," Schaefer exclaimed, taken aback. "You make drawing blood sound like an act of violence."

Lilah nodded mischievously. "Hey, who knows what buttons it might push?"

"I'd like to know what's pushing yours."

"My genes," she replied with a laugh. "Come on, this thing's been controversial from the get-go anyway."

"I don't know. It's an extremely risky concept."

"You make that sound like a negative," Lilah joked, her eyes glowing with enthusiasm. "I didn't get where I am by playing it safe. Neither did you."

Schaefer studied her for a moment, captured by the infectious spirit and willingness to take risks that had first attracted him to her, then broke into a wry smile. "You know, Lilah, as mad scientists go—"

"I'm the maddest. I know. Come on, what do you say?"

"Well," Schaefer mused, warming to the idea, "it could provoke some intriguing behavioral dynamics." Lilah was beaming in triumph when he glanced at his watch and began to slide from the booth. "I have to make a call."

"Use my cellular."

"Thanks. Need to make a pit stop too."

He's calling his wife, Lilah thought as Schaefer moved off. She was toying with a piece of grilled shrimp when snippets of conversation about "tissue sections" and "mast cells" drew her attention to a group of medical students who had entered the restaurant. The cavelike darkness and thickets of plastic vegetation allowed her only fleeting glimpses at first, but as the students made their way to a table, the glow from a cluster of illuminated grapes raked their faces, confirming that the lean, curly-haired guy hitting on his twenty-something classmate with the pouty lips and perky breasts was exactly who Lilah thought it was.

Thankful for the garish divider that concealed her, Lilah sighed and stared at the shrimp impaled on her fork. Nothing could fill the hollowness now. Nothing could satisfy the gut-wrenching emptiness that rocked her. Not even Mario's legendary gamberetti a l'aglio. She knew it was childish, knew Kauffman was a meaningless roll in the sack. Even he was mature enough to know all she was doing was getting her rocks off. She was a grown woman who'd survived more than her share of busted relationships. Why did it always hurt so much? she wondered. Why did she always feel so vulnerable and anxious? Why this overwhelming sense of impending doom that always came over her when she felt rejected, or found herself manless?

She was still lost in her thoughts when Schaefer emerged from the restaurant's dingy recesses. "I've got piles of work to do before Monday," she said, anxious to leave before Kauffman spotted them. "And I'm dying for a cigarette. Cover the check, and we'll settle up later. Okay?"

Lilah left the restaurant, digging the pack of Virginia Slims from her briefcase. She lit up as she walked, and charged down Weyburn oblivious to the glow of wildfires streaking skyward behind the mountains. The winds were still blistering hot, and the streets were jammed with students seeking refuge in the movie houses and eateries. After several blocks she flicked the half-smoked cigarette into the gutter and took an air-conditioned shortcut through Bullock's. Like most Southern California department stores, the longtime Westwood landmark—which had recently been bought by, and renamed, Macy's—remained open till nine P.M.

Its 1950s fieldstone facade spanned the entire block on two levels, with entrances from Weyburn on the lower, where Lilah entered, and Le Conte on the upper—devoted to women's clothing, accessories, fragrances, and the like—where Lilah exited opposite the Stein Eye Institute. The latter, one of UCLA's many prestigious medical facilities, had been founded by Dr. Jules Stein who—personifying the Hollywood adage that everyone in L.A. has two businesses, their own and the movies—had also founded MCA/Universal Studios.

Lilah crossed the street, taking another shortcut between a brick wall and a towering stand of pines to where a section of fence had been removed, providing mid-block access to the campus. The respite from the heat was momentary, and she was drenched with perspiration by the time she arrived at Mac-Med.

"Been shopping again, Dr. Graham?" the security guard said cheerily, drawing her attention to the Macy's shopping bag clutched in her fist.

Lilah stared at it for a long moment, having no recollection whatsoever of making a purchase, then forced a confused smile and entered the elevator. The instant the door closed, she reached into the bag and removed something wrapped in tissue paper, something that appeared to be shiny and red. She was about to tear off the tissue when the elevator stopped and the door opened to reveal Serena striding down the corridor toward her. Lilah quickly shoved whatever it was back into the shopping bag and hurried from the elevator.

"Lilah . . ." Serena called out cheerily in her mild accent; then, never missing an opportunity to needle her boss, she added, "I can't remember the last time I ran into you here at this hour."

"Sounds like the onset of Alzheimer's to me," Lilah teased without breaking stride.

"Really? I distinctly recall leaving a consent form on your desk—a blank one," Serena said pointedly. "Ruben said you'd take care of it straightaway."

"Straightaway," Lilah echoed, too distracted by the mysterious purchase to talk shop.

"I flagged it in the computer in case you . . ." Serena let it trail off and shrugged resignedly as Lilah turned the corner, heading toward her office.

Lilah went straight to her desk, without noticing the package with the bold angry printing that Cardenas had put on the table beneath the bookshelves. She set the shopping bag down and removed the contents. Wrapped in the tissue she found a silk, fire-engine-red teddy. It had a peekaboo bodice, fluttery side slits, and a $350 price tag that made her gasp. She pinched the thin straps between thumb and forefinger and held the slinky garment out in front of her as if she'd never seen it before, let alone purchased it.

Stunned and shaken, she stuffed the teddy back into the shopping bag, then dropped into her chair, steadying her hands long enough to light a cigarette. Her lips were pursed to blow out the match when her eyes became drawn to the flame, and she began rocking back and forth like a hyperactive child unable to sit still in class; then she began swiveling left and right until it seemed as if the chair was spinning one way and the room the other—spinning faster and faster in opposite directions until everything began to blur in horizontal streaks that ended with a headlong rush into the all too familiar explosions of colored light, leaving her dazed and disoriented.

The next thing Lilah knew, the cellular was in her hand—she'd evidently already made some calls: among them, one to her service and one to the answering machine in her condo, because there was a short list of messages jotted on a pad—and now it dawned on her that she must have also just autodialed her parents' number because she could hear her mother's voice saying, "Hello? Hello, is anyone there?"

"Oh—oh yeah . . . hi, Mom, it's me," Lilah said, blinking at the fluorescents as she came out of it. "Is Daddy there?"

"Of course. Hold on a sec."

"No, no don't bother him, it's okay."

"I don't understand, Lilah. You asked for your father but you don't want to talk to him?"

"I just wanted to know if he was there."

"Where else would he be?"

"How would I know?" Lilah replied weakly, feeling confused. "Listen, I have to go," she said, suddenly struck by an overwhelming desire to get out of there. "Yeah, I'm still at the office . . . No, no don't worry, I won't."

She hung up and was taking a moment to pull herself together when she thought she smelled something vaguely familiar, something she couldn't place. She dismissed her concern with a glance to the ashtray, and was crossing to the door when she smelled the acrid, fuel-like odor again. She began sniffing the air, finally zeroing in on the package. She had no idea what it contained, no idea that the fire bomb had just been activated, that the lightbulb filament had ignited the book of matches, that the fuel-sprinkled excelsior was already aflame inside. She was reaching for the carton to open it when the phone on her desk rang, startling her. She froze momentarily, then scooped the receiver from the cradle. "Genetics—Dr. Graham."

"Hey, what do you like on your pizza, Doc?"

"Kauffman?" she wondered, displeased by the elation she heard in her voice.

"Your own personal pizza man, who else?" he replied with a cocky chortle. "I can handle anything but pineapple."

Yeah, and med students with pouty lips and perky boobs, she thought, tempted to reveal she'd been at Mario's and tease him that he was calling her because he'd struck out. "You're something else, you know?"

"Hey, all the professors I sleep with say that."

Lilah laughed in spite of herself, and glanced over her shoulder at the carton. "Yeah," she said, deciding not to play hard to get, "but this one means it."

"Agggh," the kid groaned, pretending that he was crushed. "I knew it. I'm nothing more than a sex object."

"A sex object who got into med school. Not bad for a guy with three strikes against him."

"Three?"

"You're white, you're male, and you're Jewish."

"How do you know I'm Jewish?"

"I had the misfortune to acquire intimate knowledge of your shortcomings, remember?" They were both laughing when Lilah suddenly screamed, then screamed again, startled by a deafening pop and blinding flash that erupted behind her when the combustion inside the box had amassed enough pressure to blow it apart at the seams. The Ziploc bag had already melted, exposing the incendiary mixture to the oxygen-rich air that rushed into the carton. Lilah whirled just as it ignited in a fireball. The intense heat vaporized the corrugated board like flash paper. Sheets of flame raced up the wall to the ceiling. Waves of fiery sludge rolled across the table and onto the floor like molten lava.

"Kauffman! Kauffmannnn!" Lilah screamed, her voice trailing off in a terrified wail.

"Lilah? Doc? Doc Graham?" Kauffman shouted into the phone. "Doc, what's going on? You okay?"

CHAPTER ELEVEN

The wail of sirens and throaty bark of Klaxons echoed off Westwood's glass-walled towers as a caravan of fire trucks thundered down Wilshire Boulevard.

Moments earlier, Mac-Med's detection system had automatically set off internal fire alarms, broadcast an evacuation announcement over the intercom, and transmitted a signal to the fire station on Veteran Avenue a quarter mile away. Within thirty seconds every piece of equipment in its arsenal was rolling.

Kauffman had dashed from the restaurant and was sprinting north on Westwood Boulevard toward UCLA's main gate when the fire trucks rumbled past him. From there it was a straight two-block run to Mac-Med. The chunky six-story building, wrapped in bands of harsh red brick and waffle-iron window grids, sat atop a forbidding concrete bunker. A sweeping staircase cut into one side led to an entrance plaza above. The entire area was being cordoned off with barricades by campus security when Kauffman arrived.

Emergency flashers swept through the darkness. Radios hissed and crackled with the detached voices of dispatchers. Firemen in their clunky boots, protective coats, and helmets ran in every direction. Some were connecting pumpers to hydrants and pulling hoses into the lobby; others were extending an aerial ladder and its platform-mounted water cannon to a window in Lilah's office that had shattered from the heat. Flames shot from the opening and licked at the facade, which was blackening from billowing smoke.

The chaotic scene confirmed Kauffman's fears that Lilah was in extreme danger. Drenched with sweat, gasping for breath, he fought through the crowd of onlookers, eluded a security guard, and vaulted the barricade. The guard pursued him to a group of firefighters who were reviewing blueprints that were spread across the hood of a campus security cruiser.

Captain Singer was in charge. A soft-spoken man with decisive eyes, he was noting the location of biohazard and radioactive symbols when Kauffman arrived. He held off the guard long enough for the kid to tell his story; then he assembled a rescue team and led the way into the building in search of Lilah. They trudged up four flights with their equipment and clumsy air tanks, then down a hazy corridor into the genetics lab. Thick smoke and torrential rains from the sprinkler system cut visibility to almost zero.

"Dr. Graham!" Singer called out. "Hello? Dr. Graham! Doc! Doc, you in here?"

There was no reply; no sound other than the rush of water and sharp crackle of fire. The sprinklers had contained it but hadn't come close to extinguishing the inferno that was still raging in Lilah's office. Several walls had already crumbled, and rhythmic waves of blue-orange flames were washing over the debris, threatening to engulf the entire lab.

The firefighters moved between the workstations, knocking down flames and flare-ups as they searched for

Lilah. Several made their way to the administrative area and found her at a wall of file cabinets. She was soaked to the skin and choking on the heavy smoke despite the scarf tied over her nose and mouth; and in defiance of the screaming alarm, raging flames, and intense heat, she was frantically trying to save the precious OX-A data from being destroyed. Lilah had already filled her briefcase with boxes of computer diskettes, and was now slipping packets of autorads into the Macy's shopping bag.

"Dr. Graham!" Singer shouted, grasping her shoulders. "Time to get out of here!"

"This data hasn't been archived!" she replied as she pulled free and whirled to the files. "And we've got all these subzero reefers. The temperature's critical—years of work—I mean, if the emergency power hasn't kicked in—"

Singer and several of his men picked her up and carried her from the lab along with the briefcase and shopping bag. Between protests and gasps for breath, Lilah told the captain about the box that had exploded and burst into flame.

Kauffman was beside himself with anxiety by the time the firemen escorted Lilah from the building and turned her over to paramedics. Relieved that she was safe, he decided discretion was the better part of valor this time and kept his distance. She was being treated for minor burns and smoke inhalation when Captain Singer poked his head inside the van. "Thought you'd want to know the fire's been knocked down, and the emergency power *is* on."

"Thanks. Can I go back up there now?"

"Not till it cools down. Besides, we're still checking for radioactivity." He noticed a vehicle rumble to a stop on the far side of the paramedic van and hurried toward it.

A short time later Lilah was sitting in the open door of

the van with a cigarette—despite a paramedic's advice that she lay off for a few days—when a shaggy, broad-shouldered man came toward her. An attaché case hung from his fist. His face was strained and smudged with soot. Massive rings of perspiration radiated from his armpits, darkening his shirt.

"Dr. Graham?"

Lilah nodded, squinting at the reflection that came from his badge.

"Lieutenant Merrick, Arson Squad. How're you doing?"

She sighed and mumbled, "Rotten."

"Me too." Merrick took a family-size bottle of Tums from a pocket and pulled the cap. He tossed a few into his mouth, then offered it to her.

"No thanks, but I'll have one of *those*," she replied, pointing to his cigarette.

Merrick slipped the pack from a pocket and thumbed the top. "The captain tells me somebody mailed you a hot potato."

Lilah lit one cigarette from the other and nodded.

"What'd it look like?"

"A box," she replied, sizing it with her hands.

"Addressed to you?"

Lilah nodded again.

"Scribbled? Printed? Neat? Sloppy?"

"Neat. Bold, black printing."

"Any idea who sent it?"

She shrugged forlornly, then exhaled, filling the space between them with smoke. "I just want to get back into my lab, Lieutenant. I've got a conference in less than a month and—"

"It's a crime scene, Doc," Merrick interrupted. "Nobody goes in there till I check it out; and I can't do that until it—"

"Cools down. I know," she said wearily.

"You have any enemies?"

"Not that I know of. I guess I rub my share of people the wrong way, like everybody else."

"Any of 'em loners?"

Lilah shrugged, then shook her head no.

"Low self-esteem, poor verbal skills?"

"This *is* a university, Lieutenant," she replied with a smile.

"Yeah, well," Merrick grunted impatiently. "Pyros are loaded with problems. Some are real good at hiding them. You ever get any threatening calls or mail?"

"No, never," she replied, baffled by it all.

Merrick was mulling it over when Captain Singer joined them. "We can go in now."

"We can?" Lilah said, brightening.

"It's your call, Dan," Singer said.

"No, it's mine," Lilah corrected. "It's my lab, and I have to get in there." She pushed past Merrick and strode toward the entrance. The determination in her voice moved him, but it was the matter of life-and-death plea in those soulful blue eyes that convinced Merrick not to stop her.

In the lobby, a fireman directed them to an elevator that had been cleared for use. "You teach?" Merrick asked as they got in and it started to rise.

"Uh-huh."

"Ever flunk anybody?"

"Came close a couple of times."

"What about a Dr. Kildare wannabe who couldn't get into med school?"

"There are jillions of them, but I'm not involved with admissions."

"What do you do in your lab?"

"Bench research."

"You use animals?"

"No. Humans." She cocked her head, reconsidering, and smiled. "Some of them might qualify."

"I was thinking the animal rights gang."

"I know. They broke into some labs here a couple of years ago. Contaminated all the experiments . . . a disaster."

"You think of any groups who have it in for *you*?"

"Other than large segments of the psychiatric and sociological communities, neuroscientists, all major religions, and most minority and antidefamation groups, no."

"That narrows it. What're you into, kiddie porn?"

"Molecular biology." She sensed his uncertainty and added, "Genetics. You know. The crazies who are going to make two-headed monsters with rat tails and shark's teeth."

"Are you?"

"Naw," Lilah replied with a pregnant pause. "We already have enough politicians."

Merrick had become preoccupied with a thought and nodded blankly; but Captain Singer laughed. He was still smiling when the elevator came to a stop. The door rolled open, and the acrid smell of fire hit them with an intensity that made their eyes glisten and burn. A smoky haze was drifting in the corridor. Water was gushing from under doors and rolling across the carpet.

"Genetics a competitive field?" Merrick prompted.

"They all are."

"What about jealous colleagues?"

"Ditto. You suggesting it was sabotage?"

"What do you think?"

"Anything's possible, I guess."

Merrick nodded pensively and led the way into the lab. Steam hissed from piles of smoldering rubble. Charred debris floated in inch-deep water. Columns of smoke twisted upward, mushrooming against the ceiling in the dim glow of emergency lights. The lab was a mess, but the sprinklers had saved it from being completely incinerated.

Lilah paused briefly, taking it all in, then, ponytail swinging from side to side, she ran to a room at the far side of the lab where the freezers were located. The digital thermometer on each control panel read -70, as did the circular graph—visible through the Plexiglas window that protected it—on which a stylus had charted temperature variations over the entire incubation period. This meant that, like the contents of standard household refrigerators, which often survive fires, the hundreds of DNA samples that the laboratory freezers contained—the painstakingly prepared blots that had been made radioactive and sandwiched with X-ray film to produce autorads—hadn't been destroyed. Lilah sighed with relief and crossed toward her office.

Twisted and misshapen by the intense heat, the steel door frame stood alone amid heaps of rubble that had once been walls. It looked more like a coal mine that had caught fire than an office. Lilah was shocked by the extent of the destruction, and stared into the cavern of charred surfaces, smoldering hulks of furniture, and mounds of sopping wet gunk. Most of the ceiling panels had vaporized; sections of the aluminum grid had sagged or fallen, causing lighting fixtures to hang from their cables at odd angles. The shattered window perfectly framed the fireman atop the ladder outside. Manning work lights and water cannon, he seemed to levitate in the darkness, ready to pounce on any flare-ups.

Merrick was standing amid the debris, sniffing the air, when Lilah entered. "Real careful, Doc," he ordered. "Don't touch anything." He sniffed the air again, nose wrinkling curiously at a whiff of something familiar.

"Gasoline?" Lilah ventured.

Merrick shook his head no. It had the same head-clearing impact of most petroleum-based accelerants but a more pronounced nose-burning sting. "Napthalene."

"What?"

"Napthalene. Probably from mothballs. They're a popular ingredient in home-brewed incendiaries."

Lilah raised a brow in tribute.

Merrick produced a small flashlight and studied the burn pattern that radiated from what had once been a wall of bookshelves. The table that had stood in front of them—the one that had held the incendiary device—had been destroyed by the fire. The granite top had broken into pieces when it crashed to the floor. Merrick put the flashlight in his mouth to free his hands and used a telescoping pointer to gently poke through the charred debris, uncovering remnants of the corrugated box, a few bits of wire, the shattered casing of the battery that had exploded, and an unidentifiable blob of melted black plastic from which a length of wire protruded.

"Find something?" Lilah prompted.

Merrick waggled a hand and took the flashlight from his mouth. "Might be part of a timer or triggering device. What's left of it anyway. This wasn't some nut tossing a book of matches into a canyon to get his rocks off."

"Pardon me?"

TOUCHED BY FIRE

"Sorry, I didn't mean to be crude."

"I'm not offended, Lieutenant," she said. "I was just curious what you meant."

"Well . . ." He paused and slipped an evidence bag from his attaché case. "A lot of arsonists are sexually stimulated by fire."

"Really?"

Merrick nodded matter-of-factly.

"Are you?" Lilah prompted flirtatiously, making eye contact when he looked up.

Merrick held her gaze. "I get off by catching them, Doc," he retorted smartly, his lip curling with a mixture of discomfort and disdain.

Lilah did a little double take, certain she'd seen that expression before. "You know," she said, trying to place him, "you look kind of familiar."

"Lots of people say that."

"The TV," she said as it dawned on her. "You're the guy who saved those firemen up in Malibu, aren't you?"

Merrick nodded humbly, then picked up the lump of melted plastic with tweezers and slipped it into one of the evidence bags. He was filling in the data block when his cellular phone started twittering.

It was Gonzalez calling from the Ops Center.

"Come on, Gonzo. I'm still at UCLA for Chrissakes . . . Where? . . . Calabasas? No, dammit, it's not on my way home, and you know it . . . Yeah, yeah, yeah . . . Fuck . . . Okay . . . Hey, take yes for an answer, okay?" Merrick clicked off, then crossed to Captain Singer, who was supervising the cooling down operation. "I got another call, Cap. You're gonna have to seal this place off for me."

"He's your man," Singer replied, introducing Merrick to Chief Copeland, director of campus security. A retired deputy LAPD commander, he was having dinner at his home in Simi Valley—an hour's drive from UCLA—when notified of the fire, and had just arrived.

"I've already ordered the C.S. be secured," Copeland said in a tone that rang with territorial imperative.

Merrick sized him up, then nodded. "Just out of curiosity, your surveillance cameras tied in to VCRs?"

"Exterior units only. We'll run the tape for CRD and let you know if anything turns up."

"Appreciate the offer," Merrick said, deciding that if there was any crime-related data on the tape, he'd find it himself. "But I'm gonna need a copy. Leave a message with dispatch, and I'll pick it up."

Copeland nodded grudgingly.

"By the way, nobody touches anything in there until I say so. Dr. Graham included."

Lilah was staring numbly at the black hole that had been her office when she noticed Merrick leaving the lab. She hurried past Copeland and dashed between the workstations in pursuit, bursting into the corridor to see Merrick entering the elevator. "Hey! Hey, Lieutenant, wait!" she called out, managing to slip inside just as the door was closing. "Where you going?"

"Another fire."

"What about this one?"

"It's on hold for a while."

Lilah's eyes clouded with disappointment.

"Sorry. Hot weather brings all the weirdos out of the woodwork. It looks like one of them tried to turn you into a french fry." Merrick fished a business card from a breast pocket and handed it to her. "Give me a call if you think of anyone who'd want to kill you."

A surge of adrenaline set Lilah's heart pounding wildly

in her chest. She was thunderstruck by the remark and was staring at him in stunned silence when the elevator stopped. Merrick bolted through the door before it had fully opened. A few seconds passed before Lilah pulled herself together and ran after him, hurrying across the lobby and through the door into the plaza. Merrick was on the far side pushing through a group of reporters who had converged on the Blazer. He climbed behind the wheel, started the engine, and set the emergency flasher on the roof. Lilah pressed on undaunted. She was a few feet from the vehicle when Merrick slammed it in gear and drove off without so much as a nod.

Lilah recoiled at the ear-piercing screech of tires, then watched numbly as the Blazer's taillights vanished in the distance. The wail of its siren rose in intensity along with the unnerving feeling in the pit of Lilah's stomach. She swallowed hard to keep from wretching, then looked about anxiously at those around her. Merrick's offhanded remark had pierced her armor, shattering her carefully crafted denial; and she had suddenly realized that her reckless disregard for her own safety, her obsessive concern for her work, her initial hostility toward Merrick, her subsequent attempts at levity and coy flirtations had all been part of a subconscious diversion, a way to avoid coping with the terrifying knowledge that someone had tried to kill her.

CHAPTER TWELVE

Serena Chen and Paul Schaefer had been at the security desk in the lobby when Lilah ran from the elevator after Merrick. They were among a group of researchers who'd heard about the fire and were trying to get up to their offices and labs. Only those with Mac-Med ID were being allowed inside, and even *they* were told to wait in the lobby until the building was declared safe. Lilah had been too intent on her pursuit to notice her colleagues, but they saw her dash past. The Blazer was long gone and she was still standing at the curb, staring blankly into the darkness when they caught up to her.

"Lilah?" Schaefer called out. "Lilah, what happened?"

She turned toward him but was blinded by lights mounted atop TV cameras as a jostling mob of reporters encircled her, elbowing her two colleagues aside.

"What *did* happen up there, Dr. Graham?" one of the reporters demanded, thrusting a microphone in Lilah's face.

"Was it an accident?" another shouted.

"We heard an arson investigator was here!"

"Was the fire intentional?"

Lilah looked confused and overwhelmed. "I don't know," she replied weakly, too shaken to explain.

The questions were still coming rapid-fire when Serena

knifed her wiry frame between two reporters. "That will be all for now," she announced, her voice ringing with clipped British authority. "Dr. Graham will have an official statement tomorrow." She took Lilah's arm and smoothly extricated her.

Schaefer ran interference as they crossed to the entrance. One of the security officers cleared them into the lobby; others kept the media from following as Serena impulsively pulled Lilah into an embrace. "Good heavens," the junior researcher exclaimed. "Are you all right?"

Lilah nodded and clung to her tightly. Her colleague's reaction was clearly heartfelt, and more than welcome, despite their professional jousting.

"I'd just arrived home when security called," Serena went on breathlessly. "Have we lost everything?"

"No, thank God. The reefers are okay, and I saved most of the—" Lilah stopped abruptly and looked around as if she'd misplaced something. Spotting Captain Singer standing amid the tangle of hoses that covered the floor, she rushed toward him. "My briefcase, my shopping bag? What happened to them?"

The captain smiled reassuringly and directed her to the security desk, where he'd stashed them for safekeeping. Lilah was just rejoining her colleagues when she glimpsed Kauffman peering through one of the windows and averted her eyes.

"I know this isn't a good time, Lilah," Schaefer said, "but what do you want to do about Monday?"

Lilah appeared puzzled. "Monday?"

"The prison . . ."

Lilah shrugged, obviously unable to deal with it.

"Why don't you let us arrange a postponement?"

Schaefer offered. "You know, a few days, until you're back up to speed."

Lilah smiled numbly and nodded.

"Well," Schaefer said, sensing she was hoping for a bit of chivalry he couldn't provide, "I'd like to see you home, but I've really got to get going."

Lilah nodded and tried to contain her emotions. Schaefer's instincts were right. She felt vulnerable and alone, and had wanted him to escort her. And, more than ever, she wished she had someone to come home to.

"I've a thought," Serena said brightly. "Why don't *I* drop you off? I'd be happy to keep you company for a while. Perhaps we can catalogue this data you've rescued? Take your mind off things . . ."

Lilah hesitated, wondering if Serena had an ulterior motive, but petty animosities paled in comparison to her fragile state. "Thanks, that would be nice."

Kauffman watched from a distance as they left the building and hurried through the windy plaza toward the parking structure. He knew the nature of their relationship kept Lilah from acknowledging him, but he still felt empty as he slung his backpack over a shoulder and started down the broad staircase.

A short time later the two women were in Serena's Mazda, winding up the hill to the condominium complex. They parked on the street and were walking through the courtyard when Lilah's eyes darted anxiously to the bank of mailboxes. Several were adorned with a yellow slip of paper, indicating a package in the receiving room; but none had been taped to hers.

Greatly relieved, she led Serena into her apartment, then excused herself to shed her damp clothes, take a quick shower, and pull on some sweats. When she returned, Serena was sitting on the living-room floor hunched over a laptop computer. She'd removed a packet of autorads from the Macy's shopping bag and was logging the bar-code numbers.

Lilah fetched a couple of beers and began removing the boxes of computer diskettes from her briefcase. "That was quick thinking before. Thanks for getting me out of there."

"I didn't think a whit, believe me," Serena confessed, typing in another bar code. "I just did it. By the way, who was that grungy fellow who drove off?"

"The arson investigator."

"An arson investigator, driving a *Blazer*?" Serena exclaimed incredulously. "Takes his work seriously, doesn't he?"

Lilah nodded glumly. "He thinks someone tried to kill me."

Serena's jaw slackened. "You're quite serious, aren't you?"

"Quite."

"My God, Lilah, I'd no idea. Really, I thought perhaps a bit of levity might . . ." Serena let it trail off and shuddered at the thought. "Good heavens . . . why?"

Lilah shrugged, and pulled her knees up under her chin. A long silence passed before they resumed cataloguing the items. They'd been at it for almost an hour when Serena got to the bottom of the shopping bag and came upon the bright red teddy.

"Lilah!" she exclaimed, whisking it out of the bag.

Lilah shrugged. "It's going back," she said, preferring not to get into the details.

"Really? I find it rather fetching." Serena eyed her as if making a decision, then dangled the slinky lingerie in front of her. "And I daresay, I'd find it all the more fetching on you."

Lilah took a moment to comprehend what her protégée seemed to be suggesting. "Something tells me there's a side of you I don't know about, Serena."

Serena peered from within the shiny black mane that framed her face and smiled seductively. "We all have one, don't we?"

She did have an ulterior motive, Lilah thought, but it was more personal than professional. Lilah exhaled a long stream of smoke, then slowly put out her cigarette. "Sleeping with the boss seems to be taking on a whole new meaning these days, doesn't it?"

Serena moved closer and put an arm around Lilah comfortingly. "It could," she said softly.

An intrigued smile betrayed Lilah's thoughts. Usually, her sense of adventure and appetite for danger would have prompted her to consider taking such a risk, but tonight it was her need to be held, to be comforted, to feel protected; and there was a surprising tenderness in Serena's moist, almond-shaped eyes, and a softness to her touch that sent a rippling sensation to the tips of Lilah's extremities.

Lilah's eyes darted about in search of a mirror, as they always did when she was in need of reassurance. She caught sight of herself in the one in the entry and studied the image, making her decision. "I really appreciate everything you did for me tonight, Serena—" she said, her voice breaking slightly.

Serena smiled thinly, knowingly. "Something tells me that teddy *is* going back, isn't it?"

Lilah nodded. "I just don't think I could handle it. I hope you understand."

"Of course," Serena replied, lowering her eyes contritely. She was flustered now, and took a moment to collect herself. "I don't know what to say, Lilah. I'm afraid I was more than a bit out of line. I can't imagine what came over me."

"An impulse," Lilah offered generously. Then, glancing with concern to the teddy, she added, "We both seem to be having trouble resisting them tonight."

CHAPTER THIRTEEN

Lilah was exhausted, but her brain refused to shut down, and she'd been lying awake in the darkness for several hours. Her eyes had just begun to close when the phone rang. "Yeah?" she whispered sleepily, fumbling with the receiver.

"Lilah? Oh, I'm so glad you're there!" Marge Graham shrieked excitedly.

Lilah bolted upright in the bed. "Is it Daddy?" she asked, assuming the worst because of the hour.

"No, he's fine. What about you? I couldn't sleep, so I put on the TV. They had something about a fire at UCLA. The genetics lab. *Well*, you can imagine what I—"

"Mom? *Mom* . . . I'm fine . . . Uh-huh, you're right, I should've called . . . No, just exhausted. I'll fill you in tomorrow, okay? . . . Promise."

Lilah hung up, sagged against the headboard and lit a cigarette. The flare of the match brought the evening's events back in a numbing rush. She inhaled deeply and shuddered at the words that were ringing in her head.

It wasn't her mother's shrill chatter that she heard, but Dan Merrick's dispassionate probing: You have any enemies? Genetics a competitive field? What about jealous colleagues? Any enemies? Competitive field? Jealous colleagues? Enemies? Competitive? Jealous? Colleagues? Colleagues? Colleagues?

Her eyes darted from one mirror to the next, and then the next; and then to the sweep of black hair beside her. Despite their awkward moment, Lilah really hadn't wanted to be alone, and she'd insisted that Serena keep her company. Now, she watched Serena's chest rise and fall in a steady rhythm.

The phone rang again, snapping her out of it.

The caller apologized for the hour and identified himself as a reporter. Lilah hung up and unplugged the phone, then sat staring into the darkness until the first rays of light painted the room a dusty pink and the rising wind rattled the windows in their frames.

The morning news shows led with the wildfires and Santa Ana winds that were still fanning them. A reed-thin fellow sporting a boutonniere was strutting across the TV screen doing the five-day forecast. "That's right, folks, we're looking at *more* dry air, *more* gusting winds, and *more* double-zero digits!" he exclaimed with the goofy enthusiasm that afflicts L.A.'s all-male corps of weather reporters. "We're talking a hundred-plus degrees out there today! And *no* end to the fire season in sight! Marta?" he prompted cheerily, handing off to one of L.A.'s many double-minority newsreaders.

"Thanks for putting it all in perspective for us, Lannie." She lowered her voice and in a grave tone repeated, "*No end in sight*. Indeed, despite the heroic efforts of firefighters, the Las Flores, Trancas, and Calabasas wildfires are still burning and are *all* of suspicious origin." She turned to a monitor where a wind-lashed field reporter was standing in front of the Health Sciences Center. The words LIVE UCLA appeared on the screen as she prompted, "This is the time of year when L.A.'s Arson Squad earns its keep, isn't it, Skip?"

"It sure is, Marta. Especially when you consider there are only nineteen investigators for a city of over three million people. Compare that to San Francisco's fifteen investigators for a fourth of the population, and you can see why L.A.'s squad is feeling the heat—but this week one of them still found time to be a hero."

Lilah was in the shower. Serena was sitting on the bed with a cup of coffee, staring at the TV. Her eyes widened when a videotape of Merrick and the rescued firemen appeared. "Lilah?" she called out. "Lilah, it seems your arson investigator is on the news."

Lilah hurried from the bathroom, drying her hair with a towel, and watched as the camera zoomed in on Merrick's weary face.

"That's right, Marta," the reporter went on, "Lieutenant Dan Merrick was in hot pursuit of an arsonist when he took action that saved the lives of five firemen; and less than twenty-four hours later, Merrick was here at UCLA investigating yet another suspicious fire." The image changed to a videotape of Lilah encircled by the media. "A fire that was started by a fire bomb mailed to Dr. Lilah E. Graham, a prominent researcher and member of the medical school faculty. Informed sources are saying the motive may be related to the controversial nature of her work—a motive that raises the specter of Unabomber Theodore Kaczynski. As you may recall, before being caught and imprisoned several years ago, Kaczynski had spent nearly two decades sending mail bombs to unsuspecting victims whose work or philosophy he found offensive. Many were university professors."

"Well," Serena sighed resignedly. "I was rather hoping it was all a bad dream."

"That makes two of us. I don't know how we're going to get it all done in time," Lilah lamented, referring to the upcoming seminar in Maryland; then her eyes clouded with fear and her voice took on a more fragile timbre. "I want to do *something*, but I don't know what. I feel so . . . so damned paralyzed."

"Well, releasing a statement would be a start. I'll rough something out, if you like?"

"Good idea, thanks. Then what?"

"I'd say you've little choice but to leave the rest to the authorities. This Merrick fellow seems capable enough."

"I'm scared, Serena. What am I supposed to do, ask him to protect me?"

"Oh, I doubt that will be necessary. He came charging to his colleagues' rescue, didn't he?"

"That's not the same."

"Really? A damsel in distress, a fire-eating prince oozing machismo from every pore—it's fair to assume he'll come charging to your rescue as well."

"Well, I'm not going to hold my breath." She lit a cigarette and exhaled thoughtfully, breaking into an ironic smile. "You know, Serena, you're the last person I thought I'd ever be talking to like this. I mean, I don't know why I feel so comfortable with you, but I do."

"That's because you don't give a bloody damn what I think of you."

"Not a bloody damn," Lilah said, mimicking her as they both began laughing.

"Good, because to be brutally honest . . . all these mirrors, really. I can barely stand looking at myself in the morning, let alone dozens of you."

The laughter brightened Lilah's spirits. She fetched Merrick's business card from her briefcase and called headquarters. When told he hadn't come in yet, she left her cellular number, said it was important, and asked that he call as soon as possible. Then she got dressed, in jeans, T-shirt, tennis shoes, put on a few dabs of perfume, and gathered her things.

Serena dropped her at Macy's and headed home for a shower and change of clothes. Lilah took the escalator to the lingerie department on the second floor. She still couldn't recall buying the teddy and, along with returning it, hoped the clerk who made the sale might recognize her and provide the details and circumstances.

Lilah was drifting between the racks of lacy undergarments when a well-dressed woman who seemed vaguely familiar broke into a knowing smile. "Hi there, how'd that teddy work out for you?"

"Oh, hi," Lilah replied. "Actually, not too well."

"Decided red wasn't for you, huh?"

Lilah removed the teddy from the bag along with the receipt. "The fact is, I just can't spend this much."

"Oh," the sales clerk exclaimed, clearly surprised. "You gave me the opposite impression yesterday."

"I did?" Lilah prompted.

"Uh-huh. I remember because, well, it took me years to stop buying cheap underwear, you know?" She leaned closer to Lilah and shifted into a confidential tone. "Of course, soon as I did, I started seeing this man who had a thing for tearing it off me. It gets a little expensive sometimes, but hey, ten years, three kids, and don't ask me how many teddies later, we're still mad about each other."

"He doesn't have a brother, does he?"

The clerk laughed, then ran Lilah's MasterCard through

the imprinter and returned it with the refund slip and a pen. "Anyway, when I showed you what I had, you went right for this one."

"Gosh, I can't imagine what I was thinking."

"Well, you did seem a little scattered," the clerk offered. She was about to staple Lilah's copy of the credit slip to the sales receipt when her eyes narrowed in confusion. "Yeah, I'd say you were having a pretty off night." She set them side by side on the counter and pointed to the signatures.

They were totally different.

An eerie chill went through Lilah and set her mind racing. How could she explain to the sales clerk what she couldn't explain to herself? "Some people get a craving for chocolate," she finally said, forcing a laugh. "Me, I get extravagant, and my signature changes. What can I tell you?"

Before leaving the store, Lilah took the cellular phone from her briefcase and called Merrick's office. "It's Dr. Graham again. I left a message earlier . . . In the field? Thanks . . . No, no need to page him."

She hung up and hurried across the street toward the campus. If Merrick was in the field, she was fairly certain she knew where to find him.

CHAPTER FOURTEEN

The elevator door had barely opened when Lilah slipped past it and dashed into the corridor. Water squished from the carpet with each step, and the musty odor of mildew mixed with the pungent odor of smoke. She ducked beneath the yellow tape that proclaimed POLICE LINE DO NOT CROSS, and headed for her lab.

A campus security officer stood at the entrance. "I'm sorry, this is a crime scene," he explained, stepping in front of her. "Authorized personnel only."

Lilah pointed to the ID badge clipped to her T-shirt. "See that? Dr. L. Graham. UCLA. Department of Human Genetics."

"I'm sorry, Dr. Graham, I can't let you in there. My orders are that nobody is—"

"Then you'll have to shoot me." Lilah lunged through the door and dashed toward her office.

Logan was standing outside the fire-ravaged cavern, taking photographs. Merrick was crawling beneath the collapsed ceiling grid in search of evidence. The twisted aluminum, charred ceiling panels, electrical cables and lighting units created an obstacle course that hampered his movement. At the moment, he was examining a piece of burnt cardboard that he'd plucked from the ashes with a pair of tweezers. He heard the commotion and peered back over his shoulder through the labyrinth to see Lilah hurrying toward the office.

"Sorry about this, Lieutenant," the officer said as he caught up, taking hold of Lilah's arm.

"It's okay," Merrick mumbled, preoccupied with his find. He crawled out from beneath the grid and showed the blackened shard to Logan. "What do you think?"

The forensic expert's crinkly eyes narrowed, then he shrugged. "Could be writing or something."

Merrick nodded. "Can we enhance it?"

Logan shrugged. "Tag it, bag it, and I'll get somebody to run it." He turned away and resumed taking photographs.

The officer had released Lilah, and she was standing there, blinking at the strobe flashes. "Hello? Anybody home?" she called out, knocking on an imaginary door.

Merrick slipped the piece of cardboard into an evidence bag. "What can I do for you, Doc?"

"You can start with an apology."

"For what?"

"Not returning my call."

Merrick jotted something on the evidence bag and put it in his attaché. "You're on my list, Doc; but the last thing I need right now is a watchdog."

"I beg to differ, Lieutenant. This arsonist, torch, whatever you call them, has already done—"

"Pyromaniac," Merrick corrected.

Lilah winced at the term.

"Torches are businessmen. They play for pay. Burn to earn. They're not into homicide, and they don't go around mailing people fire bombs."

"Well. As I was saying, this *pyromaniac* has already

done enough damage. I don't want you and your people making it worse."

"We know a little about lab procedures too."

"I'll be the judge of that."

"Whatever you say," Merrick conceded wearily. He was operating on a couple of hours' sleep and wasn't up to a confrontation. "Long as you're here, what time does the mail get delivered in this place?"

"Mid-morning. Why?"

"The fire bomb came in the mail, right?"

"To my condo."

"Condo?" Merrick echoed with surprise. "Why didn't you say that last night?"

"I don't know," Lilah replied, flustered. "I was upset. I had other things on my mind."

Merrick let out a long breath. "What time does it get delivered to your condo?"

"Before noon. Usually," Lilah replied, explaining that the package had arrived the previous day, remained in the receiving room until morning, and finally ended up in her office. "I spent the afternoon teaching class," she concluded. "Then I went to the gym, had dinner with a colleague, and did a little shopping. It was after eight by the time I got here. Ten minutes later it went off."

Merrick's brows went up. "Almost thirty-six hours after it was delivered," he said, suggesting this was significant. "Pete, you get a chance to check out that lump of plastic I found last night?"

"I have people working on it. Nothing definitive yet. Why?"

"Well, since it wasn't rigged to detonate when it was opened, like most package bombs, I figure it was probably some kind of timer."

Logan nodded patiently.

"So, why wasn't it set to go off sooner? The pyro didn't know the doc wouldn't pick up her mail, or that she'd bring the package here, let alone be out of her office all day."

"Good question," Logan mused. "We're either talking pure luck or detonation by remote control."

Merrick nodded in emphatic agreement.

Logan smiled and fired the camera.

Lilah squinted at the blinding flashes. "You mean, they waited until I was here?"

"Well, yeah, that, or they got lucky. Either way, most homicides are committed by someone the victim knew. Any idea who *they* might be?"

"Well, let's see . . . there were four—no, no five—people who knew I was here: the guard in the lobby; my junior researcher, Dr. Chen; Dr. Schaefer, over in Neuro-psy—that's who I had dinner with—and one of my students, a kid named Kauffman. We were on the phone when it went off. Oh, and I called my mother."

Merrick jotted down the names on a pad. "Any of them have a motive you can think of?"

"No."

"Think some more. If I'm right about it being detonated by remote, and they're the only ones who knew . . ." He let it trail off, implying the conclusion was obvious. "You get along with your mother okay?"

"My mother?" she echoed incredulously. "She needs my father to light the barbecue."

"Okay. Put the guard and your mother on hold for now, and talk to me about the rest."

"Well, for openers, there are times when Serena—Dr.

Chen—thinks I'm out to torpedo her career; but that's normal in this business."

"In every business. What else?"

"She's ambitious, driven, competitive . . ."

Merrick emitted a dismissive grunt after each and scanned his notes. "What about Schaefer? You said all the shrinks hate your guts?"

"No, he's one of the enlightened few. We're actually working together." Lilah paused, making a decision. "What if I said we had an affair?"

"Did you?"

The strobe flashed again before Lilah had a chance to reply. She blinked back the spots, then nodded. "I'd like some privacy if we're going to talk about it."

"Gonnahaveto," Merrick grunted, running it into a single word.

Lilah led the way to an enclosed conference area, dropped her briefcase on the table, and leaned against the window ledge. "I know I should've mentioned it last night," she said defensively. "But before you jump down my throat, I didn't because Dr. Schaefer is married. He's also a highly respected psychiatrist, and I wasn't about to damage his reputation."

Merrick dropped into a chair and swiveled to face her. "You said 'had.' That mean it's over?"

Lilah nodded.

"How come?"

"He didn't want to lose his wife and kids."

"Good for him," Merrick mumbled, feeling a little stung. "For the sake of clarity, he dumped you, not the other way around?"

Lilah waggled a hand. "It cuts both ways. He started telling me how to run my life."

"Like how?"

"Well, he kept insisting I should see someone."

"You mean a shrink?"

Lilah nodded.

"Why?"

Lilah ran her hands through her hair and smiled demurely. "You have no qualms about prying into a girl's innermost secrets, do you?"

"None whatsoever. Shoot."

"No, I don't think so, Lieutenant. Suffice to say I didn't take his advice."

"He get pretty pissed off?"

"We argued about it."

"Okay." Merrick made a note and closed the pad. "I'll start with him."

"Because we had an affair?" she challenged.

"Because passion is a powerful emotion that drives other powerful emotions: anger, jealousy, revenge . . ."

Lilah nodded thoughtfully. "Then I guess you'd want to know about Kauffman too."

Merrick's eyes flickered with intrigue. "Good guess. That still going on?"

Lilah nodded and lit a cigarette. "It's a new thing."

"How's he doing in class?"

Lilah bristled at the innuendo. "He's very bright."

Merrick grinned. "You're some piece of work, Doc."

"Piece of work?" Lilah mused, exhaling a stream of smoke. "Really, I'd have thought one of those macho firehouse metaphors, the one with the three letter word that starts with A and ends in S, for example, would be more your style."

Merrick tilted back in the chair and swept his eyes over

her, then nodded in approval. "Yeah, that too. Now, where were we?"

"Relationships."

"Right. Does Schaefer's wife know he was sleeping with you?"

Lilah shrugged. "You think she might've done this as a revenge thing?"

"Depends."

"On?"

"Aptitude. You said three kids. She a housewife?"

"Research scientist," Lilah fired back with a laugh. "Biochemical engineer. One of the best."

Merrick took a breath, digesting the implication, then glanced at his notepad. "Let's go back to that lab tech. The one who brought the box up here."

"Cardenas?"

"What's his story?"

"Bright. Inner city. Wants to be a doctor real bad. I'm sponsoring him."

"Okay, we can draw a line through his name."

Lilah nodded, then her expression darkened with concern. "Whoever it was, you think they'll try again?"

"Depends on what triggered it. I had this pyro, once—a kindly old widow—she puttered in her garden, spoiled her grandchildren, and every year on the anniversary of her husband's death she started a wildfire. Took me damn near six years to catch her."

Lilah shuddered at the thought. "I don't think I could live with this for that long, Lieutenant."

"I won't lie to you, Doc. There are no quick fixes in this game. Arson has the lowest arrest and conviction rate of any felony."

"I guess that's what you were trying to tell me last night," she said obliquely.

"Run that by me again, will you?"

"You were the one doing the running," she replied, trying to keep her composure. "You—you told me someone tried to kill me, and took off."

"I'm an arson investigator, Doc, not a bodyguard."

Lilah sagged with disappointment and turned to the window. Gritty smoke hung in the sky, casting a pall across the landscape. She was twisting a length of flame-red hair around a finger and trying to come to grips with all that had happened to her—with what was still happening to her—when she sensed Merrick's presence and turned. The light caught his eyes at an angle that seemed to soften them.

"I can't give you what you want, Doc."

"You really think you know?"

"Protection. Personal attention. An A.I. who'll drop everything until this nut is busted. That's what I'd want. Unfortunately, it doesn't work that way—"

Lilah frowned and nodded weakly.

"—but I'll do my job."

"And in the meantime, I live in terror, waiting for this nut to—to"—her voice faltered and broke with emotion—"to turn me into a french fry?"

Merrick's brow furrowed with a thought. "You know, that's been bugging me."

"I certainly hope so," she said softly.

"I meant, the incendiary device. Why a fire bomb? You ever thought about that? Why not a knife, a gun, a hit-and-run?"

"That's not funny, Lieutenant."

"I'm not trying to be funny, Doc. Maybe there's a reason; then again, maybe there isn't."

"I guess I'm supposed to find that comforting, but I don't."

"Hey, if you're looking for an up side, keep in mind that they took their best shot and missed. Blew the element of surprise too. That tilts the odds in our favor." He gave her a thumbs-up and slipped his cellphone from its sheath. "And I know just the guy who can help tilt them even more."

Odds? Lilah wondered forlornly as Merrick circled the conference table, dialing a number. I don't want odds. Odds are what doctors give cancer patients.

CHAPTER FIFTEEN

"Right—a hold for X-ray stop," Merrick barked into the phone. "Correspondence, packages, junk mail, the works. Name's Graham, Dr. Lilah E." He spelled it out along with both addresses. "Effective immediately."

"Immediately . . ." the postal inspector mused. His days were long, his efforts unappreciated, but Old Glory, on the pole outside the federal building in South Pasadena, was a symbol of authority Tomas Jesus Tlahualilo knew couldn't be denied. "Two conditions: First, since we're talking federal law here, anything we hold, *we* X-ray; any evidence we seize, *we* analyze in our lab; and anybody we bust, *we* prosecute."

"Come on, T.J. You said two. That's three."

"No no, that's *one*," T.J. retorted with a self-satisfied chuckle. "Two is, the hold kicks in soon as I have her J.H. on a stop order."

"Chrissakes," Merrick exploded. "I don't want her turning into a crispy critter because of some paperwork glitch. She'll sign enough forms to wallpaper your office, but you have to do this for me now."

"Damn, that's gonna be a major hassle."

"I know, T.J., I know. That's why I'm calling you. Kings and Mighty Ducks next week. What do you say?" He and

T.J. had been making deals for years, and as Merrick expected, his offer closed this one. He and Logan spent the rest of the weekend wrapping up the field investigation, then released the crime scene to the university.

First thing Monday, Lilah gathered her staff and set them to cleaning up the lab, then made some revisions in the statement Serena had drafted. "Better?"

"Better. How do you want to handle it?"

"By the numbers," Lilah replied, staring with disbelief at the black hole that had been her office. "Get it over to Public Affairs and let them run it up the chain of command."

That same morning, Merrick turned his attention to questioning suspects. He caught up with Serena as she left the Health Sciences Center after delivering the press release.

"Ah, yes, Lilah's knight in shining armor," Serena said, eyeing Merrick's badge. "I'm quite pleased she took my advice and sought you out."

"Unusual for her, huh?"

"On the contrary. Lilah's not at all timid when it comes to pursuing men."

"I meant the advice," Merrick said, lighting a cigarette as they exited the lobby. "Way I hear it, you two don't get along."

Serena leaned into the searing wind and nodded. "Quite frankly, we have been clashing as of late."

"Over what? Money, men, career?"

"Imprisoned sex offenders," Serena replied dryly. "We're genotyping them. I'd worked quite diligently on the protocol, and just prior to commencement, Lilah took it over. She seemed... *driven* to personally confront these felons. It was all rather strange."

"Really pissed you off, huh?"

"You certainly have a lovely turn of phrase, Lieutenant."

"Did it?" he persisted.

"Of course," Serena replied bluntly. "Now, if you'll excuse me, I've a ten o'clock lecture." She forced a smile and hurried in the direction of the medical school.

Merrick was right on her heels. "Were you at the lab that night when Dr. Graham got back?"

"Just leaving, actually. I reminded her to fill out a form I'd left on her desk. She seemed terribly distracted." Serena stopped at the entrance and pointed to his cigarette. "I'm afraid you can't go in there with that."

Merrick took a deep drag and directed her aside. "When you were in her office, did you happen to see a large box on the table beneath the bookshelves?"

Serena nodded curiously.

Merrick arched a brow. "The fire bomb may have been detonated by remote—which suggests the pyro knew both Dr. Graham and the box were there."

"I'm not at all amused by your insinuation," Serena replied coolly. "The truth is, I rescued Lilah from the media, drove her home, and spent half the night cataloguing data."

Merrick nodded thoughtfully, then slipped his notepad from a pocket and handed it to her with a pen. "Home address and phone number, if you don't mind."

Serena broke into a flirtatious smile. "I'm not quite sure how to take that, Lieutenant."

"Quite seriously," Merrick advised.

Serena frowned and printed the information in bold decisive strokes that caught Merrick's eye. He had no way of knowing if it matched the printing on the fire bomb, but it was a candidate.

"Thanks," he said, concealing his reaction. "I need to get somebody out of class. Can you swing it for me?"

Minutes later, Serena had fetched Kauffman from one of the lecture halls and pointed him toward a bench outside where Merrick waited. The kid came loping over, lugging his backpack, and remained standing as Merrick brought him up to speed. "The box you put in Dr. Graham's car—what'd it look like?"

"Like a box," Kauffman replied flippantly, sizing it with his hands. " 'Bout so big."

"Addressed to Dr. Graham?"

"Uh-huh, real large printing. Couldn't miss it."

Merrick placed his thumb over Serena's name and showed him the notepad. "Sort of like that?"

Kauffman studied it for a moment. "Yeah, sort of . . . but it was much bigger, bolder. You know, one of those markers." He shrugged. "Hard to say for sure."

"Did you know the doc was taking the box up to her office?"

"I guess. Why? What're you getting at?"

"Chances are the fire bomb was remote detonated. You called her just before it went off. Whoever sent it would want to know she was there before hitting the switch."

"That's really lame," Kauffman said, tossing his backpack onto the bench in protest. "If it was me, I could've hit the switch soon as she answered."

"Did you?"

"No," the kid exclaimed indignantly. "We were shooting the bull about pizza and getting into med school and stuff. Ask her."

"I will." Merrick's gaze shifted to the backpack. "Can I

see one of those?" he asked, indicating the spiral-bound notebooks.

Kauffman shrugged indifferently.

Merrick removed one, swept his eyes across a page of tight, tiny scrawls, and put it back, thinking he'd have disguised his handwriting if he mailed someone a bomb. "I hear you're scoring pretty good . . . in her class."

Kauffman's eyes widened in reaction. "I don't like what you're insinuating, Lieutenant. I was getting an A in Genetics way before we started to . . . before I 'became involved' with Dr. Graham."

"In that case, I'd be worried if I were you."

"About what?"

"That grade." Merrick flicked the last cigarette he'd lit to the pavement and ground it out with a heel. "It's got nowhere to go but down." He grabbed the backpack from the bench, tucked it into Kauffman's gut like a football, and walked away.

Overhead, a yellow-brown splotch of light marked the position of the sun. Merrick wandered the campus for a while, replaying the two conversations in his mind. He ended up at the falafel stand on Weyburn, washed down a pita bread with a diet Coke, then headed for Schaefer's office, draining the melted ice from the container as he walked.

A secretary, working on a computer, explained the therapist was just finishing a session and suggested Merrick take a seat. He was more interested in the handwriting that filled the margins of a letter she was typing. "Those Dr. Schaefer's notes?"

"Patient data is confidential, Lieutenant."

"Sorry, I've just got this thing for penmanship," Merrick said, eyeing the graceful script. "Is it?"

She was nodding when the intercom buzzed. The office had a rear exit to ensure departing and arriving patients wouldn't cross paths; and it was Schaefer's way of informing her a patient had left. He was caught off guard when she told him Merrick was there.

"Hope you haven't been waiting long, Lieutenant," Schaefer said, ushering him into the office. "You should've made an appointment."

"I don't know about *your* game," Merrick said, noticing that whoever had just finished spilling their guts left a lipstick imprint on a coffee cup and wore heavy perfume. "But spontaneity usually produces the breakthroughs in mine."

"We're talking painstaking introspection and analysis here," Schaefer replied with a glance at his watch. "I have ten minutes before my next patient."

"Put me down for five. I've got limited coverage."

Schaefer laughed, then fetched his remote. "I'd like to get this on tape, if you don't mind? I always record sessions."

"Hey, we're picking *your* brain here, not mine."

The therapist smiled thinly, then sat in his chair and gestured to the lounger. "Make yourself comfortable."

Merrick remained standing. "You're a close friend of Dr. Graham's, that right?"

"We're colleagues," Schaefer replied, displeased with the defensive timbre he heard in his own voice.

Merrick rocked back on his heels and eyed him. "She used another word."

"Lovers?" Schaefer sighed in concession, cringing at the specter of phone sex coming up. "I don't know what Lilah told you, but *I'm* the one who ended it."

"I've found it usually cuts both ways."

"Well, *she's* the one who has an ax to grind."

Merrick nodded thoughtfully and picked up the photograph of Schaefer's family: three blond, blue-eyed cherubs hugging a striking woman with intelligent eyes and hair pulled back into what Merrick imagined was a bun, maybe a ponytail. "What about your wife?" he asked, observing Schaefer's reaction in the ornately framed mirror. "Did *she* have one? Did she find out what was going on?"

"Of course not." Schaefer smoothed his mustache with a fingertip and swallowed. "What if she did?"

"Jealousy's a provocative emotion. Revenge is a powerful motive. Together they make one hell of a—"

"I don't need a lecture on psychodynamics, Lieutenant; and I resent what you're insinuating."

"You and everyone else. Brings another popular saying to mind: 'Hell hath no fury like a woman scorned.' You've heard that one?"

"William Congreve, *The Mourning Bride*," Schaefer recited, removing his glasses in a little gesture of triumph. "Often wrongly attributed to Shakespeare. My wife is neither a bride nor in mourning, Lieutenant. She didn't know about the affair. She still doesn't."

"As far as you know."

Schaefer toyed with his glasses, then pinched the bridge of his nose and sighed.

"You want to ask her? Or should I?"

Schaefer stiffened, then nodded resignedly. "Leave it to me."

"Sure," Merrick grunted, unleashing the first in a series of rapid-fire jabs to further unhinge him. "I hear she's into chemistry, that right?"

"Yes, Dr. Fiona Sutton-Schaefer is a highly respected *professor* of biochemistry, and a scientist who—"

"Her work put her in competition with Dr. Graham?"

"No."

"The doc told you she was going back to her office that night, didn't she?"

"Yes, over dinner. She said she had some—"

"You tell your wife?"

Schaefer scowled. "Fiona's been out of town at a seminar. There's no way she could have—"

"Where?"

"Santa Barbara."

"You call her?"

"Of course. To tell her about the fire; but she wasn't in her room, so I beeped her."

"She call back?"

Schaefer groaned, losing patience. "Immediately. What's it matter? It was after the fact; and neither of us knew anything about the package, so—"

"I didn't mention a package."

"It's been all over the media, Lieutenant."

"Not last night."

"I just said, I wasn't aware of it that night."

"I wouldn't expect the nut who sent it to admit he was. Would you?"

"I resent that, Lieutenant!" Schaefer exclaimed, almost leaping to his feet. "I am not a nut and I won't tolerate being called one!" He angrily spun the chair on its base and sent it slamming against the desk.

A bemused smile turned the corners of Merrick's mouth. "How about a shrink with a hair-trigger temper?"

Schaefer reddened sheepishly and took a moment to settle. "I was letting off steam. It's a normal human response under the circumstances. A healthy one, I might add. Are you finished?"

Merrick nodded.
Schaefer clicked off the recorder.
"Mind if I borrow that?"
"The tape?"
"No," Merrick replied with a thin smile. "The remote."

CHAPTER SIXTEEN

Lilah spent most of the day getting the lab back up to speed, then went about processing the group of blood samples that had been collected prior to the fire—the group that included Kauffman's and her own.

It was mid-afternoon when Serena returned from her lecture and blew into the lab where Cardenas and other staffers were working with a crew of General Services personnel. Some were moving office equipment and records to a suite down the corridor. Others were removing the collapsed ceiling grid from Lilah's office. Serena saw her standing outside the charred cavern and quickened her pace. "I must say," she said in a cutting tone, "he does possess a certain animal magnetism."

Lilah looked puzzled. She glanced at a workman hacksawing the twisted aluminum and mouthed, *Him?*

"Hardly," Serena scoffed derisively. "Your favorite arson investigator. You really think I had a bloody hand in this?"

"No, of course not," Lilah replied defensively. "He asked questions and I answered them, Serena."

"Oh? Did you tell him about Jack Palmquist?"

Lilah's hand went to her mouth. "Gosh no, he completely slipped my mind."

"Mine too." Serena's eyes took on a sly feline glint. "We'd all like to forget him, wouldn't we?"

"Hey, boss," Cardenas called out, emerging from the maze of workstations before Lilah could reply. "Your dad's CBC and plasma came back." He handed her the printout, then added, "And Knoble's office just called. He wants to see you ASAP."

"Well," Serena intoned, "it seems they ran our press release up the chain of command straightaway, doesn't it?"

Lilah nodded apprehensively as she slipped the printout into a pocket in her lab coat and headed for her boss's office.

Dr. Raymond Knoble was the embattled director of UCLA's Center for Health Sciences. Burdened with a health care system demanding that providers reduce charges for their services, he was also responsible for funding the medical school, neuropsychiatric institute, and research programs. A gifted cardiologist, he had the action-oriented personality of a surgeon and a reputation for unfailing integrity. "Lilah," he cooed as she entered the wood-paneled office. "Thank God you're all right."

Lilah shrugged with uncertainty. "Some patients are a lot sicker than they look, Ray."

Knoble hugged her affectionately, then escorted her to a chair. "This put you out of business?"

"Yeah," Lilah sighed. "But not for long."

"Good. By the way, I appreciate the look-see," he said, holding the press release by the corner as if it were contaminated. "The authorities concluded this fire bomb was directed at you."

Lilah nodded glumly. "Lieutenant Merrick thinks someone tried to kill me."

"And you concur."

"The damn thing blew up in my face, Ray," Lilah snapped, her eyes softening with remorse the moment she said it. "Sorry, it's been a tough couple of days."

Knoble absolved her with a nod. "You're certain it wasn't directed at the university or at your lab?"

"Your guess is as good as mine. Either way, the lieutenant thinks it's a possibility. Serena just reminded me about Jack Palmquist."

"Palmquist," Knoble ruminated. "Tall, ascetic-looking fellow . . . from Sweden. A bit of a misfit as I recall. You think he's capable of this kind of behavior?"

"I never ran his DNA, Ray," Lilah quipped.

Knoble's stone face cracked a smile. "Seriously."

"Well, he was an outspoken critic of OX-A, figured that meant he'd never get tenure, and resigned."

Knoble stepped to a file cabinet. "I vaguely recall he'd returned to Europe. Signed on with one of the big drug companies." He slipped a piece of correspondence from a folder and scanned it. "Here it is. He used this office as a reference. It was well over a year ago."

"Sort of rules him out, doesn't it?" Lilah prompted with a mixture of surprise and short-lived relief. "Though I guess he could've come back."

Knoble nodded pensively, deciding if he'd go the next step. "While we're on the subject, any chance we're into something like this Imanishi-Kari/Baltimore mess at MIT a few years ago?"

Lilah looked stunned. Dr. Thereza Imanishi-Kari, a gifted immunologist at MIT, had been accused of publishing an article supported by faked test results. She and her coauthor, Nobel laureate Dr. David Baltimore, forced the junior researcher who made the allegation to resign from the lab; but National Institutes of Health investigators verified her claim. Imanishi-Kari lost her funding, and Baltimore was reprimanded for not giving the charge an honest hearing. The incident rocked the entire research community.

"I'm confused," Lilah finally replied. "Are you saying someone's accused me of fudging data?"

Knoble crossed his arms and studied her. "Have you?"

"You know me better than that, Ray," she replied, sounding hurt. "I'm not out to prove a pet theory. I turn over stones, and whatever crawls out is fine with me. I'm sorry you had to ask."

"So am I," Knoble said softly. "But like it or not—and you know damn well I don't—I'm the guy in charge of damage control."

Lilah shrugged resignedly. "The media's gonna say whatever it wants anyway."

"Screw the media," Knoble snapped in a rare loss of composure. "I have to deal with the regents, the chancellor, the provost, Congress, not to mention well-heeled alumni who are more picky about the research they're willing to fund than the NIH...."

Lilah nodded vulnerably. She didn't need to be reminded NIH was funding the OX-A study.

"Off the record," Knoble resumed, "sources tell me NIH is coming down hard on informed consent violations, especially where politically sensitive protocols are involved."

"We do it by the numbers in my shop, Ray."

"Good. While I'm at it, have you conducted any unauthorized protos."

"No."

"Pushed the envelope beyond NIH guidelines?"

"No."

"Played games with research funds?"

"No."

"What's in the OX-A hopper these days?"

"Convicted sex offenders."

Knoble brightened with intrigue, then frowned at a thought. "Neuro-psy is involved in that, isn't it?"

"Uh-huh. I'm working with Paul Schaefer."

A dismayed hiss came from between Knoble's perfect teeth. "The place is a political hornets' nest. The top guy over there resigned months ago, and I'm having a hell of a time getting someone to sign on."

Lilah nodded warily. "You're not going to get politically correct on me, are you, Ray?"

"I may not have a choice. This is the last thing I need at Neuro-psy now. I'm tempted to pull the plug on the whole damn thing."

"On OX-A?" Lilah asked, astonished.

"Genetic predisposition to antisocial behavior," Knoble corrected. "This compulsion to prove that medicine can explain and, as many are suggesting, *cure*, crime and violence is a lightning rod for controversy, and you know it."

"You're starting to sound like Jack Palmquist," Lilah said, stung by the blow. "Has it occurred to you that OX-A may *dis*prove it? My staff worked their butts off. I've landed a key slot at GRASP to present our findings, and—"

"Don't remind me," Knoble interrupted with a scowl. "The infamous conference on 'Genetics and its Relevance to the Anti-Social Personality.' As you may recall, it generated so much outrage when first proposed, NIH pulled the plug on funding."

"Well, they're not pulling it this time; and I have to be there. Don't do this to me, Ray. Please?"

Knoble gave her a moment to settle. "Could that be

what it's about? Some zealot who's out to stop you from making that presentation?"

Lilah shrugged forlornly, then she reached up to her hair, twisted into a neat bun, and with practiced grace gradually undid the precise spiral until it came free in a flaming column, which she shook out with several snaps of her head.

Knoble watched the fiery waves cascading across her shoulders. He'd seen the performance before—at official dinners, fund-raisers, and seminars—where heads turned until all eyes were on the woman who ran his genetics lab. "I'm sorry, Lilah," he said softly. "I sense you feel *personally* threatened by all this."

"Yes, I do. Some wacko sends me a fire bomb; you're on the verge of flushing my career—how else can I feel?"

"No, I meant, it's as if you have another—for want of a better word—agenda, that's also being endangered."

"I've no idea what you're talking about, Ray."

"I'm sorry, I can't quite put my finger on it."

"Neither can I," Lilah said, clearly baffled. "Can we get back to OX-A? I mean, if this is an internal thing, you're playing right into their hands. If it's not, why should it have any impact on my work?"

"Good question," Knoble conceded, steepling his fingers in thought. A suspenseful moment passed before he nodded. "Okay, you're still in business; but you're on the bubble. The NIH starts firing warning shots across my bow, that protocol is history."

"Thanks a bunch," she said flippantly, turning to leave; then paused, and, with a perky grin, added, "Of course, you could always fire back."

Knoble smiled and put a concerned hand on her

shoulder, his fingertips grazing the waves of flame-red hair. "Take care of yourself."

Lilah nodded and left the office, trying to clear her head. She was getting into the elevator when she called Schaefer on her cellphone.

"Well, we'll always have phone sex, won't we, Lilah?" Schaefer cracked when he came on the line. "Or did you tell the lieutenant about that too?"

"Paul, please. I just had a meeting with Knoble. He threatened to shut me down. We need to—"

"My kind of guy," Schaefer snapped, slamming the phone into the cradle.

"Paul? Paul, don't hang up on me! Paul?" She clicked off, and slipped the phone into her briefcase. The floor indicator was emitting a steady stream of chirps like a monitor in an intensive care unit; but it was Lilah's spirits, not her vital signs, that were plummeting. By the time the elevator reached the lobby, she was paralyzed with anxiety. A long moment passed before she realized the door had opened and the people waiting for the elevator were staring at her. Lilah took a deep breath and propelled herself past them, then hurried outside, walking in the direction of Wooden Center. Vigorous exercise had a way of reinforcing her sense of well-being and ability to cope; and if they ever needed reinforcement, they needed it now.

The last rays of light streamed skyward, turning the smoke from the wildfires into deceptively picturesque clouds of pink cotton candy. Lilah didn't notice them as she charged down the pathway, her attention drawn to a tall figure running toward her in the darkness. The man's powerful strides closed the distance between them more swiftly than she expected. He was almost on top of her before she made out the headband and running shorts. No sooner had the jogger passed than she became aware of another, shorter, bulkier figure lumbering in her direction on an intersecting walkway; and, lastly, of fast-moving footsteps behind her. Could one of them be the lunatic who had tried to kill her? Was she being stalked? Every sound, every shadow, every movement intensified her anxiety. Lilah quickened her pace, then broke into a run. Her face was glistening with perspiration by the time she arrived at the gym.

A short time later she had changed into workout gear and was giving one of the Nautilus machines a run for its money when she sensed she was being watched. Her eyes swept across the crowd of flushed, sweat-slick faces and found Kauffman's.

The kid had just arrived and was standing inside the entrance, glaring at her. He held her look briefly, then broke it off with a disgusted scowl, did an about-face, and went through the double doors.

Lilah disengaged from the apparatus and went after him. "Kauffman?" she called, running down the corridor. "Kauffman, wait up!" He didn't flinch, didn't hesitate, didn't acknowledge her in any way. "Joel! Joel, come on, let me explain!"

He accelerated, chin thrust upward, eyes straight ahead, as if she weren't there. She caught up and grabbed his arm. Kauffman yanked free without breaking stride, exaggerating the movement to communicate the depth of his anger; then, without so much as a glance, he charged through the exit into the darkness, letting the door slam in her face.

Lilah stood there feeling humiliated and confused. She hadn't done anything wrong, she thought; she hadn't hurt anyone. Hadn't engaged in any maliciousness. On the contrary, she was a victim, an innocent victim of a heinous crime. Yet, friends and colleagues had taken to treating her like a leper, her boss had threatened to ruin her career, and whoever had marked her for a fiery death was still on the loose. She felt persecuted and frightened and terribly alone, and longed to crawl into bed and pull the covers over her head.

She was driving home to do just that when, instead of angling up the hill, she impulsively made a left into Gayley and headed west toward Santa Monica. Traffic was moving at a crawl. Her stress level was already off the scale, but instead of further unnerving her, the slow movement of cars gave her time to sort her thoughts. Before she knew it, the Jaguar's headlights were sweeping across her parents' driveway.

"Hi, it's me," Lilah called out, letting herself into the house. She closed the door and peered into the den. Her father had nodded off watching television and was slouched in his slipcovered lounger.

"Lilah?" Marge Graham called from the kitchen. She'd been washing cookware, and stood in the doorway in apron and rubber gloves. "What are you doing here?"

"Oh, just thought I'd drop by."

"Try dropping by some morning . . ." she said with a suspenseful pause that belied her chatty tone, "and come with me to see your sister."

"You know mornings are hard for me," Lilah replied, as if her mother had suggested they go shopping at the mall. "I have all I can do to get here for Daddy's checkups. By the way," she went on, changing the subject, "his tests were fine. He's holding his own."

"And then some," Marge cracked, peeling off the

rubber gloves. "You should've seen him today ranting and raving."

"About what?"

"His slipcover. It's filthy. I made a special effort to get home early to wash it. He wouldn't let me near it. Made such a fuss."

"It's his security blanket, Mom. Let it be."

"Security blankets are for children, Lilah, *grand*children."

"Spare me the guilt trip, okay?"

"Just a reminder," Marge replied, her voice rising in the way parents have of saying, *Don't say I didn't warn you,* without saying it. She began emptying the dishwasher, automatically handing the plates to Lilah, who just as automatically put them in the cupboard. Marge cocked her head knowingly and caught Lilah's eye when she turned. "Did it again, didn't you?"

"Wrong shelf?"

"No, parked behind my car."

"Mom," Lilah groaned. "It's almost nine-thirty. Where would you be going at this hour?"

"Lucky's."

"You're going to the supermarket now?"

"Why not? It's the only time I have to do my marketing. Even if I wasn't, it's the principle of the thing, Lilah, and you know it."

Lilah nodded contritely to mollify her. "You know, you don't sound very happy to see me."

"How can you say that? Your father and I were worried sick after what happened. He got right on the phone to his cronies in County to make sure they put a priority on the investigation."

"Yeah, they're totally ignoring the wildfires just for me," Lilah said facetiously.

Marge sighed. "I'm relieved just to see you're in one piece."

"Well," Lilah replied, smiling at what she was about to say, "the Lord giveth, and the Lord taketh away."

Marge nodded and studied her with disapproving eyes. "And one of these days, if you don't get it cut, He's going to come after that hair."

CHAPTER SEVENTEEN

Merrick was driving north on the Harbor Freeway—the twelve-lane slab of concrete that split the city's core like a seismic fault. He took the Sixth Street off-ramp into a mirror-walled canyon of skyscrapers, and turned into the parking garage beneath L.A.'s World Trade Center. Its impenetrable granite base and concrete pedestrian bridges perfectly suited a building that housed the Bureau of Alcohol, Tobacco and Firearms laboratory.

The whir of processors and scent of ozone came from the Computer Imaging unit, where the piece of charred cardboard that Merrick found in Lilah's office—the piece that seemed to have printing on it—was centered beneath the lens of a video microscope tied in to a computer. The greatly magnified image looked like a black-on-black relief map of the Grand Canyon.

Logan and Pamela Dyer, an ATF computer technician, had spent the afternoon engaged in a two-step process designed to visually separate the charred printing from the charred cardboard.

The first step, Spectrophotometric Analysis, used the light absorbent properties of substances to differentiate between them. The cardboard didn't react in the ultraviolet band, but the black marker, used to print the address, did;

123

and fragments of printed letters began slowly emerging on the monitor.

The second, computer Image Reconstruction, refined the bits and pieces so they could be read. Video line by video line, it scanned them until they resolved into a distinct character or digit. The painstaking process took hours to spell out the letters: P.O.

Logan didn't have to wait for the word that would eventually follow. "Son of a bitch—a post office box."

"A fire bomb with a return address?" Dyer exclaimed incredulously. A straight-A DeVry graduate with a sexy, counterculture eccentricity, she spent her off hours playing backup guitar in her boyfriend's rock band. A tiny tattoo that proclaimed WIRED, the name of the magazine of the Internet elite, could sometimes be glimpsed above the lacy edge of her bra. She stared at the monitor anxiously; but the digits she hoped would follow had defied reconstruction and were illegible.

"Great," Logan grumbled. "It could've been mailed anywhere in the goddamn country."

Dyer widened the field of view. A line of craggy, oddly spaced letters filled the screen: –A–TA––––NICA

"A, B, C, D," Logan recited, searching for the missing letter of the first word, "E, F, G, H—"

"Try Santa Monica," Merrick said from the doorway, where he'd been watching with bemused detachment.

"Smart-ass," Logan growled, winking at Dyer.

"But you still don't know the number," Merrick chided. "You have any idea how many post office boxes there are in Santa Monica?"

Dyer shrugged. "Why would this nutcase put a return add on a fire bomb anyway?"

"Nuts do things that are nuts," Logan replied.

"Did a nut do this?" Merrick opened his attaché and removed the remote he'd borrowed from Schaefer.

Logan slipped it from the plastic evidence bag and gave it a once-over. "Your standard universal remote. You can program it to turn on your TV, VCR, stereo, open your garage, brew coffee, mix martinis—"

"How about detonate an incendiary?"

Logan's eyes widened with curiosity. "Take another whack at that number, Tattoo," he said, heading for the door.

"Better make that plural, gramps," she cracked.

Logan paused. "You got another one?"

Dyer nodded coyly.

"On your butt, right?"

"Down south," she replied with a saucy grin. She hooked her thumbs in her jeans, letting her hands frame her pelvis. "I'd show you, but your hard drive might crash, and then where would we be?"

"In heaven," Logan quipped under his breath.

Merrick laughed and followed him down a corridor to the Forensics unit. The glass-partitioned space contained diagnostic equipment, detection gear, and tools designed to work within the miniature universe of electronic devices. In moments Logan had the remote apart and was scrutinizing the components with an illuminated magnifier. "Nada."

"No modifications? The range hasn't been extended?"

"Doesn't look that way."

"His office is a block from hers. There's no way it could have been used to detonate this damn thing?"

"I didn't say that."

"Then it could?"

"I didn't say that either. Gonna have to run the circuits in the chip to be sure. This guy a prime?"

"Could be. Busted affair, cheating on his wife . . ."

"Then I'd be looking real hard at *her* too."

"I'll bet," Merrick teased. "Hubby claims she was out of town, so . . ." He was splaying his hands to imply the conclusion was obvious when Fletcher came through the door and announced, "WAR came up empty on that Las Flores print." Earlier, a technician had lifted the thumbprint from the charred matchbook that Merrick found in the ashes of the wildfire; and Fletcher had just run it through the Wildland Arson Response program. WAR contained computerized personal profiles of known arsonists along with their modus operandi. Statewide in scope, the data was used to identify repeat offenders, or unknown arsonists with similar profiles.

Merrick sagged with disappointment. "You run it through APP?" The Arson Profiler Program was an index of arsonists who had been apprehended and interviewed by ATF agents, and was national in scope.

"Naw, I figure our guy is a local and—"

"Don't figure, Billy-boy. We know it's not the Unabomber, but running his profile might help."

Fletcher nodded, appropriately chastened.

"Might as well run the fire-bomb-in-a-box M.O. while you're at it. Might be something in their weirdo file. Oh, before you do that, get hold of that guy Copeland, and see where my videotape's at." Merrick watched him go, then shifted his glance to Logan. "Anything on the blob?" he asked, referring to the lump of black plastic he'd also found amid the debris in Lilah's office.

Logan slipped three X rays onto a light panel. Captured within the ghostly outlines were the remains of an electronic device. The intense heat had vaporized most of the microchips and circuitry, fusing the rest into a globule of silvery gray silicon. "Nada."

"I can see that for myself, Pete," Merrick said. "No idea what kind of gizmo we're looking at?"

"Gizmo, geegaw, gadget—call it what you like. Not enough left to tell what it is. My money's on some kind of timer."

"Great. I had it down to whoever knew the doc and the hot potato were both there. Now it could be damn near anybody."

"Yup, damn near anybody," Logan echoed.

Merrick groaned wearily and headed for the door. "I've got to crash for a while."

Traffic was lighter now, and the Blazer was soon heading west on Rosecrans, one of several streets in Manhattan Beach that led to the ocean, though the sound of crashing surf was well out of earshot when Merrick pulled into the carport beneath his apartment. He had moved into the place a couple of years ago when he and his ex-wife separated—a temporary situation that gradually became permanent.

The Santa Anas were still gusting, and the door blew open with a bang when he unlocked it. A blast of stale air rushed from within to greet him. Merrick glared at the struggling air conditioner, then winced at the empty cans and fast food containers on the table. He stepped over the dirty laundry and fell on the bed fully clothed. The light on the answering machine got his attention, and he reached over and slapped at it, lighting a cigarette as the tape rewound. There was a message from his dentist, scolding him for being months overdue for a cleaning, followed by Jason's adolescent squeak, which made him smile. "Hi, Dad, I'm calling about the game. We're going, right? Oh, and I need a little help with my algebra. Talk to you later, okay?"

Merrick pulled the phone onto the bed and dialed. He hated talking to his ex, and hoped Jason would answer. "It's me," he said coolly, exhaling smoke into the phone when he heard her voice. "Put him on, will you?"

"He's doing his homework," Joyce Merrick replied.

"Good. We're working on his algebra this weekend."

"Too little too late, as usual. Steve's helping him as we speak."

Merrick winced, then, unable to resist the opening, said, "Really? I didn't know cops could spell algebra, let alone teach it."

"That's not all they're good at," Joyce taunted.

"Can I talk to my son, please."

"Hold on," she said curtly.

Merrick pictured her crossing to the table where Jason did his homework, pictured him nodding admiringly at his tutor's mathematical prowess. He was reflecting on Jason's comment that "Steve's okay," when the kid's voice pulled him out of it.

"Hi there, tiger," Merrick said cheerily. "Take it from someone who's been there. There's life after algebra."

Jason chuckled. "So . . ." he asked hesitantly. "We still on for the game?"

"You know it," Merrick replied. They were bemoaning the Kings lack of scoring when the call-waiting signal beeped. Merrick put Jason on hold and clicked to the other line. "Merrick."

"I don't know how she did it," Logan growled, "but Tattoo came up with the number for that P.O. box."

Merrick bolted upright and lunged to the night table for a pen. "Okay, shoot."

"It's either seventy-four twenty-*three* or seventy-four twenty-*eight*."

"Two?" Merrick wondered, writing on his palm.

"She couldn't resolve the last digit. You'll have to get your buddy at postal to run 'em both."

"No way I'm gonna get hold of T.J. now."

"Tomorrow's another day, Dan. Take a couple dozen Valium and call me in the morning."

Merrick grunted wearily and hung up. The last thing he remembered was thinking he had to call Jason back. Twelve hours later he awoke with a start. He took a few minutes to get his bearings, then, with a cup of cold coffee in one hand, P.O. box numbers jotted on the other, he called T.J. and had him run them.

"Seventy-four twenty-*three* hasn't been rented for over six months," T.J. finally reported.

"Then it's gotta be twenty-*eight*, right?"

"Right."

"Rented to?"

"Woodlawn Cemetery in Santa Monica."

CHAPTER EIGHTEEN

"Woodlawn Cemetery?" Lilah said, baffled. She was sitting on the floor of her blackened office, looking up at Merrick. The workers who removed the collapsed ceiling grid had also replaced the shattered window with plywood and erected some temporary walls. Outfitted in surgical gloves, mask, and protective eyewear, Lilah was unhappily picking through the sooty debris for the remains of books, research papers, and personal effects. She had just unearthed a charred strip of plastic that still faintly proclaimed LIKE BEGETS LIKE when Merrick arrived and briefed her on the return address. "Woodlawn Cemetery in Santa Monica?"

Merrick nodded. "Ring any bells?"

"No," Lilah replied, brushing herself off as she got to her feet. "Should it?"

Merrick grinned at a thought. "Wouldn't happen to have any patients planted there, would you, Doc?"

Lilah shed the glasses and mask and began peeling off the gloves. She hadn't slept well after trading barbs with her mother, and the smudges of ash on her cheeks heightened the appearance of fatigue. "You're making fun of me," she said with a weary smile.

"Well, doctors, med schools, cadavers . . . you know. I

figured maybe there was an odd chance. I mean, this is no time to pooh-pooh an off-the-wall connection."

"A cadaver with a return address?" Lilah wondered. "I mean, why would this creep even use one?"

"Because the post office won't accept a package without one. Could be that simple."

"But a cemetery? It doesn't make sense."

Merrick retrieved a charred binder from the debris and handed it to her. "I guarantee you it makes sense to your favorite pyro."

"You mean, like a symbol or something?"

"Like a sick joke, Doc. Like that's where you were supposed to end up. In the cemetery."

Lilah shuddered, took a breath to settle herself, then put the binder into one of the file boxes that held the items she'd salvaged. "Grab one of these, will you?"

Merrick made a face but hefted an overstuffed box and followed her through a newly installed door. It opened into the reception area of an adjoining suite where administrative functions were being moved.

Lilah's temporary office was about half the size of the burned-out one. The furnishings were utilitarian at best. The windows overlooked the brick facade of the adjacent building, not the plaza, and there was little natural light. The thought of spending months working here soured her mood. She set the box on the desk and stared at Merrick. "You've got a big mouth, you know?"

He set his box down, confused by her sudden change in attitude. "What're you talking about?"

"They all knew I talked to you. The least you could've done was use a little discretion."

"Discretion doesn't cut it in my business, Doc. I was baiting them."

"Any bites?"

Merrick shook his head, dismayed. "Couple of nibbles, but this angle I was working got blown out of the water. So, back to square one."

Lilah sighed with disappointment. "Which is what?"

"The target."

"Me?"

"Yeah. You. What you do. You said it was controversial, but we never got into it. Give me something I can sink my teeth into."

"Well, it's a cause and effect kind of thing," Lilah explained. "A certain genetic defect may be the cause. Impulsive, antisocial behavior the effect."

"Violence, no?"

"Violence, yes; but it takes many forms."

He nodded and studied her for a moment, making a decision. "You ever been to a hockey game?"

"Hockey?" Lilah echoed in an incredulous tone. "I'm afraid I have no interest in blood sports per se."

"Don't knock it till you've tried it," Merrick advised with macho enthusiasm. "We're talking fast and furious; and the squad has a box right on the glass. If you're into violence, you have to get into hockey."

"I'm into science, Lieutenant. Whether or not genetic defects predetermine antisocial behavior."

"Yeah, like arson and pyromania. Keep talking."

"Okay, think of the human genotype as a computer program that affects everything: your health, intellect, temperament. If it has a glitch someplace . . ." Lilah paused, fetched some autorads, and spread them on a light table. "This little marker means breast cancer," she resumed, using the point of a pencil to indicate specific bands. "This little marker sickle cell anemia. And *this* little marker—well, we have reason to think it may set off violent and/or sexually abusive impulses. In other words, we know some people have a higher risk for certain diseases. It may be true for certain behavior. Of course, you need an environmental trigger to set it off. You can be genetically predisposed to melanoma, but you won't get it if you never go in the sun."

"Impulses . . ." Merrick grunted, visibly agitated. "You saying that killers, rapists, child abusers aren't responsible for their actions?"

"Well, for example, there's a family in Holland. For five generations, most of the men were in the habit of sexually abusing women. DNA typing of their remains revealed they all had the same genetic defect."

"Doesn't answer my question. Are they responsible or not?"

"I have to finish my study and run it past the scientific community first; then you and the rest of the mucky-mucks get to decide."

"What mucky-mucks?"

"Law enforcement types, legal scholars, social scientists. It's dicey, but some people think genotype should be taken into account when sentencing criminals."

"You're going to give these creeps an out?" Merrick bellowed in protest.

"Not me. The mucky-mucks. Though I suspect you'll side with those who believe that since genetically programmed 'creeps' can't be rehabilitated, why not just lock 'em up and throw away the key?"

"Great idea."

"There are those who believe there's a difference between being programmed to do something and choosing to do it of your own free will."

"You really think the pyro who tried to kill you couldn't help himself?"

"Well, if he has certain markers, it's possi—"

"Come on! Anyone who makes a fire bomb knows what the payoff's going to be! It's bad enough every weirdo from the Menendez brothers to O.J. and McVeigh are claiming *they're* the victims! By the time *you're* done, they'll all be saying—"

"Hold it," Lilah interrupted. "Emotionally, I agree, but intellectually, there's nothing wrong with keeping an open mind until—"

"Bullshit!" Merrick erupted. "I'm sick and tired of open minds and bleeding hearts telling these animals it's okay to hurt people!"

Lilah recoiled at his outburst, then collected herself, sensing that Merrick's anger wasn't personal, wasn't as driven by her or what she said as by some inner turmoil; and it wasn't the first time it had occurred to her. "What's your problem, Lieutenant?"

"Problem?"

"Yes," Lilah replied gently, her soft soulful eyes finding his. "Who hurt you?"

"Nobody," Merrick muttered. He came within a blink of replying, *Her name is Joyce,* but the words stuck in his throat. "I was about to say, by the time you're done, every serial killer and pedophile on this planet will be saying, 'Don't blame me, blame that guy my great-great-grandmother married.'"

"Hey, we've already identified a genetic marker that's a predictor of violence—give you one guess."

Merrick shrugged with indifference. "I wouldn't know where to begin."

"Right there," Lilah said, her Doug Graham smile tugging at the corners of her mouth as she pointed to Merrick's groin. "An X-Y sex chromosome. The marker that produces a male. Men commit violent acts nine times more often than women."

"Twenty times when it comes to arson."

"Then I guess we're looking for a man, aren't we?"

"Yeah, and when I bust him and he says, 'This naughty gene made me do it,' you're gonna say, 'No problem. Let him walk'? *You're* the victim here! Don't forget it."

Lilah nodded vulnerably.

"You're like two people, you know?" Merrick went on, baffled. "One wants me to nail this pyro's ass. The other's working overtime cooking up excuses for him."

"It's called conflict," Lilah explained, unsettled by the exchange. "Not everyone's heart and head are in perfect sync like yours." She looked around, as if trying to get her bearings, then fetched a vacutainer kit. "Roll up a sleeve. I want to take a blood sample."

"For what?"

"My study."

"No thanks. No way you're turning me into some guinea pig. Like I said, get into hockey."

Lilah was about to reply when something dawned on her. She hadn't seen the potential when he said it earlier; but this time, as she stood there studying the vacutainer, the mention of hockey struck an intriguing chord. "Was that an invitation to a game?"

"Why?"

"I think you might have something there."

"Don't patronize me, Doc."

"Not what I'm doing, Lieutenant."

"Could've fooled me."

"That's nothing to brag about."

"Okay, okay," Merrick said in mock surrender. "What's your problem?"

"Same as yours," Lilah replied with a laugh. "I'm dying for a cigarette."

"Tell me about it," he said, laughing with her. "So what's your angle on hockey?"

"The players," Lilah replied, fetching her briefcase. "They're like a population subgroup. It'd be neat to profile an entire team's DNA."

Merrick nodded, taken by the scent of her perfume as she brushed past him and headed for the door.

"I'm starving," Lilah went on. "What do you say we get something to eat while we're at it?"

"Where? There's no place left in this town where you can chow down and light up at the same time."

Lilah laughed knowingly and entered the reception area. "There's this funky little falafel stand over on Weyburn. Why don't we—" She suddenly stiffened and bit off the sentence.

"Been there," Merrick replied. He was feigning indigestion when he saw Lilah's reaction and realized the woman waiting in the reception area was the cause of it. Her hair wasn't swept back the way it was in the photograph, and she was taller than he'd imagined, but her lab coat and the icy stare she was giving Lilah confirmed she was exactly who Merrick thought she was.

"Fiona," Lilah finally said, trying to sound friendly. "What brings you by?"

"You're Lieutenant Merrick, aren't you?" the woman declared as if Lilah weren't there. "Fiona Schaefer. My husband thinks we should have a chat."

"Right," Merrick grunted, caught off guard. "I figured he might."

TOUCHED BY FIRE

"I hope you don't mind my dropping by like this?" Fiona went on coolly. "I called your office to make an appointment, and they said you might be here."

"No problem," Merrick replied with a pained glance at Lilah. "Doc, would it be okay if we—"

"Use the conference room? Of course. I'll be in my office when you're finished." Lilah turned to Fiona with uncertainty and added, "I don't blame you for being angry, Fiona. It . . . it just happened. I'm sorry. I don't know what else to say."

Fiona's glare hardened, then she broke it off, turned to Merrick and said, "I think whoever tried to kill her had a perfectly good reason, don't you?"

CHAPTER NINETEEN

"I didn't know," Fiona said smartly, leveling a forthright gaze at Merrick. They sat on opposite sides of the conference table, Fiona straight-backed and forward in her chair, Merrick in his weary slouch.

"Know what?" he prompted, knowing the answer.

"That my husband was having an affair with her. Isn't that what you asked him, to find out?"

Merrick's shoulders hunched. "Someone tried to kill the lady; and I had to know if you had a motive."

"I do now, thanks to you," Fiona said calmly. "But I'd have resorted to civilized discourse, not violence, had I known."

Merrick nodded as if accepting it. "Your husband said you were up in Santa Barbara that night."

"Exactly," Fiona said, implying it cleared her.

"You could've come back," Merrick challenged. "Drive takes about an hour and a half, right?"

"I was attending a workshop. It lasted well into the evening."

"Bomb-making one-oh-one?"

"No, the electrochemical absorption and processing of lecithin and choline by neurons."

"Joint-rolling one-oh-one."

"For your edification," Fiona lectured without cracking a smile, "it is the process by which synapses metabolize the enzymes that make our brains function."

"Ah," Merrick intoned as if he understood, but it had nothing to do with synapses. After three children, Dr. Fiona Sutton-Schaefer still had the freshness and figure of a fashion model, and he couldn't imagine why her husband—despite Lilah's charms—would fool around. Now he knew. She was humorless. "How well into the evening did this workshop last?"

"It was scheduled to end at eight," Fiona replied. "They always go longer."

"So, you have all these choline junkies who could testify you were there the entire time?"

"The *participants* come and go, Lieutenant, but I'm sure there are some who—"

"Names and numbers," Merrick said smartly, sliding pad and pen across the table. "All of 'em."

Fiona shrugged, then took an address book from her purse and began writing. "You know," she said, sounding like a preoccupied child, "I wouldn't have this problem if I were a praying mantis." She said it as seriously as if she'd said, *if I had paid more attention to my marriage* and it took Merrick a moment to process it.

"Why? Their husbands never cheat?"

"No, the female kills him after mating," Fiona replied matter-of-factly. "I did a high school biology project on it. It won a Science Award from NOW."

Merrick was about to make a wisecrack about the National Organization for Women when it struck him that something had driven Fiona to come looking for him, not to mention to invade Lilah's territory and infer she deserved what she got. It was gutsy, assertive. Right out of the NOW manual. But she'd been too cool, too composed since they'd made the move to the conference room. He waited until she finished the list, then, trying to rattle her, said, "I don't believe you didn't know what was going on."

"Well, I didn't."

"Come on, nobody who just found out her husband's been having an affair is this laid-back."

"I'm not a yeller and screamer, Lieutenant. I don't lose my temper and throw things."

"How about in the reception area before? You were dying to scratch her eyes out, right? It's only human. I mean, when this guy I know caught his wife cheating on him, he wanted to tear the other guy's head off."

"Did he?"

"No, he . . . he went to a hockey game."

"The defense rests."

"Come on, she's been sleeping with your husband for a year, and you're Little Miss Calm, Cool, and—"

Fiona's jaw dropped. "A year?" she repeated, eyes flaring with anger. "It was going on for a year?"

"Give or take," Merrick replied taunting her.

"That bastard! That miserable son of a bitch! I'd cut his heart out—if he had one! He said it was just a fling! A little fling!"

"If you'd known that, you would have sent Dr. Graham an even bigger bomb, huh?"

"That's ridiculous!" Fiona shouted, jumping to her feet, Merrick's pad and pen clutched in her fist. "This interview is over!"

"Hey—hey!" Merrick called out as she started for the door. "I think those are mine."

Fiona whirled and threw them on the table.

The pen bounced off, whizzing past Merrick's ear like a

tiny missile. "Atta girl," he chuckled. "As your husband said, it's healthy to let off steam."

"Good," Fiona snapped. "I'll be the healthiest person on campus by the time I'm finished with him."

"Hold it," Merrick ordered as she headed for the door again. "I need a phone number."

Fiona bristled with impatience. "I'm in and out," she warned, digging a business card from her purse.

"That's why God made beepers," he replied, noticing the one clipped to her lab coat.

"It's on there," Fiona snapped, referring to the number. She dropped the card in Merrick's palm, then left, slamming the door so hard the partition rattled.

Merrick scanned the business card then retrieved his pad. Fiona's frenetic, almost childlike mix of printing and script brought an amused smile to his face; but the names and phone numbers quickly wiped it off: the seminar was international in scope; and only one of the dozen or so scientists she had listed lived in the United States, let alone in the area. Merrick grunted in disgust and headed for Lilah's office. His cellphone started chirping before he got there.

"It's me," Logan growled when he answered. "We got us an ID on the print from that matchbook."

"Way to go," Merrick enthused. "APP?"

"DMV," Logan replied. The California Department of Motor Vehicles thumbprints and photographs driver's license applicants as a matter of protocol. "Billy ran their files. Guy's name is Eagleton, James D."

Merrick flinched. "Eagleton? Son of a bitch. That's the guy who put us on to the flash point."

"The homeless guy in Las Flores Canyon?"

"Uh-huh."

"The homeless guy in Las Flores Canyon that you could've busted?"

"Ditto," Merrick replied gloomily.

"I'll put his mug on the wire. We just pulled a copy from his D.L."

"Okay, in the meantime I'm going to get my dumb ass up there and see if I can flush him out. Hold on a sec." He rapped on Lilah's door and opened it. "Doc?"

Lilah had spent the time setting up her temporary office. "All set?" she said brightly, assuming they would now be heading off to lunch, not to mention discussing Merrick's one-on-one with Fiona.

"What's your fax number, Doc?" Merrick went on. He repeated it into the phone as Lilah recited it, then instructed Logan to send him a copy of Eagleton's driver's license photo.

"Lost her cool, didn't she?" Lilah prompted as Merrick hovered over the fax machine.

"Can't get into it now. Break in another case." Merrick took the fax the instant it appeared and made a beeline for the elevators. His thumb was pummeling the call button when Lilah caught up with him.

"What about the hockey game?"

Merrick looked at her blankly. "Oh, yeah, right." The floor indicator dinged. "Call me," he commanded, stepping into the elevator. "We'll work something out."

"Okay, but is there another number where I—"

The elevator door rolled closed.

Lilah had the Ops Center number, but wanted his cellphone or apartment so she could call him directly. She'd been excited about having lunch with him, though she wasn't sure why. His manner was brusque, he made no effort to be charming, his rumpled appearance was a bit of a turnoff, *and* he was a hockey nut; but she couldn't deny that she found herself drawn to him.

Was it the circumstances? The hope, despite his admonitions, that he'd become her protector? Didn't Serena say, "He came charging to his colleagues' rescue , it's only natural he'll come to your rescue as well"? Then again, maybe it was as simple as finding each other on that sliver of common ground smokers have been driven together to defend. There *was* something symbiotic about it. Something deliciously ironic about both of them being cranky from nicotine deprivation and breaking into laughter, finally breaking the ice.

Whatever, not fifteen minutes ago Lilah sensed he was becoming interested in her, not just in her case. Now, despite Fiona's appearance, he'd shifted gears to another case, and she was standing in the corridor feeling alone and wholly demoralized.

The floor indicator dinged again, startling her.

Paul Schaefer strode out of an elevator. "Lilah?"

She stepped back and glared at him. "What're you doing here?"

"I want to apologize. I overreacted when you called, and I—"

"Tell me about it." She turned on a heel and charged down the corridor.

Schaefer went after her. "Lilah? Lilah, listen. I've been in touch with the prison and—"

"Good. Your wife may be spending time in one."

"Seriously, Lilah, they've rescheduled the prison thing for Friday. If you're up to it, I'll confirm and—"

"Call me," she commanded, pushing through the door into her office. "We'll work something out."

CHAPTER TWENTY

The Pacific Coast Highway was still closed to traffic as Merrick turned off onto the blacktop that snaked through Las Flores Canyon. Teams of weary firemen were wetting down hot spots, and here and there residents who had been allowed to return to their homesites were sifting the ashes for whatever they could salvage.

None recalled seeing a man with a ponytail and the beaten look of the homeless; and the fax of Eagleton's photo failed to jog their memories. Merrick proceeded deeper into the canyon in search of his quarry. Dusk was falling and he was about to call it a day when the Blazer's headlights picked up a figure walking along a heavily treed area near the crest, which had been spared by the fire. He had caught a fleeting glimpse of worn jeans, rumpled jacket, and ponytail whisking across hunched shoulders.

It was Eagleton. Had to be. Merrick had no doubt of it as he angled onto a scorched hillside dotted with blackened boulders and tree stumps. The sight of the zigzagging vehicle sent Eagleton dashing into the trees, plastic bag with his belongings swinging from a hand. Merrick bolted from the Blazer and charged up the slope in ankle-deep ash. He paused at the tree line, then heard the distant rustle of leaves and sprinted through the overgrowth into a small clearing. A massive rock formation walled off the uphill side.

Eagleton was nowhere in sight.

Merrick was circling the rocks when his phone started chirping. It shattered the silence like a wailing siren, spooking Eagleton, who bolted from his hiding place. Merrick brought him down with a diving tackle and went sprawling across the rocky terrain. Both men jumped to their feet. Merrick got hold of Eagleton's arm, spun him around, and found himself face-to-face with a woman, a bizarre-looking woman with a ponytail.

She had rouged cheeks, spooky eyes caked with makeup, a lipstick-smeared mouth, and a large hunting knife in one of her gloved hands. "Don't try it," she said in a raspy voice, slashing the air. "The last asshole who tried to fuck me without paying got cut real bad."

"Your name wouldn't be Joyce, would it?" he quipped under his breath, sidestepping the blade.

"You got some beef with this Joyce bitch?"

"You could say that," Merrick replied softly. "Look, I just want to talk. So why don't you chill out and put that away?"

The bizarre woman eyed him warily, then sensed her fear was unwarranted and sheathed the knife. "My friends call me Rene," she whispered, trying to sound sexy.

"Rene what?"

"Rogers. Rene Rogers." She took a snapshot from a pocket and offered it to Merrick. "I used to dance at the Get Wet."

Merrick had no doubt the youthful face was hers, but, like the snapshot, it had become cracked and creased with age, and the body wrapped around one of the poles in a topless dance club had become emaciated from hard living and drugs. "I could wrap myself around you like that," Rene offered in her pathetic whisper.

"Thanks, but that's not what I'm after, Rene," Merrick said, lighting a cigarette.

Rene's eyes widened. "Spare one of those?"

"They're yours," Merrick said, handing her his box of Marlboros; then he showed her the fax of Eagleton, which made her eyes flicker with recognition. "Ever see this guy around here? Wears his hair like you now."

"You're a fucking cop, aren't you?"

"County Arson Squad," Merrick replied, deciding he'd be better served by the truth.

Rene looked threatened and began drifting away.

Merrick slipped a twenty from his billfold, which lured her back. "He a friend of yours?"

"His name's Jim," she said, her eyes riveted to the money. "Haven't seen him since the fire."

"Any idea where he might be hanging out?"

Rene shrugged. "He used to go down to Santa Monica sometimes."

"He has friends there? A place where he stays?"

Rene's face screwed up in thought. "His mail—that's it—yeah—yeah, he had to pick up his mail!" she exclaimed in little bursts, grabbing for the money.

Merrick pulled it back. "His mail?"

"Yeah, homeless people get mail. They rent boxes and stuff. You know, in those postal places?"

"No, I didn't," Merrick said, giving her the twenty.

Rene stuffed it into a pocket, then went about picking up items that had spilled from the plastic bag when Merrick tackled her: sunglasses, paperback, keys, several tubes of lipstick, a few coins.

"By the way, what are you doing up here?"

"Selling information," Rene replied with her twisted grin as she moved off.

Merrick watched her vanish into the trees, then returned to the Blazer and drove to ATF headquarters. By the time he arrived, Logan had already left for the day, but Fletcher was still there, cleaning up some paperwork.

"Well, Billy-boy," Merrick bellowed as he entered the lab. "Every dog has his day."

"That mean you nailed Eagleton?"

"Nope, but I got a serious line on him; got me a prime in the Graham case too: Fiona Sutton-Schaefer, research nerd, top dog in brain chemistry. The doc was boinking her husband. She swears she didn't know."

"You already Q and A'd her?"

"Uh-huh. I think she's lying through her teeth."

"Raging jealousy, high-tech chemistry . . ." Fletcher mused. "Sounds like the lady's got motive and means."

"She's got the temperament too. She was Little Miss Composure till I started tweaking her. Turned out she could rant and rave with the best of 'em, but—"

"She's got an alibi," Fletcher added knowingly.

"Yep, seems she was at some seminar up in Santa Barbara the night the box went boom."

"Santa Barbara? That's not exactly airtight, Dan. I mean, she could've easily driven back."

"Easily, but she swears she didn't." He opened his pad, slapped Fiona's list facedown on the Xerox machine and thumbed the button, then handed Fletcher the copy. "Get on the horn and see if any of them back her up."

"Looks like roll call at the U.N.," Fletcher joked.

"Start with the guy in Baltimore."

"Still gonna take some time."

"I know," Merrick replied, heading for the door. "That's

why I'm giving it to you." Darkness had fallen and the Santa Anas were gusting again as he wheeled the Blazer onto a southbound freeway for Manhattan Beach.

It was another sweltering night in Los Angeles; another one of those autumn nights taut with unnerving tension; another one of those nights when the pressure to seek revenge peaked and safety valves failed.

To the clerk in the all-night supermarket on the other side of town, it was one of those nights when shoppers in the checkout line acted like it was feeding time at the zoo. To make matters worse, his fellow checker had succumbed to the autumnal madness and called in sick; and he was working the surly crowd by himself. It was sometime after midnight when he had a vague sense of déjà vu.

"Two fifty-nine," the computer voice said. The clerk swept the next item across the laser. "One forty-nine." And the next. "Ninety-nine." He couldn't quite place the customer, and the half dozen or so items didn't seem more familiar than any of the others he'd rung up that evening, but that last one sparked his curiosity. Why, he wondered, would someone be buying a fireplace log in the middle of a heat wave?

Several hours later the customer's hands—the hands that had emptied the supermarket cart and set the items on the checkout counter—were sheathed in rubber gloves, putting the finishing touches on a homemade incendiary device. A fire bomb in a box—identical to the first. They closed the flaps and, repeating the obsessive packing tape ritual, sealed every edge, seam, and corner of the box, making absolutely certain that its explosive secret would be contained. When finished, they grasped a black marker and, with the same festering hatred and bold strokes, addressed the package to LILAH E. GRAHAM.

CHAPTER TWENTY-ONE

Several days had passed since Merrick left Lilah standing at the elevator. She spent them settling into her new office and tentatively opening her mail. Each piece had stickers proclaiming INSPECTED, X-RAYED, OK TO DELIVER. As instructed, she called him to "work something out" for the hockey game. Though he hadn't called back, she briefed Serena on her idea to genotype the Kings players, and asked her to contact the team doctor. With luck they might have results in time for the GRASP conference. In the interim, Schaefer called, and they "worked something out" on the prison study.

Early the next morning, they caught a flight to Sacramento, then rented a car and drove to Vacaville State Prison, a drab edifice west of the capital. As in most prisons, sex offenders were isolated from other inmates, who, despite their own hideous offenses, could become righteously indignant over sex crimes.

Lilah sat at a table in an interrogation room, her head filled with the odor of sweat and testosterone that comes from locking hot, angry men in cages. There was an empty chair next to her and another opposite at the focal point of spotlights, video cameras, and a one-way mirror through which prison guards and members of the psychiatric staff were observing. A side table held vacutainer kits, inmate files, and Schaefer's voice-activated recorder. Schaefer stood off to one side so that, on entering the room, each inmate would have the impression he was alone with a woman.

And Lilah *was* terribly alone when the first one appeared. His hard-packed body filled the doorway as he ducked his shaved head and turned his shoulders to avoid the jambs. He sat glaring at Lilah through lidded eyes that gave him a chilling malevolence. Indeed, if he was intimidated on finding a woman waiting for him, it was news to her. Esoteric theory had become hard core reality, and it wasn't anxiety in her eyes, imploring Schaefer to come forward, but sheer terror. He took a deep breath, then crossed the room and sat next to her. "This is Dr. Graham, I'm Dr. Schaefer," he said nervously. "We appreciate your taking part in this study. May I ask why you volunteered?"

"Get my ass out of the cage," the inmate growled with disdain. "Why the fuck else?"

"I see. But you do know what the study is about."

The inmate nodded sullenly. "Jeans. They said somethin' about jeans. I get mine at the Gap."

Looks darted between Schaefer and Lilah. Was he ignorant or incredibly quick-witted? "Can you roll up your sleeve for me?" she finally asked.

The inmate grunted and rolled up a cuff, revealing a powerfully muscled arm crisscrossed with bulging veins. There'd be no need for a tourniquet, Lilah decided, as she opened a vacutainer kit and uncapped the needle.

The inmate's eyes darted to the gleaming steel.

"According to your file," Schaefer said, scanning the pages of data, "you were convicted of sexually abusing your daughter. Is that right?"

"It's a bad rap. I never done nothin' to her."

"Never?"

"That's whut I said, asshole."

"Okay . . ." Schaefer conceded evenly, signaling Lilah with a veiled glance.

She took the inmate's arm, aligning the needle with a purple knot inside his elbow. "Make a fist, please?"

"For the sake of discussion," Schaefer went on as the inmate complied, "let's assume you did abuse her."

Lilah stabbed the needle hard into the man's flesh. He concealed his reaction to the pain, then grasped her wrist tightly with his free hand. Lilah had no doubt he could snap it with a flick of his own. Her adrenaline surged. Her pulse rate soared. Her eyes blinked to avoid his threatening stare. "You can open your fist now," she said as calmly as possible. *"Both of them."* A tension-filled moment passed before he released her.

"Did that hurt?" Schaefer wondered, pretending to be unaffected by the confrontation. "You think it hurt as much as what you did to your daughter?"

"How the fuck should I know!" the inmate bellowed.

"How old is she?"

"Shit, man, I don't know . . . ten, maybe eleven."

Schaefer toyed with his glasses. "I have an eleven-year-old too," he said in a conciliatory tone. "They tend to be full of themselves at that age, don't they?"

"Damn right. The sassy bitch was always dissin' me when I come by to be with her mama. I tol' her I'd shut her up, and that's whut I did."

"By forcing your penis into her mouth . . ."

"You got a better way?"

Lilah shuddered. She felt paralyzed, like in one of those dreams where you can't move no matter how hard you try;

but she recovered and managed to take his blood. When finished, she went about determining if the men in his family were candidates for a genetic linkage study. "You have two sisters, don't you?" she asked softly.

The inmate nodded.

"Do you know if your father treated his daughters the way you treated yours?"

"No idea who the dude was," he replied with a scornful snort. "Betcha them bitches don't either."

Lilah nodded with clinical detachment and scanned his file. "Let's talk about your brother. Does *he* treat his daughter the way you treated yours?"

"Can't say, but I remember askin' him if I could bust her cherry when she was ready. You know, keep the prime pussy in the family? You know whut the little shit went and done? Punched me out, that's whut."

"So, the answer to my question is no," Lilah said, smiling at Schaefer, who signaled her with a slight nod. "Were you sexually abused as a child?" she asked.

"Was I whut?" he challenged, his eyes flaring.

"Sexually abused, molested. Did someone in your family or, perhaps, someone in a position of—"

"Whut the fuck is this?" He leaped up in an angry rage and threw his chair across the room. Lilah and Schaefer ducked as it smashed into the wall behind them. They were both thinking they'd be next when three guards charged through the door and gang tackled the inmate, cuffing his hands before wrestling him out of the room.

Schaefer and Lilah sat in stunned silence. "Wow!" she finally exclaimed. "That was something else."

"Wow?" Schaefer echoed, his heart pounding. "He damn near beheaded us and you're getting off on it?"

"Nobody's going to fault *this* study for being light on

behavioral data," Lilah replied spiritedly. They spent the remainder of the morning interviewing inmates. Some responded. Others refused to be engaged: unmoved by Lilah's presence, Schaefer's preamble, or the pain of being rudely stuck with a needle.

After a break for lunch—during which Lilah left another message for Merrick—a pale youth with wispy blond hair entered the room. His sleeveless shirt revealed three tattoos: a rose that said MOM, a heart that read MOTHER, and a broken heart that proclaimed MOTHER FUCKER. He slouched in the chair, studying Lilah out of the corner of his eye.

"You were convicted of rape?" Schaefer prompted, moving in from his position next to the door.

The young inmate grinned smugly and nodded.

"It says here you bound your victims' wrists with guitar strings, then painted their faces with white makeup and bright red lipstick. Can you tell us why?"

" 'Cause I'm addicted to love," he replied in a drawl that made him sound like Texas senator Phil Gramm.

"Love?" Schaefer echoed with contempt. "Rape has nothing to do with love. Rape is an act of violence."

The inmate guffawed in disbelief. "Y'all ain't ever seen it, have you?" he challenged, his voice rising with each successive query. "The music video? Robert Palmer? 'Addicted to Love'? Been on MTV for years!"

"Oh, yes, MTV, of course," Schaefer bluffed unconvincingly. "I believe I did catch it once."

The kid eyed him skeptically. " 'Addicted to Love,' man. Check out the backup band. We're talking some serious pussy. All tens. Totally fuckable."

"Oh? What makes them so . . . so desirable?"

"Fuckable!" the inmate corrected, his eyes turning to

predatory slits, his lips curling to reveal his incisors. "Like, they all have these skintight dresses cut right up to their beavers like my mom's? And they ain't wearing no panties either."

A little look passed between Lilah and Schaefer. "Your mother dressed provocatively?" she prompted gently. "You want to tell us about her?"

"N-n-nothin' to tell."

"Nothing?"

"Nothin'. I split when I was thirteen."

"Thirteen . . . How come?"

" 'Cause'a C-c-cattus. That's my old man. He—he—he used to—to—to do s-s-s-stuff to me."

"He was sexually abusing you?"

The inmate bit a lip, nodding in shame. "Smacked us around too. I was always catchin' it 'cause'a her."

Lilah winced. "Because of your mother?"

"Bitch was a slut. A punch board for any redneck with a hard-on." He made a fist and jerked it back and forth rapidly. "Turn 'em upside down, they're all sisters, right? I mean, we're talking fucking quintuplets."

"Quintuplets?" Schaefer prompted, confused.

"The pussies in the video, stupid. They got these white faces and huge red lips, and these great cheekbones." His eyes took on a crazed sparkle as he touched Lilah's face with a fingertip. "Kinda like hers."

Lilah held her ground until he removed it, then began peeling the wrapper from a vacutainer holder.

"And they just stand there," the inmate went on, "you know, grinding to the music—with this fuck-me-if-you-can attitude." He snorted and made the jabbing motion with his fist. "So, I did! Punched 'em right in the honey pot. Punched me dozens of 'em."

"Thirty-nine of them," Lilah said sharply as she grasped the vacutainer holder and uncapped the needle.

"And soon's I get out, I'm punchin' me thirty-nine more. I mean—" His eyes darted to the needle in terror, then they rolled up into his head as he passed out and slumped forward onto the table.

Moments later, when he came to, Lilah had already drawn his blood, and two guards were waiting to escort him from the room. "That slut ain't wearing no panties, man. I want to eat that slut's pussy," the inmate said, making a slurping sound that made Lilah's skin crawl. Rather than give him the satisfaction, she forced a smile and held up the needle. The young inmate recoiled like a vampire confronted with a silver cross. It was almost comedic, and she and Schaefer stifled nervous laughter as the guards hustled him from the room.

They went through several more inmates before a grayhaired man in his mid-sixties appeared. He had a healthy vigor that reminded Lilah of her father before he became ill; but there was a refined aura about him in contrast to Doug Graham's earthy persona. "Welcome to Vacaville," the inmate said with an amiable smile. He had just taken his seat when Schaefer came forward and launched into his preamble.

"Oh yes," the old fellow replied brightly when asked if he'd been briefed on the study. "Actually, I know quite a lot about the subject."

"Really?" Lilah prompted.

The inmate nodded. "I found several articles on genes and antisocial behavior in the library. We have an excellent one here, thank God."

"Ah, yes," Lilah exclaimed, indicating his file. "You were an English teacher, weren't you?"

"Yes, at a Catholic elementary school."

"A boarding school for girls, wasn't it?"

The old fellow nodded glumly; then brightened and began rolling up a sleeve. "I'm hoping those articles turn out to be right."

"Why?" Lilah asked. "Because you wouldn't have to accept responsibility for what you did?"

"Oh, I accept it, fully; but even after all these years of therapy, I'd go right back to my old habits. If I have a genetic defect—if my biological soul has been stained by some sort of original sin—it might be accepted as proof that I can't be rehabilitated, and I wouldn't have to worry about being paroled."

Lilah nodded, almost unable to believe that this articulate and apparently decent fellow was a chronic pedophile who'd molested untold numbers of schoolgirls.

"Do you have any idea why?" Schaefer asked.

"Oh, yes, I recall being taken by their purity. It was as if a sense of mission would suddenly come over me . . . a calling to carry out God's will."

A look passed between Lilah and Schaefer. "God wanted you to molest these children?" Lilah asked.

"Of course not. You see, I've always despised the way men use women and discard them like trash. It's the sort of behavior responsible for our lovely language being marred by all those horrible D words: deviant, degenerate, demented, despicable, disgusting—yes, *disgusting* . . . that's the one that troubled me most." He let it trail off, and then, with dramatic eloquence, recited: " 'A first experience of loving or being loved may be enchanting, desolating, embarrassing or even boring, but it should not be disgusting.' You know who wrote that?"

They both shrugged.

"Quentin Bell."

"Yes, of course," Schaefer intoned professorially. "Virginia Woolf's biographer, wasn't he?"

"The best of several. He was also her nephew."

"So, you were going to save these innocent girls from a horrible experience," Schaefer concluded.

"Someone had to," the old fellow replied with frightening sincerity. "It tortured me to think that one of these animals would sexually brutalize them."

"So you beat them to it," Schaefer taunted.

"I beg to differ," he said, keeping his composure. "I taught them that, like the Blessed Virgin, their sexuality was sanctified."

"You're a devout Catholic, aren't you?"

"Yes, I've attended mass daily since I was a child. I receive Communion as well."

"Did you ever confess any of this to a priest?"

"Weekly. Like Augustine, there was a part of me that knew my mission was unholy."

"And you expected them to treat what you told them as a privileged communication."

"Of course. As I recall, they always seemed so mortified—save for this one fellow who wanted to know: Which girls? Where did I touch them? Did they derive pleasure from it? Well, I never went back to *his* confessional again."

Lilah suppressed a smile, then tied a tourniquet around the inmate's biceps and began swabbing the bend of his arm with alcohol.

"What about your victims?" Schaefer prompted. "Weren't you concerned they would tell someone?"

"Always," he replied, then paused, as if deciding whether to go on. "Years before I came to the academy, one of the students drowned in the lake; and as so often happens, it became legend—replete with dark religious overtones, of course. A legend, which I'm ashamed to admit, served me well. I simply implied that anyone who revealed our little secret might suffer a similar fate—if God so decreed."

"Yes yes," Schaefer gushed haughtily. "This mode of psychoemotional terror is quite common in these situations. It's a highly effective technique that—"

"Christ!" Lilah snapped, glaring at him. "This isn't a lecture hall. The man threatened children with a horrible death to keep them from talking! Some of them are probably still mute!"

Schaefer recoiled, taken aback by the outburst. "Just an observation, Dr. Graham," he finally said evenly. Then he leaned over and, through clenched teeth, whispered, "Come on, Lilah, lighten up."

Lilah nodded contritely and sighed with fatigue. "Sorry, it's been a long day." She unwrapped a vacutainer, then looked up at the inmate and forced a smile. "You're an only child, aren't you?"

The old fellow had been visibly unnerved by her condemnation and just nodded grimly.

"Would you happen to know if your father had a similar 'calling'?" she asked, grasping his arm.

"Not to my knowledge. Though I have no way of—"

Lilah tightened her grasp and stabbed the needle into the inmate's flesh, stabbed it hard.

He squirmed in pain and let out a yelp.

Schaefer gasped in astonishment.

"I'm sorry. I must've missed the vein," Lilah said calmly. "I'm afraid I'm going to have to try again."

CHAPTER TWENTY-TWO

The lead on Eagleton had shifted Merrick's focus from Lilah's case to the Las Flores wildfire. Rene might've been spooky and weird, but if she was right, if Eagleton did have a postal box, Merrick was going to find it and bust him when he picked up his mail. He called T.J. and had him run a computer search of Santa Monica's routes. T.J. came up with:

> James D. Eagleton
> P.O. Box 739
> 2231 Wilshire Blvd.
> Santa Monica, CA 90403

Rene *was* right. The address turned out to be the Pack-Tel Business Center. It offered packaging and shipping services along with postal box rentals. The owner's eyes brightened with recognition when Merrick showed him Eagleton's photo. "Haven't seen him for weeks," the husky fellow said, explaining homeless people use postal boxes to receive unemployment checks and replies to job applications.

"Any idea when he might show?"

The owner shrugged, then checked Eagleton's box for mail. "Couple of pieces in there. Hard to say."

"Maybe I'll get lucky," Merrick said cynically. That was three days ago, and since then, from eight in the morning to seven at night, he'd been hunkered down in the Blazer, staking out Pack-Tel from various vantage points. But Eagleton hadn't appeared.

Today, Merrick was parked in front of Madame Wu's, a once classy Cantonese restaurant where Hollywood's elite gathered in the sixties and seventies. Like Chasen's and the Brown Derby, it had lost its clientele to cholesterol, and its cachet to the Wolfgang Puck craze for cuisine "Indochine." Merrick slouched behind the wheel munching on a doughnut he'd have gladly traded for an order of moo-shu pork. It was almost four o'clock when Fletcher arrived to relieve him. He had just enough time to buck Friday traffic, pick up Jason, and get to the Kings game before face-off.

"How goes it, boss?" Fletcher asked, settling next to him in the Blazer.

"I'm putting on a lot of weight," Merrick joked, offering him a doughnut.

"Thanks, but Ellie would kill me."

"Must be taking lessons from my ex."

Fletcher chuckled, then handed him a sheaf of pink message slips. "Dispatch sends their regards."

"Anything on that videotape yet?" Merrick asked, noticing one of the messages was from Lilah.

"Nada. I called over there a couple of times."

"What about my prime's alibi?"

"Ditto." Fletcher produced his now well-annotated copy of Fiona's list. "Three are still traveling and unreachable. I'm playing phone tag with three more in Europe 'cause of the nine-hour time warp; but I did get hold of the guy in Baltimore."

"And?" Merrick prompted impatiently.

"Well, he confirmed Dr. Schaefer was at the workshop, but was foggy on the time. Said he doesn't wear a watch 'cause it reminds him of his mortality."

"His mortality?" Merrick cackled incredulously.

"Yeah, something to do with the erosion of the ozone layer. Don't ask about the lady in Bombay."

Merrick questioned him with a look.

"We had a conversation—in English—and I have absolutely no idea what she said."

"Well, stay on it, Billy-boy," Merrick said with a snicker. "Fiona Sutton-Schaefer is as prime as they get." He briefed Fletcher on the stakeout, and headed for the freeway, thinking about Lilah. He owed her a call on the hockey game. He'd crossed a line into dangerous territory when he invited her. Half of him wanted to scurry back to safety, the other half wanted to explore it no matter how treacherous. After a few moments of reflection, he decided he could never have a thing for a brainy redhead, no matter how attractive—and promptly called her office. He got Lilah's voice mail and sat there thinking about whether or not he'd leave a message.

About an hour and a half later Fletcher was still slouched in his car across the street from Pack-Tel. There was nothing more boring than a one-man stakeout, and he was glad to have Fiona's list to keep him busy. He was dialing one of the numbers when a figure came loping through the darkness. The gaunt, shabbily dressed man was gnawing on a sparerib as he stepped off the curb. He paused and looked left and right for a break in traffic, sending a long ponytail sweeping across his shoulders.

Fletcher figured he'd gotten lucky; but Eagleton had been a regular at Madame Wu's during the years he was employed, and was a regular still, stopping by the back entrance for leftovers prior to picking up his mail.

Traffic had eased and Eagleton was crossing the street. Fletcher resisted the impulse to dash after him, and took a moment to call the Santa Monica police for backup. There was no need to rush. No need to take him now. Merrick had told him about the pieces of mail in Eagleton's box. Eagleton would be preoccupied with them when he left, and Fletcher would be waiting for him.

CHAPTER
TWENTY-THREE

That same afternoon, in Sacramento, Lilah and Schaefer boarded United's four-thirty shuttle to Los Angeles. She'd been shaken by her loss of composure, and hadn't said a word during the drive from the prison to the airport. Barely a week had passed since the fire bomb erupted in her office. Considering the stress she was handling, it was more than possible that the incidents at Vacaville—the violent and degenerate behavior of those "fucking rapists and child abusers"—had put her over the edge. Still, she couldn't fathom why she'd taken it out on an affable old man, and a subliminal awareness that she'd felt more threatened by him than the others kept nagging at her.

Schaefer had respected her silence until now, but his concern and curiosity finally got the best of him. "Want to talk about it?" he prompted gently as the plane climbed into a darkening sky.

She studied him as if considering it. "I think you've probed enough psyches for one day, don't you?"

"I meant as a friend."

Lilah's eyes softened. "Thanks, Paul, I don't think I'm up to it right now. Something to drink would be nice, though. Something alcoholic."

Schaefer flagged a passing steward, and Lilah was soon

settling back with a glass of chardonnay. She was staring out the window when her eyes were drawn to the running light on the tip of the wing, which seemed to beckon in the darkness like a twinkling star. Suddenly it was joined by a second light. And then a third! *Three bursts of light, strobing in hypnotic cadence! Bursts of colored light! Blinding bursts of violet, yellow, and white! Violet, yellow, and white!* Faster and faster, they exploded across the suede-black canvas of sky, painting it with nightmarish images: images of neon-green tentacles threatening to ensnare her; images of her smooth naked body plunging headlong through the darkness, pale skin aglow with eerie holographic translucence as it raced alongside the jetliner.

Though a combination of exhilarating sex and trance-like slumber were usually required to unleash the nightmare's full-blown fury, other stimuli were capable of setting off disturbing flashbacks. Until this moment, Lilah had no recollection of the one in her office the night of the fire; but now it came back in a series of fleeting bursts that further unnerved her. She finally tore her eyes from the window and lowered the shade. The entire episode lasted less than ten seconds, but its mind-numbing effect lingered as she slipped the phone from her briefcase and dialed a prestored number. "Hi, it's me. Daddy there?"

"Of course. Where else would he be?" Marge Graham replied, sounding puzzled, as she always did whenever Lilah asked. "Just a sec, I'll put him on."

"No. No, it's okay, I'll—" Lilah looked up when a passing flight attendant pointed to the phone.

"I'm going to have to ask you to stop using that, immediately," the stewardess said smartly, enforcing the announcement the captain had made prior to takeoff. "FAA regulations."

TOUCHED BY FIRE   165

The woman's tone wrenched Lilah out of her stupor, leaving her embarrassed and confused. She'd heard the announcement, and had no idea why she disobeyed it; but whenever she had one of these episodes, she was on the phone when she came out of it. Lilah quickly ended the call, then drained the glass of wine and had Schaefer order her another. She drank the second glass even more quickly than the first, and it seemed to relax her.

The Los Angeles airport was teeming with the Friday evening crush of passengers when their flight arrived. Lilah had been forced to endure it without a single cigarette, and she exited the terminal digging in her briefcase for the pack of Virginia Slims.

"Well," Schaefer said wearily as they crossed to the parking structure. "It's been a very long day."

"Now I know why I didn't go into psychiatry," she said in a voice that rang with renewed energy.

"Afraid you'd be crazier than your patients, huh?"

"You oughta know," she said, lighting a cigarette.

"My lips are sealed."

Lilah held the match to her mouth and blew him a kiss that extinguished the flame, then exhaled seductively and said, "Call me if you want to chat."

Schaefer laughed good-naturedly at her allusion to phone sex and, as taken as ever by the rhythmic sway of her hips, watched as she walked to the Jaguar and drove off. She seemed spunky, more like herself, he thought; but the incident at the prison wasn't the first time Schaefer had seen Lilah have difficulty modulating anger, nor the first time he'd seen what therapists referred to as inappropriate behavior. He'd experienced her insatiable sexual appetite firsthand; not to mention the risk-taking, impulsive extravagance, and sudden mood swings that sometimes came over her. Most of the time they struck him as facets of a unique personality that had the potential for exceptional professional achievement and personal fulfillment. On occasion, as symptoms of a neurosis that had the potential to incapacitate her, and had resulted in his suggestion that she see someone. As of late, he attributed it to post-traumatic stress caused by the pyrotechnics that destroyed her office and had almost taken her life.

Lilah circled out of the airport and headed north on the 405. Traffic was heavy, and the twenty-minute drive took almost an hour. The Jaguar was approaching the Westwood exit when she pulled the phone from her briefcase and dialed Kauffman's number. Lilah had no plans for the weekend, and was hoping they might spend it together patching things up. She was thinking about going directly to his apartment when she sighed with disappointment at the sound of his answering machine. She left a brief message, then called the lab for her phone mail. "Okay, Doc, listen up," Merrick's voice commanded. "Hockey game. Tonight. Inglewood Forum. Season box entrance. Seven-thirty sharp. Bring your appetite for violence."

Not on your life, Lieutenant, she thought, put off by his last minute timing and cocky tone; but try as she might, she couldn't deny she was drawn to him. The Jaguar accelerated up the off-ramp, then quickly slowed, merging into heavy traffic streaming along Wilshire. With a little luck she'd have just enough time to shower, get into some fresh clothes, and drive to the Forum.

A car was pulling away as she turned into her street. She whipped the Jaguar into the vacated spot, then dashed through the courtyard toward her condo. The bank of mailboxes went past in a blur. She didn't glance at them, let alone notice the slip of yellow paper taped to hers, indicating she had a package; and she wouldn't have taken the time to fetch it from the receiving room even if she had. She wasn't frightened; she wasn't using time pressure as an excuse. She'd been getting mail at home and in the lab for almost a week, and there wasn't a single piece that hadn't been X-rayed and so labeled. She had no reason to think, nor any way of knowing, that this one hadn't. Furthermore, Merrick's call had buoyed her spirits; and a sense of security, a feeling that the pyro was his problem now, not hers, suddenly came over her.

CHAPTER TWENTY-FOUR

In Kings cap and prized Enforcer jersey, Jason Merrick was bouncing with anticipation as his father made the turn into Manchester, the main thoroughfare that led to the Forum. They were within sight of it when his cellphone started twittering. "Merrick."

"Dan?" Fletcher said excitedly. "Dan, I got him. I got Eagleton."

"Way to go, Billy-boy!" Merrick exclaimed, wishing he'd been there. "You take him downtown?"

"No, SMPD's baby-sitting him for us."

"Okay, have 'em keep him on ice till morning. We'll get up close and personal with him first thing." Merrick hung up and pumped a fist in triumph. To Jason's relief, his father continued straight down Manchester. The Forum's marquee proclaimed: KINGS VS. DUCKS 8:00 P.M. They parked in the reserved lot, then met Logan and T.J. at the season box entrance.

"Good news, guys!" Merrick bellowed jubilantly, briefing them on Eagleton's capture as they headed inside. "Hey, hang on a sec," he called out, realizing Lilah wasn't there. "We have to wait for somebody."

"Anybody I know?" Logan asked with a sly grin.

"Yeah," Merrick replied grudgingly. "I think you met her once."

"A girl?" Jason blurted in a tone that rang with equal amounts of surprise and disapproval.

"A woman," his father corrected.

"Don't stop now," T.J. chided.

"Yeah, the world's waiting for you to explain the difference," Logan said with a smutty snort.

Jason scowled, looking at them with the wise-beyond-their-years disdain children have for adults who are acting like children.

By the time Lilah arrived, located a parking space, and made her way to the season box entrance, Merrick and the others were long gone and the game was in progress. She stood there forlornly, listening to the muffled roar that came from within the arena.

"Excuse me?" the guard at the security kiosk called out. "You wouldn't be Dr. Graham, would you?"

"Yes," she sighed hopefully. "Yes I am."

"Thought so," he said, handing her a ticket. "The lieutenant said to keep an eye out for a—a—" He realized he was about to say something he shouldn't and paused. "To keep an eye out for you."

"No, you said, keep an eye out for *a*," Lilah prompted suspiciously. "For *a* what?"

The guard squirmed, wishing he'd never said it, wishing he was inside listening to the slap of stick against puck, the whisk of sharpened steel against ice, the thud of powerful men slamming into the boards.

The Kings had just scored when Lilah entered the arena. The fans were on their feet cheering wildly, bells were ringing, sirens screaming, and the red light behind the net that signaled a goal was strobing like crazy. Lilah's eyes went right to it. Less than four hours had passed since the light on the wingtip had triggered the episode on the plane. The nightmarish images had since receded, but they were still close to the surface, and it wouldn't take much to unleash them again. She paused in the aisle and steeled herself against the onrushing wave until it subsided, then continued down the steps until she reached the front-row box.

"Hey, Doc!" Merrick exclaimed. Then, crushing any thought that she might be the cause of his exhilaration, he added, "You just missed a fantastic goal!"

"Just like a flaky redhead, huh?" she prompted with a knowing smile.

Merrick feigned puzzlement.

"Come on, fess up. You told the guard to keep an eye out for a flaky redhead, didn't you?"

"He said that?" Merrick countered, thinking fast. "No no—*foxy*. I said foxy redhead—who kinda looks like Nicole Kidman. He left that last part out, huh?"

"Very quick on your feet, aren't you, Lieutenant?"

"Foxy, flaky, whatever. He found you, right? I mean, what'd you want me to say?"

"Well," she said, eyeing him flirtatiously, "fantastic would've been nice ..."

Merrick was about to reply when a screaming shot on goal brought a roar from the crowd. The goalkeeper slapped the puck aside. Players from each team raced after it and slammed into the boards in front of the squad's box. The local rivalry had them fighting for the puck with playoff-like intensity. One threw an elbow, another a punch, and sixteen-thousand-plus surly fans began chanting, "Fight! Fight! Fight!"

"Dad!" Jason exclaimed as a player vaulted onto the ice from the Kings bench. "Dad! The Enforcer!"

"The who?" Lilah asked.

"The most violent goon in the game," Merrick replied pointedly.

The Enforcer came screaming across the ice, stick held high, and slammed one of the Ducks into the boards. Both benches emptied. Sticks and gloves were all over the ice. Everyone was throwing punches, everyone except the Enforcer, who was pinned by the mob, his face flattened against the glass right in front of Lilah, Merrick, and the others.

The officials finally broke up the free-for-all and began assessing penalty minutes, allowing the Enforcer to part company with the glass. Lilah's eyes darted to the blood cascading from a gash over his eyebrow. The Kings' feared hit man was a kid with innocent eyes and a peach fuzz beard. He was looking for his stick when he sensed Lilah's gaze and winked. He shook his head as if trying to clear it, sending a spray of blood into the air, then skated toward the penalty box for his two-minute exile.

Lilah recoiled as the bright red drops spattered across the glass. A group of photographers were working in the adjacent box, and several drops had arched through the camera port nearest Lilah, landing on her bare arm. She stared at them for a moment, then rummaged through her briefcase for some tissues.

Jason watched curiously. "You really a doctor?"

"Sure am," Lilah replied brightly.

"My mom's a nurse."

"Good for her," Lilah enthused, noticing a line of glistening red spots on the youngster's jersey. "Looks like the Enforcer got you too."

"He did?" Jason blurted excitedly, pulling it away from his body so he could see them.

"Maybe we can get them off before they dry," Lilah offered, reaching for the jersey.

"Wait," Jason protested, backing away. This wasn't an autograph, or a puck that had sailed into the crowd; nor was it something that could be purchased; no, this was a priceless souvenir. "Dad! The Enforcer's blood!" Jason exclaimed in a tone that meant this jersey would never be washed again.

When play resumed, a series of blinding fast passes had the Kings swarming around the Ducks goal. Players poked and slapped at the puck as it ricocheted off skates and sticks until it finally streaked over the goaltender's glove, tying the score.

The crowd went wild; the sound and light show erupted; and once again Lilah's eyes locked on to the strobing red flasher that sent the wave of images rolling toward her. Once again she steeled herself against it; but this time it crested and broke over her, unleashing a deluge of flashbacks. As always, she was on her cellphone when she came out of it. By the time Merrick noticed, she had already called her mother, checked the messages at her condo, and was about to dial another number.

"What're you doing, Doc?" he chided. "Take the night off, will you? Have some fun!"

"I *am* having fun," she replied, concealing the episode's aftermath. For the next hour or so she got caught up in the fast-paced action and was cheering and pumping her fist with the others.

The Kings had a man advantage and were mounting an attack when Merrick's cellphone twittered. "Merrick . . . Don't do this to me, Gonzo. The score's tied, we're on a power play, and . . . Yeah, yeah, I know I'm on call. Can't you get somebody to cover me? I mean—"

"No can do," Gonzalez interrupted. "We're already handling a warehouse downtown and a nasty wildfire in Laguna Canyon. I sent my last crew up there a couple of hours ago. I'm fresh out of A.I.'s. This baby's yours."

Merrick arranged for Logan to take Jason home after the game, then turned toward Lilah. "Doc? Doc?" he called out over the crowd. "Sorry, I've got to split."

"Another fire?"

Merrick nodded glumly.

"Guess I'm being relegated to the back burner again," Lilah quipped. "Can't someone else cover it?"

"Naw, I'm it. Besides, I'm on call."

"Oh, we doctors know all about that. Well, thanks again for the invite."

"Anytime," Merrick grunted, turning to leave.

"Hey there?" she called after him. "It was really . . . fantastic." She thought it was corny the instant she said it, and was relieved to see him smiling as he hurried off.

About a half hour later the Kings scored the winning goal with seconds to play. Jason, Logan, and T.J. were ecstatic as they headed for the exit.

Lilah remained and asked an usher for directions to the Kings clubhouse. He swept his eyes over her appreciatively, assumed she had an invitation from one of the players, and led the way to the entrance, where an odor reminiscent of Vacaville State Prison greeted her. She presented her UCLA identification to the security guard and explained she was there to see the team doctor. A clubhouse attendant directed her to one of the training rooms, where a natty man in shirt, tie, and suspenders stood at an examining table. He was working on a player who had a towel around his waist and sat with his back to the door.

"Dr. Spicer?" Lilah asked.

"You're off-limits," he replied sharply. "The media room is down the corridor to the right."

"I'm not a reporter. I'm a doctor. Lilah Graham? UCLA Department of Human Genetics?" she prompted expectantly.

"Oh? Oh, of course," Spicer said, waving her in. "Sorry, I didn't mean to be rude. They're always in here looking for an angle."

"I should have called," Lilah said, surprised to find herself face-to-face with the Enforcer, who grinned as Spicer took another suture in the gash above his eyebrow. "But I had a last minute invitation to the game and thought I'd introduce myself."

"Good idea," Spicer said brightly. "Your assistant, Dr. Chen—very sharp, by the way—she brought me up to speed on your study. Sounds intriguing. I brought it up at the players' meeting yesterday."

"And they've agreed to cooperate?"

"A majority of them," Spicer replied. "I still have to run it past the front office. Maybe even the league. That's where it could get dicey."

The Enforcer eyed her knowingly. "So, like you're the one who wants to tap our veins, huh?" he said, still sounding like the sophomore from North Dakota State who turned pro barely a year ago.

"I'm the one," Lilah replied as Spicer tied off the last suture. "Nice work."

"Practice makes perfect."

"That's why we nicknamed him the Zipper," the Enforcer joked, referring to the scar left by the sutures.

A trainer leaned into the room. "Doc? Doc, we need you next door ASAP."

"Won't be a minute," he replied, taking a large adhesive bandage from his suture kit.

"Save you the time?" Lilah offered.

"Thanks." Spicer handed it to her and packed up his gear. "I'll be in touch."

Lilah removed the wrapper and went about applying the bandage. "The Zipper, the Enforcer . . . you have nicknames for everyone around here," she observed, trailing a finger across his cheek when she finished. "No doubt you'll come up with one for me too."

The Enforcer's eyes twinkled mischievously. "Let's see, what if we called you the . . . the Blood Sucker?"

Lilah broke into a suggestive giggle.

The Enforcer grinned and slid off the table. He was standing right next to her now, his baby face inches from hers, his gentle eyes blinking vulnerably in contrast to his macho swagger, his bow-shaped mouth trembling in anticipation as Lilah's fingertip traced over his lips. "So, like, maybe we could get into this study right now."

"Crossed my mind," Lilah replied in a sassy whisper, burying her hands in his hair and pulling his mouth to hers. He shuddered and soared with passion as she worked around to his ear. "But I don't think the front office would approve of this phase, do you?"

"Who cares?" he moaned, losing control.

"I do," Lilah replied, holding him off. "We can be at my place in twenty minutes."

A short time later they were heading north in the Jaguar. The erotic nibble had given the Enforcer an insatiable hunger for more, and he was all over Lilah with childish impatience as she drove, nuzzling her neck, working his hand beneath her skirt, causing her to squeal and squirm like a hormone-charged teenager.

The freeway was moving at this hour, and the Jaguar was soon snaking through Westwood's streets. It was on the hill that led to the Spanish-style condominiums when his finger found its mark. Lilah was biting a lip in an effort to maintain her concentration, making the turn into her street at the same time. She saw something out of the corner of her eye, slammed on the brakes, and brought the car to a stop inches from a barricade adorned with emergency flashers that proclaimed: POLICE LINE DO NOT CROSS.

The Enforcer bolted upright and blinked in confusion at the scene. Lilah clung to the wheel, stunned by the fire trucks angling this way and that in the street, the rainbow of lights raking the putty-colored facades, the smoke curling into the darkness, the firemen dashing in every direction, the TV reporters and camera crews doing their live-at-eleven reports.

Moments later she was backing into a parking space when a familiar voice called out. "Doc? Hey, Doc!" Lilah turned to see Merrick lumbering toward her. He looked weary. Sweat rolled down his face and ringed his armpits. Smudges of ash and soot darkened his hands, face, and clothing.

She shuddered in disbelief. Hadn't the odds been tilted in her favor? Hadn't all her mail been X-rayed? Hadn't the pyro become Merrick's problem, not hers? She left the Enforcer in the car and ran toward Merrick hoping he had an explanation, any explanation, other than the one that had sprung to mind, but his somber eyes left no doubt what had happened. Her worst fear had come true—whoever had targeted her for a fiery death had struck again. She ran into his arms, nestling her head in the curve of his neck. "I'm scared, Merrick," she said, her voice trembling with emotion. "Hold me. I'm really scared."

CHAPTER
TWENTY-FIVE

The receiving room at the condo complex was awash with burned parcels. The flames had been knocked down, but firefighters still had several hoses going, and rivers of water gushed from within, carrying a flotsam of charred debris along with it.

Lilah was sitting on a courtyard wall, smoking a cigarette and staring blankly at the bank of mailboxes. The yellow message slip taped to hers was fluttering noisily in the searing winds that made her skin glisten with perspiration.

Merrick was pacing nearby, talking animatedly on his cellphone. "I thought you guys were supposed to X-ray everything?"

"We did," T.J. fired back. The postal inspector's home was almost an hour's drive from the Forum, and he had barely gotten in the door. "I personally checked off on every package, every letter and piece of—"

"You saying the pyro used another shipper?"

"Damn right I am. UPS, FedEx? Who knows, maybe he delivered it personally?"

"Come on, these wackos never change their M.O. Ten victims, twenty years, the Unabomber did it by the numbers every single time."

"He never went after the same target twice, Dan. Maybe this pyro isn't your normal wacko."

"Maybe. And maybe he just slipped one past you."

"I'm telling you he didn't, man," T.J. protested. "Let me get into it, okay?"

"Yeah, keep me posted." Merrick hung up and went in search of Captain Singer, who was overseeing this operation with characteristic decisiveness.

"Still too hot in there," the captain said, seeing the question in Merrick's eyes. He advised that the Arson Squad hold off until morning and ordered the area be secured as a crime scene.

Merrick nodded, then crossed to Lilah and settled on the wall next to her. "How're you doing, Doc?"

Lilah shrugged and sighed. "You think it's Fiona?" she asked in a childlike voice.

"Yes—and no," Merrick replied. "She's my prime; but it's all feeling and no fact. She could have a fire bomb factory in her kitchen, still no way I'd get a search warrant. Whoever it is, they've swung and missed twice. Chances are they're feeling real frustrated. I'm thinking maybe you shouldn't stay here tonight."

Lilah nodded glumly. "I don't think I could."

"Be happy to drop you someplace. There a friend you can stay with? Your folks?"

"That'd be nice," Lilah replied, clearly relieved. "But maybe I'll just throw a few things together and check into a hotel."

They crossed the grounds to her condo. Merrick led the way inside. There was no sign of package or pyro in the entry, nor in the kitchen or main living area, though a blinking light, which turned out to be the answering machine, gave him a moment's pause. It was well past eleven. Lilah had no intention of returning calls, and headed for the bedroom. Merrick entered first to check it out. The darkness came alive with a flurry of startling, almost heart-stopping images when he turned on the lights. Dozens of Merricks moved in perfect synchronization on every wall, surface, and shelf. The visual effect was mesmerizing, and almost as intriguing as the collection of mirrors that produced it.

Merrick's eyes darted from one mirror to another and then another, and finally to Lilah. He was about to make a crack about excessive vanity but thought better of it. "Get your stuff, Doc."

A short time later, overnight bag in hand, Lilah followed him to the Blazer, passing the Jaguar on the way. The Enforcer was long gone. Their encounter in the training room a vague memory, as if days, not hours, had passed. She activated the car's burglar alarm, which emitted a series of chirps.

Merrick whistled softly. "Sure wouldn't keep that out here if I was making the payments."

"You would if your garage was busting at the seams like mine." She got into the Blazer, gazing forlornly at the fire bomb's aftermath as Merrick drove off.

"So, what'd you think of the game?" he asked, trying to get her mind off it.

"I'd be more interested in what your son thought of it if I were you."

Merrick groaned. "You sound just like his mother."

"He mentioned she's a nurse."

"Yeah, a real angel of mercy."

"Something tells me I struck a raw nerve there."

"Oh?"

"Mm-hmm. I think you just answered my question. *She* hurt you, didn't she?"

Merrick responded with a halfhearted shrug and headed east on Sunset. He glanced at the rearview mirror and noticed the headlights of a car making the same turn. The driver was the only passenger, and one of the parking lights seemed slightly dimmer than the other. "Yeah, I guess," he finally conceded, tromping on the gas. The Blazer accelerated, its knobby tires rumbling loudly on the boulevard's serpentine curves. "The divorce became final a couple of months ago."

Lilah leaned into the stream of cold air blasting from the dash. "There are a lot of broken marriages in law enforcement, aren't there?"

"Yeah, most guys blame the job. You know, the wife couldn't handle the tension, didn't like being alone at night, wondering if the phone was going to ring with bad news."

"That's understandable."

"Yeah, well, I don't have that excuse."

"You lost me, Lieutenant."

"She's living with a cop, Doc," he replied with an ironic snort. "In my house."

"Oh boy," Lilah empathized. "So what happened?"

"Tofu."

"Tofu?"

"Yeah, and alfalfa sprouts and rice cakes. She lowered our cholesterol and killed our marriage." His eyes darted to the mirror. Despite the Blazer's speed, the headlights were still there. "Couple of years ago she starts working at Pritikin. Next thing I know, I can't smoke in the house." He made a right into Warner, a tree-lined street on the eastern edge of the campus, then glanced at the mirror again. Headlights swept through the turn behind them: single passenger, dim parking light—same car. "That was bad enough, but when she started in on the smell on my clothes from the job—I mean, I'm out there busting my hump . . ." His voice rose in anger then trailed off.

"I don't know," Lilah said with a wistful smile. "I kind of like it." She exhaled a stream of smoke, reflecting on her childhood, reflecting on how she would spend the time when her father was on duty gripped by an overwhelming fear that something would happen to him, on how she would wait anxiously for him to come home from his three-day shift, and how euphoric feelings of relief would wash over her as she ran into his arms and drank in the pungent scent of fire and smoke that mixed with his own. "Always did," she concluded. "Ever since I was a kid."

"Yeah, well she wouldn't let me in the house till I changed," Merrick went on, too fixated on the lights in the mirror to pick up on Lilah's mood. "I'd like to see you come home exhausted at three in the morning and strip to your Fruit of the Looms in the backyard."

"So would a lot of guys," Lilah said with a deadpan delivery.

Merrick burst into laughter, as she'd intended. He angled the Blazer into Hilgard, a winding street that bordered the campus. It was free of traffic at this hour, but the car with the dim parking light was still close behind. "You know, you bounce back pretty good, don't you?"

"We all have our share of equanimity."

"Good. It's going to come in handy. Hang on. We're being tailed." Merrick punched the gas, hit the brakes, and spun the wheel simultaneously. The Blazer went into a controlled skid that turned it sideways, blocking the street. Lilah cringed at the screeching of brakes behind them.

"Stay here," Merrick ordered as he popped the door and leaped out. The car that had been tailing them stopped about ten feet from the Blazer. Merrick yanked open the door and shoved his badge in the driver's face. "L.A. County Arson Squad! Out of the car now!"

Lilah's curiosity quickly got the best of her. She left the four-by and came around toward the sedan to see Merrick patting down a woman who was spread-eagled across the hood. Lilah squinted into the glare of the sedan's headlights that obscured the woman's identity. Who could it be? One of her students? Serena? Fiona Schaefer? Fiona! Of course! She was the one with the motive, with the biochemical engineering background—it had to be her. But she was out of town when the first fire bomb detonated; and the odds were twenty to one the pyro was a man, weren't they?

Her mind raced in search of other possibilities as she approached, stopping dead in her tracks on glimpsing the woman's face. "Mom?" she exclaimed incredulously. "Mom, is that you?"

"Lilah?" Marge Graham cried out in a trembling voice. "Lilah, you all right?"

"Of course I am. What are you doing here?"

"That's what *he* wants to know," Marge grumbled, craning her neck to glare at Merrick.

CHAPTER TWENTY-SIX

The Westwood Marquis rose amid stands of tall trees. Its quiet European elegance made Marge Graham uncomfortable as she followed Lilah and Merrick into the lobby, which they'd decided would be a more suitable place to chat than the middle of a darkened street.

"Okay, Mom," Lilah began as they settled in a distant corner. "You want to tell us what's going on?"

"Going on? I was worried sick. What else would I be doing out at this hour?" Marge replied defensively in her brisk cadence. "They had something on TV about a fire at your condo complex. Well, after what happened at the lab . . . I called and left several messages. I even tried your other phone."

"Sorry. I guess the battery must've run down."

Marge harrumphed impatiently. "Anyway, your father was snoring in his chair, so I decided to come over and see what was going on," she resumed in the blithe tone that made whatever she said sound like idle chatter. "I was looking for a parking spot when I saw you getting into a truck with a man who looked like a—a"—she paused and swept Merrick with disapproving eyes—"a street person. For all I knew, it could've been this animal who's trying to hurt you. I wanted to make sure you were okay."

"She's fine, Mrs. Graham," Merrick said, suddenly aware of his soot-smudged appearance, which explained the doorman's reaction when they entered the hotel. "And I'm making sure she stays that way."

Lilah smiled, heartened by his unabashed chivalry. "We decided it'd be a good idea if I spent a few nights away from the condo."

"Oh! You're so extravagant," Marge exclaimed, her anxious eyes darting about the plush interior. "What's wrong with your room at home? Your father'd love to have you, and it'd give me some time to—" She stopped abruptly in reaction to her beeper, which had just begun vibrating. "Oh my," she exclaimed, suddenly flustered. "He probably woke up and is wondering where I am." She hugged Lilah, turned on a heel, and hurried through the lobby toward the exit.

Lilah watched her go, then took the phone from her briefcase and called her father. After assuring him her mother was on her way, she went to the desk and asked for a room.

"High floor, no deliveries," Merrick added smartly.

The clerk scowled as if he were a piece of litter that had blown in from the street, then noticed the badge in Merrick's palm. Moments later a bellman took Lilah's bag and showed them to a room. It had the same elegance of fine fabrics and antique furnishing as the lobby, and a view of the campus. Merrick tipped him, then gave the place a once-over, making certain the door to the adjoining room was locked. "Should be okay . . ."

"Thanks," Lilah said with a smile. "And thanks again for the game." She struck a match and lit his cigarette, then her own. "You don't really get off on the violence, you know," she offered in that omniscient tone doctors employ when debunking imaginary illnesses. "I watched you. I can tell."

"Sure I do," Merrick protested, as if offended. "It's great therapy. I scream my lungs out and sleep like a rock. Speaking of which . . ." He let it trail off and turned to leave.

"Sleep? No way I could crash now," Lilah said with a frantic drag on her cigarette. Between the prison, the hockey game, and the fire bomb, it had been a long, nerve-racking day, and she was still wired. Her eyes went to the minibar. "There's got to be a couple of brews in there. Stick around. Have one with me."

Merrick cocked his head, deciding, then yawned and fell onto the sofa, sinking deep into the cushions. "So how'd you get into this medicine game?"

"By playing doctor with the little boy next door."

"Seriously."

"Seriously?" she echoed, fetching the beers. "I always knew what I wanted to do. My parents encouraged me. Especially my father. He's very ill. I've sort of been caring for him as of late."

"You saying you're your father's doctor?" Merrick asked, uncomfortable with the idea.

"Of course not," Lilah replied, bemused. "We've had the same general prac for years; but if having his daughter check him out once a month and tell him he's doing great makes him feel better, why not? He was the best father a girl could have. A wonderful, decent, and supportive man. I'd do anything for him." She sat cross-legged on the floor, then, setting Merrick up, added, "Saved a few lives in his day."

"Ah, so, you're following in his footsteps," Merrick said, making the obvious assumption.

She broke into that little Doug Graham grin and delivered the punch line. "He was a fireman."

Merrick arched a skeptical brow. "A fireman? You're putting me on..."

"No, really."

He sighed in amazement, too fatigued to recognize the significance of the little bell that had just gone off in his head. "So was mine."

"Figures. Fire fighting's a family thing. My dad put in forty years in Santa Monica."

"Thirty-five, L.A. County," Merrick reflected. "I spent more holidays at the station than I did at home. My mom used to say our lives were touched by fire. I mean, it just kinda gets in your blood and—"

"Well, we haven't identified *that* gene yet," Lilah said girlishly.

"You really think there is one?"

"Wouldn't be surprised. You know, we saw you on TV after you rescued those guys. My dad took one look and said, 'My kind of guy.'" She raised her arms with a dancer's grace and sensuously ran her hands along the side of her neck up into her hair, her slender fingers gathering it into a flaming column; then, as she began arranging it into a perfect chignon, she glanced up at Merrick, with soft, deep blue eyes, and said, "I always thought he was a great judge of character."

Merrick took a long swallow of beer, studying her from behind the bottle. "You wouldn't be making one of your famous medical advances here, would you, Doc?"

"Hey, don't take it personally, I'm bound by oath and training to make as many as I can."

Merrick feigned being crushed. "And I thought it was because I reminded you of Daddy."

"Well, you *do* smoke the same brand of cigarettes—like chimneys."

"Look who's talking. I mean, if anybody should know better, it'd be you, no?"

Lilah nodded. "You think I'd be indulging a two-pack-a-day habit if I didn't?"

Merrick looked puzzled. "What am I missing here?"

"Information," Lilah replied, intensifying his curiosity. She got to her feet, fetched a vacutainer kit from her briefcase, and sat next to him. "Roll up a sleeve," she commanded as she peeled off the wrapper.

Merrick shrunk back deeper into the cushions and yawned. "Not that violence thing again."

"No, I'd have to screen your X chromosome for that. The tweak I'm looking for rears its ugly head on fifteen."

"Tweak? What tweak?"

"The FHIT marker. It's a genetic defect that turns the compounds in cigarette smoke into carcinogens."

Merrick broke into a knowing smile as the pieces fell into place. "Tested yourself, haven't you?"

Lilah smiled, exhaling through her nose and mouth as she continued. "You just might be one of the lucky ninety-three out of a hundred who don't have the marker."

"Which means?" Merrick asked, stifling a yawn.

"You can smoke your fool head off without worrying about lung cancer . . . just emphysema and heart disease."

"Only seven out of a hundred have it, huh?"

Lilah nodded, then swabbed the bend in his arm and readied the needle. "Make a fist."

"I'll probably be one of the unlucky seven," Merrick said as the vacutainer began filling.

"Then you'll have to make one of those nitty-gritty decisions," she replied in a sassy tone. "You could quit cold turkey and spend a lot of time sucking your thumb. You could keep smoking and worry your ass off. You could wait until you get the big C and put in for a lung transplant, if it hasn't already spread to your nodes. Then again, you could run around with one of those metal clips on your ear. You don't exactly strike me as the earring type, but I know several people who tried it and broke the habit."

She finished filling the container, then extracted the needle, and was surprised when she looked up to see that he'd dozed off. An amused smile, infused with traces of affection and relief, broke across her face. Until tonight, he would barely give her the time of day, let alone eight cubic centimeters of his blood. Now, their playful sparring and sharing of childhood experiences had rekindled her earlier feelings that she'd gotten his attention. He *was* interested in her, not just her case. And whether he had intended it or not, she felt safer, felt he *had* become her protector, and would soon *consciously* make that commitment if he hadn't.

Merrick's eyes were closed and his breathing was steady, but he was still in the netherworld of semiconscious thought, his mind flitting from one thing to another.

Why *had* the pyro changed his M.O. and used a different delivery system? Why had the second fire bomb detonated in the receiving room, instead of after Lilah had taken possession of it, like the first one? He thought, too, of Lilah's revelation that her father had been a fireman. Merrick's mind was plunging from twilight into total darkness when that little bell started ringing again. This time it set off a flicker of insight about motive, an insight that could explain why an incendiary device, rather than a more common method, had been used. He tried to hold on to it, tried valiantly to store it for later retrieval, but the cerebral shutter slammed shut, obscuring it in trancelike slumber.

CHAPTER TWENTY-SEVEN

Merrick awakened with a start. His mind was blank, his eyes gritty, and his neck stiff from the sofa. He squinted across the hotel room where Lilah slept beneath sumptuous bed covers. The digital clock read 6:27. He stumbled into the bathroom, threw some cold water on his face, and was combing his hair with his fingers when a vague feeling that he'd had an insight about the case came over him. He racked his brain to find it, but the elusive thought defied recall.

Lilah was still asleep when Merrick left. The freeway was empty at this hour on Saturdays. He made it home in record time, showered, changed clothes, and drove to the Manhattan Beach Coffee Shop, a short-order joint that smelled of buttered toast and bacon. Jason's mountain bike was chained to a signpost out front.

"Dad! Dad, they won!" the youngster exclaimed as his father slid into the booth opposite him. He was still wearing the blood-spattered Kings jersey. "It was super. You missed the neatest goal."

"Yeah," Merrick grunted, lighting a cigarette. "Story of my life..."

"Come on, Dad, okay?"

"Sorry. I get a little cranky when I'm hungry."

The waitress came gliding up to the table with her Silex pot and winked at Jason as she filled Merrick's cup. "Maybe I can do something about that?"

"Don't get your hopes up, Faye."

"Hey, I must be doing something right. You keep coming back for more," she said suggestively. Her face had lost its surfer-girl freshness, but she still had her shape, and thrived on the banter. "The usual for cranky guy, here, and . . . ?" She nodded at Jason, took his order, and winked at him as she moved off.

"So, Dad," Jason said, affecting a casual air. "She your new girlfriend?"

Merrick cocked a thumb after the waitress. "Faye?"

"No, you know . . . last night."

"Dr. Graham? Not a chance. Why?"

"Well, me and my friend Mark at school? We were talking. I mean, about our parents . . . you know, being divorced and stuff?"

"That's okay."

"Yeah, well, we were saying how our dads get kinda weird sometimes? And Mark goes, his dad got over it as soon as he . . . you know"—Jason hesitated, then leaned across the table and whispered—"got laid."

Merrick damn near gagged on his coffee. "Hey," he scolded, unable to suppress his laughter. "Your mother hears you talk like that, she'll crucify me. Besides, Dr. Graham's a little too . . . brainy for me."

"I kinda liked her."

"Hey, go for it. By the way, I have to put that algebra lesson on hold till this afternoon. Okay?"

"Sure. Steve's been tutoring me, but there's still some stuff I don't get."

"Don't worry," Merrick said with a relieved smile as their food arrived. "We'll figure it out together."

After breakfast, Merrick headed north to Santa Monica. Police headquarters was on Main Street about a block from the ocean. Last night, after taking Eagleton into custody, Fletcher turned him over to the SMPD officers who responded to his backup call. Eagleton spent the night in the city's lockup, and in the morning was taken to an interrogation room where Merrick, Logan, and Fletcher were waiting.

"I didn't do it," Eagleton blurted as he entered. "I didn't, and I'm really pissed off that you—"

"Hold it," Merrick interrupted. "You have counsel?"

"I called one last night, but had to leave a message." He paused in bitter reflection, then added, "He's a friend. Did some estate planning for me once."

"Shit," Merrick grunted, flicking the ashes from a cigarette onto the floor. "Better bring in a P.D. No sense trying to wring a statement out of him without—"

Someone rapped on the door. An athletic man in his mid-forties, wearing shorts, polo shirt, and tennis shoes entered. "Dick Fallon. Apologies for the getup. I was halfway to the club before I checked my service." He removed his sunglasses and glanced at the gaunt figure in the threadbare clothes. "Jim?" he wondered, unable to hide the surprise in his voice.

" 'Fraid so," Eagleton said with an embarrassed smile. "Thanks for coming."

The two men stepped aside and huddled in whispered conversation until Fallon was up to speed, then returned to the table. "You have evidence to support the charges against Mr. Eagleton?"

Merrick smiled and signaled Fletcher with a nod.

The young A.I. emptied the contents of an envelope on the table. Among Eagleton's personal effects were several matchbooks from Alice's, a legendary restaurant on the Malibu Pier that served up a panoramic view of the ocean along with trendy California cuisine.

"I didn't know Alice's had a homeless special," Merrick cracked, intending to unsettle him.

"I wasn't always homeless," Eagleton protested. "My wife and I used to go with friends." He looked to Fallon, who was nodding in confirmation. "And I still do. I go in the kitchen door now. I usually grab some matchbooks from the storeroom when I leave."

"Only takes one!" Merrick erupted. "You didn't happen to hitch down to Laguna last night, did you?"

"Laguna? I was in Santa Monica all day—and all night, thanks to you. Why?"

"Somebody torched the whole damn canyon, couple of hours before you were picked up. Plenty of time to hitch back for spareribs at Madame Wu's." He tore the filter from his cigarette, slipped the unlit end into one of the matchbooks, and closed the cover. "Familiar?"

"No, dammit. I never torched any canyon."

Merrick set the igniter aside. "Come on, you're an angry, bitter guy. You wanted to take it out on somebody. Your former neighbors were handy, so—"

"No," Eagleton interrupted forcefully. "No, those people were my friends."

"Evidence," Fallon prompted. "I asked for evidence, Lieutenant. I still haven't seen any."

Merrick glanced at Logan. "Pete . . ."

Logan placed a photo blowup of a charred matchbook on the table in front of Eagleton. "The igniter that started the fire." He set another blowup next to it. "Your thumbprint—found on the igniter."

"Counselor?" Merrick taunted. "Your client ready to make a statement now?"

Eagleton's eyes darted from Merrick to the photos and back. "Yeah, I'll make a statement," he blurted angrily. "Las Flores was my home when I owned a house there. It still is. I use matches to make campfires. I must've—" He was interrupted by an explosive whoosh from the matchbook igniter, which was spitting flame.

"Familiar now?" Merrick prompted.

"No," Eagleton replied, pointing to the photo of the matchbook. "That may be mine—I mean, I must've discarded hundreds of 'em up in Las Flores—but I didn't start any wildfire in that canyon or any other."

"What say we flutter this guy?" Logan suggested in an ominous growl.

"Flutter?" Eagleton echoed apprehensively.

"A lie detector test," Fallon explained. "You don't have to take it. You can refuse."

"No way," Eagleton said indignantly. "No, no, I'm innocent. I want out of here."

Merrick challenged him with a look that Eagleton held unblinkingly. Merrick broke it off and offered him his pack of Marlboros. "Smoke?"

"Thanks. Never use 'em."

Merrick nodded, noting the absence of the telltale nicotine stain on his fingers, then directed the others aside. "There's a chance this guy's telling the truth."

Logan waggled a hand. "A chance."

"You're going to cut this guy loose?" Fletcher exclaimed in an incredulous whisper. "We got prints, we got an igniter, we got matchbooks . . ."

"It's all circumstantial, Billy," Merrick explained patiently. "Not enough to hold him."

"But it still might be him, right?"

Merrick and Logan nodded grudgingly.

"Suppose he goes out there and does it again? Why not keep him on ice for a while? I mean, what's wrong with a little guilty until proven innocent? We're the guys who represent the victims, right?"

"It ain't easy, Billy," Logan counseled. "But there are times when you just have to let go."

Merrick nodded with finality. "You found him once, you can find him again." He crossed to Eagleton and, his voice devoid of apology, said, "You're free to go." Merrick glanced at Fallon and forced a smile, then headed for the door.

"Next stop, Westwood," Merrick announced, leading Logan and Fletcher down the corridor.

"Which reminds me, boss," Fletcher said, a little too eagerly. "You're gonna have to find yourself another prime."

"What?" Merrick exclaimed in disbelief. "Fiona what's-her-face's alibi checked out?"

The young A.I. nodded smugly.

"You're kidding."

"Nope. I got hold of three guys on that list last night. They're all pretty sure she was at the workshop when the box went boom."

Merrick looked crestfallen. "She was lying about that from the get-go," he said, unwilling to accept it. "I know she was."

Fletcher nodded sagely and suppressed a smile. "Hey, sometimes you just have to let go."

CHAPTER TWENTY-EIGHT

The Santa Anas were up well before Lilah on this broiling morning, and the stands of eucalyptus outside the Westwood Marquis bent and straightened in rhythmic waves. In the distance, smoke from smoldering wildfires swirled between the high-rises that ran down Wilshire.

Exhausted from yesterday's events, Lilah had slept well-beyond Merrick's departure. On waking she realized he had left without a word or even a note.

Now, she stood beneath a steaming shower lost in her thoughts. Hadn't there been another attempt on her life? Hadn't he been so concerned that he escorted her to the hotel? Hadn't he accepted her invitation to get to know her better? She had purposely left him sleeping on the sofa, hoping to awaken and find him next to her, hoping to bathe in the tenderness she sensed beneath his coarse veneer, hoping to be caressing him beneath the water cascading over her. Yes, she longed to be lost in ecstasy now, instead of thought; but even if it was all romanticized drivel, his indifference hurt.

Lilah put her damp hair in a ponytail, pulled on a T-shirt and pair of jeans, then ordered breakfast and checked her condo for messages. She assured concerned family, friends, and staffers she was alive and well, reminding the latter that weekend or no—because of the upcoming conference—they were expected in at noon to process the blood samples from the prison. Then, to bolster her flagging spirits, she headed for Macy's. She soon had Ferragamo pumps, Nike Air-Max workout shoes, and Cole Haan loafers arrayed on the sales desk.

"Six hundred forty-two eighteen," the salesman said, zipping her credit card through the reader. He frowned curiously and tried again, then said, "I'm afraid your card's been rejected."

Lilah sighed in disbelief. Sure, it was charged to the hilt, but she made the minimum payment every month. And it had been a week since she returned the teddy. She was dialing customer service when she pictured the pile of bills on her desk, and realized, in the recent turmoil, she hadn't paid them. She didn't have enough in her checking account, but she wrote a check anyway, then headed to cosmetics to pick up some eye shadow.

Cardenas had spent the morning in the lab working on his medical school applications and fielding calls. He was just getting off the phone when Lilah arrived, briefcase in one hand, shopping bag in the other. "Been jumping off the hook, boss."

"The media," she said knowingly. "I've got two words for them, Ruben, and the first one rhymes with duck."

"I guess this isn't a good time to remind you about that letter of recommendation."

"Good guess," Lilah replied, then sighed with remorse and said, "Today, Ruben. That's a promise."

She touched base with a technician who was preparing a centrifuge, a Dupont 75B Ultra that looked like a cross between a mainframe computer and top-loader washing machine, then headed in Serena's direction.

The J.R. was at her computer scrolling through a log of numerically coded blood samples. "We're absent some C.F. data here," Serena said in her haughty British tones. She pointed to a consent form number on the monitor. The adjacent line—where the volunteer's name, Social Security number, and the date the sample was taken should have been recorded—hadn't been filled in. "I'm afraid we're genotyping a Mr. Blank."

Lilah looked genuinely baffled. "We are?"

"From the last series we processed," Serena said, referring to the one that contained both Kauffman's and Lilah's samples. As instructed, Cardenas had peeled a bar-code sticker from a blank consent form, affixed it to Lilah's sample—without knowing it was hers—and, with the stroke of a light pen, recorded it in the log. "I'm quite certain it's the one Ruben left on your desk."

"The one that went up in smoke," Lilah corrected, realizing it had been destroyed in the fire. She shifted her look to Cardenas. "Void that number, assign a new C.F. to the sample, and put it on my desk, will you?"

"I'm on it, boss," he replied, moving off.

"Leave me an indie too," Lilah called after him, thinking of Merrick's sample, which was independent of the OX-A study. Then her eyes shifted back to Serena's. "We'll just call him Mr. Blank for now."

"T minus three and counting," Serena warned. This meant that in three days the sheets of X-ray film would be developed and the resulting autorads evaluated. "We really should have that data by then."

Lilah nodded, then took a rack of vacutainers from her briefcase and set it on Serena's desk. "From the veins of convicted sex offenders."

Serena eyed the gleaming red tubes and shuddered. "So, did you get them to spill their guts?"

"Like they had morning sickness. By the way, I made some headway with the hockey thing last night. I don't know what you said to him, but Spicer thinks you're sharp. Schmooze him a little, okay? Stay in touch." Lilah turned on a heel and headed for the suite of temporary offices.

Kauffman was slouched in a chair, waiting for her. She saw him out of the corner of her eye and crossed the reception area as if he weren't there. "Hey?" he bellowed, tossing the textbook he was reading aside. "Called you last night. Came by this morning too, but the lieutenant and his flunkies were there. I split before he spotted me. Figured he'd think I was admiring my handiwork."

"Is that what you were doing?" Lilah teased as they entered her office.

"Come on, that's really lame. I wanted to make sure you were okay."

"I'm fine. See?" She did a little pirouette into her chair, then noticed the consent forms. She slipped the one for her OX-A sample into a drawer and left Merrick's on the desk. "I thought you might want to apologize," she said with a little smile.

"I might . . ." Kauffman pawed at the carpet with a Reebok. "You busy tonight?"

"I'm up to my ass. I'll have to let you know."

"Why? You hoping for a better offer?"

"Joel," Lilah admonished, concealing he'd hit the nail right on the head. She didn't know it, but at the moment the better offer was crawling around the grounds of her condo complex on his hands and knees.

* * *

Earlier, after grilling Eagleton, Merrick, Logan, and Fletcher had driven straight there. The yellow streamers used to cordon off the crime scene were snapping loudly in the hot winds when they arrived.

The deluge of water required to extinguish the fire had deposited a layer of ash gray silt in the courtyard and washed clumps of cinders against the stucco walls and into the landscaped areas beyond. Fletcher settled into a crouch and began picking through the wet debris with a pair of surgical forceps.

Logan took a camera from his field kit and took shots of the blackened exterior before working his way inside and focusing on the charred details.

Merrick entered the smoldering receiving room. The smell of napthalene was unmistakable as he began his search for the flash point. He soon located an area where everything had been totally incinerated—the area from which the inferno had radiated. He set his attaché on the scorched flooring and began looking for bits of minutiae that were once part of a homemade incendiary.

The three arson investigators spent the entire weekend sifting ashes and picking through soggy debris. Late Sunday afternoon Fletcher was still working the grounds when his eyes darted to what looked like a bent twig but turned out to be a piece of twisted wire. Its vinyl sheath had been burned to a crisp. He pulled gently with the forceps but it wouldn't come loose. After scooping the muck aside, he unearthed a charred plastic device the size of a pack of cigarettes. *Two* twisted wires pierced a seam that ran around the perimeter; and, unlike the device Merrick had found in Lilah's office, this one had been swept outside by the deluge of water before being fused into a blob.

Fletcher knew he'd found the fire bomb's detonator, and

knew it wasn't some sort of timer, but a fiendishly clever remote control device. "Guys? Hey, guys! I got something hot out here!"

Merrick was staring at the detonator in stunned silence when Logan arrived. "You know what that is?"

The old guy's brows twitched excitedly. "Yeah, looks a whole hell of a lot like a beeper, don't it?"

"A modified one," Fletcher replied, toying with the wires.

Merrick whistled in appreciation of the elegant simplicity. "Fucking pyro's been setting these things off with a goddamned phone call." He took the device and slipped it into an evidence bag. "Pete, find out who this thing is registered to and get me its number." He turned to Fletcher with a smug grin. "I think I just got me back my prime."

"Hey, when you're right, you're right," the young A.I. conceded, looking chagrined.

Merrick pumped a fist in triumph. "Billy, my boy, I'm gonna need a list of all the calls Dr. Fiona Sutton-Schaefer made from Santa Barbara."

CHAPTER TWENTY-NINE

"Yes! Yes! God! Oh God! Yessss!" The words came in a rush from Lilah's trembling lips. "Yes! Ohhhh yes—wait, wait! Joel! Joel, I'm going to fall! Joelllll!" she shrieked, her arms around Kauffman's neck, her legs about his waist as the room-service cart scooted out from beneath her. It zipped across the room, crashing into a table that held her briefcase, the remains of several meals, and a phone with a flashing message light. Kauffman was laughing so hard he could hardly stand. He had her bare bottom cupped in his palms and was looking for a surface that would support it.

Yesterday afternoon Lilah kept Kauffman on hold until she finished the letter of recommendation for Cardenas and drafted an outline for the presentation she'd be giving at the conference, all the while hoping Merrick would call. When he didn't, she and Kauffman went to the hotel and spent the night in her room.

They spent Sunday in bed watching football games and ended up in the shower, running a few plays of their own. Neither heard the phone ringing. Neither would have made an effort to answer it if they had. Having soaped each other into a passionate frenzy, they were en route from bath to bed when Kauffman impulsively lifted her onto the room-service cart.

Now, while the message light flashed and Lilah clung to him fiercely, Kauffman fell backward into a chair. She came at him with such enthusiasm that it teeter-tottered and suddenly went over. They tumbled to the floor in a tangle of arms and legs, and broke into hysterical laughter. It wasn't long before they decided they were starving. Lilah went to the phone to call room service and saw the flashing message light.

"You had a call from a Lieutenant Merrick," the hotel operator said.

"That it?"

"Yes, he just said to tell you he called."

Lilah lit a cigarette, disappointed that it had taken him the entire weekend to get around to it. A plume of smoke came from between her lips, curling gracefully upward, like a soul leaving a body. She inhaled deeply as if trying to recapture it, but the emptiness prevailed, along with an awareness that the sexual marathon had been the act of a spiteful child rather than the choice of a mature woman, and was ultimately unsatisfying.

Monday morning, Lilah awakened before dawn with the sense of uncertainty that always surfaced after she'd had sex. She decided to get an early start and headed over to her office well before nine. Kauffman went along to retrieve the textbook he'd left behind, and slouched in a chair, cramming for class. She was reviewing the outline she'd drafted when the intercom buzzed. "Yeah? . . . Okay, Ruben. Thanks for the warning."

Thirty seconds later Merrick rapped on the half-open door and entered the office. "Got a few minutes?"

"What if I said no?" Lilah teased.

"Bad hair day?"

"I've had worse," she replied, burning him with a look.

"Saturday, I had breakfast alone. My poached eggs were harder than hockey pucks. And I went shopping only to have my credit card rejected and discover my eye shadow's been discontinued."

"Ah, a bad eye day too," he observed wryly. "That it?"

"No. In case it slipped your mind, someone's been trying to turn me into a french fry." Lilah smiled and pushed a consent form across the desk. "Sign this."

"Look, Doc, I've got something real important to—"

"Make your mark," she commanded sharply. "We have a witness. I'll settle for an X if I have to."

Kauffman emitted a complacent snicker.

Merrick scrawled his signature across the bottom, then glared at him. "You're outta here, junior. Now." Kauffman stiffened in protest and looked at Lilah in search of support.

"Do me a favor, Joel, and wait in the lab, okay?"

The kid made a face, then bolted from the office.

"That was uncalled for," Lilah said, coming around the desk toward Merrick. "You have no right to—"

"It was a beeper, Doc," he interrupted, silencing her with the impact of a gunshot.

Lilah recoiled and questioned him with a look.

"The detonator. It was a modified beeper. A wire in, a wire out . . . the phone call completed the circuit, and ba-boom."

"Then it could have been set off from anywhere."

"Anywhere on the goddamned planet. Which blows Fiona Schaefer's alibi right out of the water."

"Jack's too—" Lilah blurted.

"Jack?" Merrick said. "Who the hell is Jack?"

"Jack Palmquist. Did his post doc here a year ago. Very gifted, politically naive, kind of weird. He got real upset when he didn't get tenure."

"This just occurred to you?"

"No, Serena reminded me, but I found out he's been living in Europe and dismissed it. Even with a remote detonator, there was no way it could've been Jack until you came up with this beeper thing, right?"

Merrick grunted, then grinned at what he was about to say. "So, did Jack and Jill go up the hill?"

"God, you're nosy."

"It goes directly to motive, Doc."

"I'd say the fact that he was an outspoken critic of my work is more on point. It shouldn't be hard to find out who the beeper's registered to, right?"

"It was damaged. I've got ATF working on it."

Lilah groaned in dismay. "Only half the people on the 'goddamned planet' use them—Fiona for one."

"Your mother for another," Merrick observed.

"My mother? Get serious."

"Everybody's a suspect till it's over, Doc. She really all thumbs with the barbecue? I mean, what was she doing tailing us in the middle of the night?"

"Looking out for me."

"So she leaves your sick father all alone?"

"Yeah, all the time. During the day when she's at work. At night when she does her marketing. That's why she carries a beeper."

Merrick nodded, then settled in her desk chair and lit a cigarette. "By the way, keep the beeper thing to yourself. We always leave a piece of the puzzle in the box. Gives us a way to verify confessions. That's why I kicked your pussy-whipped friend out of here."

"That gets an A for strategy and an F for bedside manner, Lieutenant. Now, to purposely change the subject . . ." She leaned across the desk, making eye contact with him. "You free later?"

" 'Fraid not. I promised my kid I'd help him with his algebra." Merrick rolled his eyes. "Talk about the blind leading the blind..."

"Hey, I got a perfect score on the SATs."

"A perfect score?" Merrick echoed incredulously.

"Uh-huh. I'd be happy to tutor him."

"And he'd be more than happy if you did."

"Am I picking up on something here?"

Merrick smiled. "What can I tell you. The kid's got a thing for, uh, foxy redheads with brains."

"Like begets like?" she ventured flirtatiously. "Sounds like he's got his daddy's genes."

"Sure as hell hope not."

"You sound just like my father," Lilah said, and laughed. "Guess firemen all have the same—"

"Hold it, hold it," Merrick interrupted, struck by a thought that propelled him from the chair. "I've been trying to think of this all weekend. You know if your father has any enemies?"

"My father?" she scoffed. "He was senior deacon at church, coached Little League . . . the guy people came to for advice. When did you cook that one up?"

"When I was crashing on you the other night," he replied with a boyish smile. "I was thinking about him being a fireman, and this little bell started ringing."

"Not loud enough to keep you awake," she teased.

"No, but it had me tossing and turning," he said, assembling the pieces. "You're the target—but maybe your father is who this pyro is out to get."

Lilah's brows arched. "By hurting me?"

"With a fire bomb," he replied pointedly. "Why not a knife? A gun? A hit-and-run? Remember that?"

Lilah whimpered affirmatively. "Who'd want to hurt a retired fireman who's dying?"

"Someone who lost a loved one in a fire and blamed it on the smoke-eater who didn't get there in time. Grief can turn real ugly. I've seen firemen spit on, threatened, assaulted—"

"My father put his life on the line more times than I can count. He has medals for heroism, bravery above and beyond the call of duty—"

"Okay, how about somebody he was on the job with? Couple of years ago we had a senior A.I. busted for torching buildings all over the state."

Lilah's jaw slackened. "If my father had an enemy on the job, I think he'd have said something by now."

"Don't let logic get in the way of common sense, Doc. You'd be amazed what people forget. You chat with them a while, push a button or two, and it all starts coming back. We do it with witnesses all the time. Can you set it up this afternoon?"

"Sure, but he's much sharper in the morning."

"First thing, then. Okay?" Lilah was nodding when his cellphone twittered. "Merrick . . . No, Gonzo, I can't," he snapped, assuming he was being assigned to another fire.

"Lighten up," Gonzalez counseled. "You had a call from Campus Security. Said to tell you they got that videotape you wanted."

Merrick hung up and turned to Lilah. "Where's Campus Security at?"

"Across the street."

"Come on, we're going to watch a video."

They were just entering the lab when Paul Schaefer came through the door. "Lilah, glad I caught you," he said, glancing at Merrick. "The tapes are being transcribed as we speak; but we better cross-reference my data with your bar-coding to make sure—"

"This isn't a good time," Lilah interrupted.

"Oh? What's going on?"

"None of your business," Merrick replied before she could answer. He looked from Schaefer to Serena to Kauffman, then broke into an amused smile. "Talk about the usual suspects . . ." He cocked his head reconsidering it. "Actually, there are a couple missing—"

"Is it one of you?" Lilah shouted. Until now she'd managed to keep her relationships in one compartment and the case in another, but Merrick's wisecrack blew a hole in the wall that separated them, and she suddenly lost it. "Is it one of you? Is it?"

"Hey, come on, Doc," Merrick said, taking her aside. "Come on, settle down, this isn't going to help."

Lilah resisted briefly, then took several deep breaths to regain her composure and nodded.

"Where was I?" Merrick prompted. "Oh, yeah, suspects." He burned Schaefer with a look and said, "Tell your wife I want to see her."

"Fiona? Why? She told you she was away."

"Her out-of-town alibi just got blown out of the water. Your office—tomorrow—five o'clock. Make sure she brings her beeper."

Merrick ushered Lilah out of the lab, then led the way to the elevators and thumbed the call button. "You really should've known better, Doc."

"Pardon me?"

"Hell hath no fury like a woman scorned."

"Shakespeare," Lilah intoned haughtily.

The elevator dinged as if indicating a wrong answer.

"Nope." Merrick followed her in, and, in a matter-of-fact tone, said, "William Congreve. *The Mourning Bride*."

Lilah shrugged, then got back to the matter at hand. "If it was Fiona—or even Jack, for that matter—they won't be on this video, will they?"

"Not unless they dropped by to see the show," Merrick replied. "Well, one thing's working for us."

"What's that?"

"Process of elimination. If it's Fiona or Jack-what's-his-face, none of the other suspects will be on it either."

CHAPTER THIRTY

"Campus Security employs a multizone video system," Chief Copeland intoned, tapping a pointer across a diagram of camera locations. "Blue-coded units cover what we call SEZs—structure entrance zones. Each provides an RTI—real-time image—to personnel manning the security desk in that structure."

Merrick squirmed impatiently. On arrival, he and Lilah had been hustled into the operations center, and now they were being subjected to a security briefing with the attention to detail Merrick imagined went into planning the Normandy invasion.

"Yellow-coded units provide GCS—general campus surveillance," Copeland droned on. "Unlike SEZs, GCS units *are* tied in to VCRs. Tapes are recycled unless they contain potential CRD like this one. If your man was in zone seven—and I have strong doubts he was—this unit would have picked him up."

"Strong doubts?" Merrick echoed, bemused. "Care to share them, or do we get to wait another week for that?"

"The incendiary device was mailed," Copeland replied condescendingly. "What would the perpetrator be doing in the target area when it detonated?"

"Getting his rocks off," Merrick replied sharply. "And

209

we'd be getting ours off if we were watching that FVT instead of talking about it. FYI, that stands for fucking video tape."

Lilah made no effort to stifle her laughter.

Copeland glared at her, then aimed a remote at a VCR. On the monitor, a grainy image of figures cloaked in silhouette and shadow began moving through leafy darkness. Date, camera location, and time counter were displayed across the bottom of the screen.

Lilah shrugged as the tape ended in a blizzard of electronic snow. "Nothing."

"Let's run it again," Merrick said smartly. "By the way, that thing have slow-mo?"

"Frame by frame if you want."

"I want," Merrick replied. He pointed at the remote, the symbol for control, the symbol that had rivalries raging in living rooms all over the country, and added, "I'll take that too."

Copeland scowled. Control was his opiate, Control Freak his nickname, which—to the dismay of the teenage daughters who gave it to him—he took as a compliment. Grudgingly, he tossed the remote to Merrick.

Merrick played the tape frame by frame. This time the obscure figures danced an eerie stop-action ballet in the darkness. He frowned in reaction to a fleeting detail that he'd missed on the first run, and froze the image. If he saw what he thought he saw, two possibilities came to mind. One was a long shot, so he decided to explore the other first. "Any idea what that is?"

Lilah leaned closer to the monitor. "Sort of looks like . . . like a ponytail, doesn't it?"

"Sure as hell does." Merrick swatted at Lilah's hair. "Like you were wearing it that night, right?"

"Yes, I remember putting it up at the gym. Why?"

"You said you got back to the lab sometime after eight." Merrick pointed to the time counter. "Any chance it was seven fifty-four?"

"No. No, I remember the clock in the lobby. It was definitely after eight. Eight-ten, eight-fifteen."

"Then that can't be you, can it?"

"Guess not."

"What about Fiona Schaefer?"

"Fiona? I thought she was up in Santa Barbara."

"That's what she claims, and some people we talked to are pretty sure she never left the place; but I've had this feeling she's been lying about it. If it is her, she never figured we'd come up with the beeper. So being out of town was the perfect alibi."

"You're thinking, beeper or no, maybe Fiona came back to . . . 'to get her rocks off.'"

Merrick nodded, then zoomed in to the figure's head. Instead of being enhanced, the image further disintegrated. "Damn. She ever wear a ponytail?"

"I guess. I mean, most women with long hair do, especially when it's hot." Lilah squinted curiously. "It sort of looks a little like a guy now, no?"

"Sort of," Merrick echoed with uncertainty.

"You think maybe it could be Jack Palmquist?"

"He have a ponytail?"

"Not when he was working for me."

"Figures," Merrick grunted, forced to consider the alternative he'd avoided earlier. There wasn't a shred of evidence to link the two cases, but it couldn't be ignored. "The name Eagleton mean anything to you?"

"Not a thing. Why, he have one?"

"Yup," Merrick replied, explaining Eagleton's link to

the Las Flores fire. "He was up there that night, and could've been down here the next. It's off the wall, but he had opportunity, and he sure has expertise."

"You're forgetting something," Copeland said with an amused smile. "It's called motive."

"What would I do without this guy?" Merrick asked sarcastically. He showed Lilah the photo of Eagleton. "James Eagleton. Any connection come to mind? Grade school? High school? College? Church group?"

"No."

"One-night stand?"

"Not a chance."

"Don't answer so fast. Maybe he tried to hit on you in a bar or something, and you told him to buzz off, and ever since he's been—"

"Who knows? A lot of guys've hit on me in bars."

"Okay . . . shifting gears, but still on motive," he said with a sideways glance to Copeland, "any chance he might have a grudge against your father?"

Lilah shrugged. "You can ask him, tomorrow."

Merrick grunted, then called Pack-Tel and asked if Eagleton had mailed any packages recently. "Large ones—bold, black printing."

The owner typed Eagleton's name into his computer. "Nope, not since we put this system in."

"Which was when?"

"Little over six months ago."

"Shit," Merrick groaned. He resisted an impulse to throw the phone, and kicked a wastebasket instead. It went tumbling across the floor, spilling its contents.

"You break it, you bought it," Copeland crowed.

Merrick muttered an expletive, then took a twenty from his billfold and tossed it on the desk. "That's for the basket." Then tossed another after it—making it an even hundred he'd doled out in recent weeks—and made a mental note to put in for reimbursement. "That's for a copy of the tape." He locked his eyes on to Copeland's. "The one I'm taking with me now."

"Now?" Copeland echoed smugly. "These things take paperwork, Lieutenant, and paperwork takes time."

"I don't have time, dammit!"

"That's your problem," Copeland said coolly. "This tape belongs to UCLA and the state of California. You want a copy of it, go get a subpoena."

Lilah stiffened with rage. "Subpoena? Lieutenant Merrick is trying to stop this nut from killing me, and you're into marking your territory? Well, pee on all the hydrants you want, but not on my time!" She stepped to the VCR, ejected the cassette, and tossed it to Merrick. "Come on, let's go."

Copeland glared at them, then shifted his look to the technician. "Make the goddamned copy," he ordered.

A short time later, tape in hand, Merrick and Lilah were walking across campus beneath forty-foot palms that were rustling in the wind. "You know, you were something else in there," Merrick said with unmistakable admiration.

"Really?" she prompted, pleased by his praise. "You don't think I overreacted?"

"No way, the jerk had it coming. The bit about hydrants was primo."

"Thanks," Lilah said, cupping her hands to light a cigarette. "But something tells me our brains were running on dangerously low levels of sero in there."

"Sero?"

"Serotonin. It's a chemical that controls impulses."

"Well, if I don't lick this case soon," Merrick growled, "mine's going to be running on empty."

CHAPTER THIRTY-ONE

Merrick was en route to ATF headquarters when he called Jason and apologized for blowing the algebra lesson. "Think you can hang in there till the weekend?"

"The weekend? What about Wednesday? There's no school. It's Veteran's Day."

"I don't know. I was talking to Dr. Graham about it. Turns out she's a math whiz, but she may not—"

"She's going to tutor me?" Jason interjected, his voice rising with excitement.

"What she said."

"So then, she *is* your girlfriend . . ."

"No, but if you play your cards right, something tells me she could be yours."

Merrick found Logan and Fletcher in the commissary. The old-timer was nursing a cup of black coffee, the young A.I. draining a bottle of Snapple. "I thought you guys were busting your ass on this case?"

"Yeah, I just got a nasty pain in mine."

"Me too," Fletcher chimed in.

"Take two aspirins, then call Passport Control and have them run a guy named Jack Palmquist. He's supposed to be in Sweden. Find out if he made any calls to this area on the nights the boxes went boom, then put out a bulletin on Eagleton."

"Eagleton?" Fletcher echoed, bemused.

"Don't gloat, Billy-boy," Merrick cautioned, "it's not what you think. Any action on the calls Fiona Schaefer made from Santa Barbara?"

"Phone company's working on it. By the way, a few more people on her list got back to me. Two of 'em swore Dr. Schaefer left the workshop before it was over."

Merrick's eyes brightened in triumph. "I knew she was lying. They say when?"

"Six-thirty, quarter of seven."

"Perfect timing too."

"What's it matter?" Fletcher prompted. "That's either her beeper or it isn't; she either called it or she didn't, right?"

"Right, neither of which we can prove."

"Yet," Fletcher corrected.

"What if it turns out we can't? What if she made the call from a colleague's cellphone or a public booth? Then the key to breaking her is going to be catching her in a lie." Merrick shifted his look to Logan. "What's the story on the beeper?"

"No prints on the case. Interior was clean. So were the guts. Tattoo is trying to come up with who it's registered to."

"She show you her other tatt yet?" Merrick teased.

Logan flicked a look in Fletcher's direction. "You know what, Danny-boy? I think you need to get laid."

"That's what my kid said."

"Smart," Logan grunted. "Took him to that bacon and egg joint again, huh?"

Merrick nodded.

"No, no, *Starbucks*," Fletcher advised, in a tone that

suggested he was dispensing profound wisdom. "You want to meet women, you hang out at Starbucks."

Merrick groaned. "I'd probably run into Joyce and her Lethal Weapon live-in."

"Then again," Logan surmised mischievously, "you might run into somebody like . . . Tattoo."

"Yeah," Fletcher said with a grin. "The rumor mill says she takes her electric guitar to bed. Think about it: She's straddling you with her Stratocaster. You're plugged in to her amplifier with a bird's-eye view of both tatts. She starts ripping off some twangy licks, gets the wah-wah pedal and whammy bar working—"

"You guys are sick," Merrick said with a lurid cackle. "Come to think of it, I need to talk to her."

"Man doesn't waste a minute, does he?" Logan said.

"Mention the word *wah-wah* and he's gone."

In the Computer Imaging lab, Pam Dyer was doing an electronic postmortem on the beeper. Her back was to the door, and her bottom, sheathed in stretch denim, balanced on the stool like a piece of ripe fruit in a still life. Merrick stood in the doorway admiring it, wondering if she thought *his* hard drive would crash if she showed him that other tattoo. "Making any headway?"

"Oh, hi," Pam chirped. The jeans were topped by a scoop-neck blouse that revealed the word WIRED tattooed on her breast in computer-style letters just below the tan line. "Pretty slow going. It's a digital Motorola. A vibrator, not a beeper. Very popular model."

"Registered to who?"

"Won't know until I come up with the cap code."

"The what?"

"The cap code. It's a number. Not the one people use to

beep you. The one that IDs you at the paging center. See, if your beeper crashes or something, its cap code is canceled; then when you get a new one, *its* cap code is assigned the same number people have been calling to beep you. That way you don't have to—"

"Give everyone on the planet your new number," Merrick interjected with a thoughtful drag of his cigarette. "If we had *that* number . . . you could come up with who it's registered to, right?"

"Uh-huh."

He gestured to the components. "Can't you get it from that?"

"I'm trying, but the chip got a little fried and the data starts breaking down when I try to extract it. So . . ." She paused and hissed in frustration.

"Sometimes it helps to get away from it," Merrick philosophized, producing the surveillance video. "Need your opinion on this." He inserted the cassette into a VCR and began fast-forwarding the tape in search of the section with the obscure figure and ponytail.

Pam watched the image streaking across the monitor. "I hear you live in Manhattan Beach."

Merrick grunted.

"You ever go Rollerblading on the bike path?"

"Not in this life," he replied, making her laugh. "I think maybe hanging out at, you know . . . Starbucks is more my speed."

"All those wanna-bes working on their screenplays? You want to loosen up, try the Sandpiper." She leaned against the table, thumbs hooked in her jeans, like a Calvin Klein kiddie porn ad. "My boyfriend's band does gigs there. I play guitar sometimes."

Merrick swept his eyes over her, making a decision. "I hear it's your favorite sleep toy."

"Who told you that?"

"Nobody. I just picked it up . . ."

"Fletcher," she guessed smartly, eliciting a boyish smile from Merrick that confirmed it. "Married guys in their twenties are the horniest. I don't get it."

Merrick was about to explain that divorced arson investigators have been known to come down with the same affliction when the obscure figure appeared on the monitor. He advanced the image frame by frame and froze it. "See that thing that looks like a ponytail?"

Pam nodded.

"Any chance we can enhance it enough to identify that—that man? That woman? That Martian?"

Pam waggled a hand. "Iffy. Give it my best shot."

"Shall I wait?" Merrick asked.

"Not unless you brought *your* sleep toys."

Merrick smiled thinly. "How long?"

"Hard to say. Coupla days, with luck."

"Coupla days?" Merrick echoed with a groan. "Come on, Tattoo, I've got a victim out there who's terrified. She damn near lost it today."

"Well, it'd go faster if I could get my hands on some snapshots of the suspects. I mean, then I could do topographic scans and computer-compare them to the image on the tape."

"You got 'em," Merrick said, making a mental list: Fiona Schaefer, followed by Jack Palmquist, Marge Graham, James Eagleton, Serena Chen, and Paul Schaefer. "Pedal to the metal, soon as you have 'em, okay? The doc's feeling the heat, but she's not a crispy critter yet. We have to nail this weirdo before he turns her into one."

Pam winced at the thought and nodded.

Merrick headed for the door. "Call me soon as that ponytail has a face or that beeper has a name."

CHAPTER THIRTY-TWO

Sunlight streamed through the blinds of Doug Graham's den, sending a pattern of bold stripes across the wall of citations and awards. He stubbed out a cigarette and leaned back in the recliner as Lilah slipped her stethoscope inside his warm-up suit.

Marge stood nearby, eyeing a glass of orange juice on his tray table. "Drink your juice, Doug," she ordered the instant Lilah finished.

Doug's eyes widened with apprehension.

"No, I'm not taking blood today, Daddy," Lilah said reassuringly. "He's not due for weeks, Mom. I thought I'd give him a quick once-over while I was here."

"That has nothing to do with it," Marge retorted. "He still needs his vitamin C, and *D*, for that matter. Remember, you're supposed to get some sun this morning."

Doug eyed her with suspicion, fingering the soiled slipcover on his recliner. "You're going to put this in the wash, aren't you?" he said, winking at Merrick, who was off to one side watching with veiled amusement.

"Oh, Doug," Marge admonished. "Why don't you and the lieutenant go out back and let me get on with this?" She undid the zipper that ran up the back, revealing a slice of the flowery upholstery beneath.

The sound of the zipper cut through Lilah like a knife. "*Mom*. Mom, he likes it that way."

"But it's grimy and smells like old socks. God knows the last time it was—"

Doug thumbed his remote as if trying to shut her off and broke into a mischievous cackle that sent her scurrying into the kitchen. "We've been through a lot together," he said, referring to the recliner. "Sort of like . . . like . . ." He sighed, unable to find the metaphor.

"An old sweater," Merrick offered.

Doug nodded emphatically. "See? Told you he was my kind of guy."

"I think it's time I left you two smoke-eaters to your war stories," Lilah said.

Doug raised his arms. "Give us a hug, princess." She embraced the bag of bones in the warm-up suit and kissed his prickly cheek. "You're my girl, Lilah."

"I know I am, Daddy." She circled behind the recliner to fetch her briefcase, deftly zipping the slipcover en route. "Call me later, okay?" she said to Merrick as she strode off.

Her mother came from the kitchen and hurried after her. "So . . ." Marge began coyly as she caught up.

"No, nothing's going on in my love life," Lilah said, before Marge could ask. "Yes, I did it again. No, I don't know why I park there; and I wish you wouldn't make such a fuss over his chair."

"Me? The slipcover was your idea, as I recall."

"That was then, this is now. He's lived in it for thirty years, and . . ." Lilah paused and lowered her voice. "If he wants to die in a recliner with a dirty slipcover, he has the right."

Doug Graham didn't hear that, though he chuckled with glee at all that preceded it; then his eyes narrowed and found Merrick's. "You gonna catch the bastard who's trying to hurt my little girl?"

"Do my damnedest," Merrick replied, lighting a cigarette. "You might be able to help."

"I'll die trying," the old fellow said with a bold gesture, ticking the recliner with his cigarette. A tiny shower of ashes and sparks fell on the upholstery and into the folds of his warm-up suit.

"Want to meet the local engine company up close and personal?" Merrick scolded in a gentle tone.

The old guy smiled sheepishly, then sighed and settled back in the chair. Merrick saw the signs of fatigue and wasted no time explaining his theory that the pyro might have targeted Lilah to get at *him*. He asked about the men he'd worked with, about notorious fires, angry victims, and arsonists he might have identified or apprehended. He poked and prodded and did whatever he could to jog Doug Graham's waning memory, but neither enemy nor vengeance seeker came to mind.

"You'll get him, son," the old fellow said, seeing Merrick's frustration. "Just like you got those guys out of that canyon. Hell, they owe you the keys to the city for that one."

"Don't hold your breath. My name's permanently engraved at the top of Decker's shit list." He saw Doug's puzzled look, and added, "He's the county B.C."

"What's his problem?"

"His brother. Senior A.I. Thirty years on the job. Made the mistake of starting half the burns he was working. I made the mistake of busting him."

Doug Graham smiled in grudging admiration. "Not easy to blow the whistle on one of your own. I spent my years on the job in the same firehouse with the same crew.

TOUCHED BY FIRE

We were close, real close. If somebody screwed up, the rest of us stood behind him." He exhaled a massive volume of smoke; then, in a raspy whisper that came from within the cloud that concealed him, he said, "Every house has its secrets. That's what we used to say." He sighed in reflection, then exclaimed, "Well, they didn't give you an award for that one, did they?"

"Looks like you collected a few in your day," Merrick observed, crossing to where the old fellow's citations and awards were displayed along with the sports trophies and photographs of Doug with his buddies in the firehouse. Photos of birthday parties. Photos of Christmas. Of him playing Santa.

Merrick was reflecting on the years he'd spent growing up in a firehouse when he noticed the wide-eyed little girl with the freckles and carrot-red hair sitting on Santa's knee. It was obviously Lilah, and, to Merrick's surprise, so was the little girl perched on Santa's other knee. Trick photography? A mirror? Two little Lilahs? He thought about it for a moment, then, thinking aloud, asked, "Lilah . . . Lilah's a twin?"

"Uh-huh," Doug Graham grunted tersely. "Marge? Marge!" he called out, bringing her from the kitchen. "Show the lieutenant the pictures of the girls."

Marge showed Merrick into the living room. It was sparsely furnished and had an almost antiseptic quality. Photographs spanning four decades were displayed on the mantel: pictures of Lilah the valedictorian, of Lilah addressing the Rotary, of Lilah at Disneyland, of Lilah in the high school play, Lilah through every age and phase until, suddenly, there were photos of two infants, two toddlers, two little girls in identical starched dresses, two identical little girls who, sometimes, even their parents couldn't tell apart.

"Lilah never mentioned she had a twin, did she?" Marge prompted, seeing Merrick's reaction.

He shook his head no, analyzing a piece of the puzzle he hadn't seen before. "Did you say *had*?"

"Yes," Marge sighed, eyes glistening with emotion. "Her name was Laura. She died when they were seven. It's very hard to lose a child."

"I know this is difficult for you, Mrs. Graham," Merrick said gently. "But can you tell me if it was the result of a fire?"

Marge smiled thinly. "Leukemia. It was a death sentence in those days. I've always thought it inspired Lilah to become a doctor."

Not what she said when *I* asked her, Merrick thought. "If I may, where is Laura buried?"

"In the local cemetery. It's just up the street from my office. I go almost every morning."

"That wouldn't be Woodlawn, would it?"

"Why, yes. Yes, it would," Marge replied, surprised he knew. "I thought you said Lilah never mentioned it."

"She didn't. Whoever sent the fire bombs has been using it as a return address."

Marge looked shocked. "You told that to Lilah, and she didn't say anything?"

"Not a word. You're sure Lilah knows she's buried there?"

"Of course," Marge sighed. "But she refuses to go with me. I can't even get her to talk about it."

"*I* won't take no for an answer," Merrick said, eyeing the beeper clipped to Marge's waistband. "By the way, how long have you had that?"

"Oh, since the summer," she replied, brightening the way she did when she had a story to tell. "You see, our church does a lot of work with inner-city kids. Wouldn't you know, the day we go to Magic Mountain is the day Doug takes a fall. When I called to check on him, the phone just rang and rang. As you can imagine, I was just beside myself. I called Lilah right away and she drove over, but . . ."

Merrick listened, thinking Doug Graham had to be a saint to cope with this for forty years. "May I see your beeper?" he finally interrupted.

"Oh, I was prattling, wasn't I?" Marge said with an embarrassed smile as she handed it to him.

Merrick thought it was very similar to the one used to detonate the incendiaries, if not the same model. "This your idea?"

"No, it was Lilah's. Why?"

Merrick was suddenly and deeply preoccupied with her response, and didn't reply. His mind had made a quantum leap—the kind born of raw intelligence and years of experience—that had him giving serious consideration to adding a new and altogether unlikely suspect to the list. Though Fiona Schaefer's profile of motive, means, and opportunity had made her his prime suspect, and several other suspects satisfied at least one or more of the three criteria, he still had no proof that any of them had tried to turn Lilah Graham into a french fry; and despite the controversial nature of her work, not a single zealot, protestor, or activist group had picketed her lab, and not a single threatening call or letter had come her way. Everybody's a suspect until it's over, Merrick thought, purposely reminding himself of the axiom; and it was far from over.

Marge Graham sensed the sudden change in Merrick's

demeanor, but she had no idea that a beeper had been used as a detonator, and didn't know what to think.

Merrick was thinking the unthinkable.

CHAPTER THIRTY-THREE

After leaving Merrick with her parents, Lilah spent the afternoon in her office working on her presentation for the GRASP conference. She was scrolling through it on the monitor when Serena stuck her head in the door.

"I'm afraid you'll have to put your hockey players on ice for a while," the J.R. quipped unabashedly.

"Great, another bummer."

"No, more like a tweener, actually." Serena saw Lilah's puzzled look and explained, "That's somewhere be*tween* rather good and could be better."

"Oh?" Lilah prompted, brightening.

"Indeed. After taking some soundings, Dr. Spicer said he expects the league will see the wisdom of cooperating—sometime next season."

Lilah spent the next hour refining her presentation, then checked the current group of probes, which included her sample and Kauffman's. The stylus-drawn chart showed that the temperature had remained constant since they'd been consigned to the freezer. "Time to go to work, Ruben," she announced. "These rads are ready to hatch."

Cardenas knew she needed the results for the conference, that the fire had put them behind schedule, and he swiftly transferred the cassettes from freezer to darkroom. He slipped the sheet of X-ray film from the first cassette and fed it into an autoprocessor. Moments later, when the developed autorad emerged, he peeled the bar-code sticker from the cassette and affixed it in the bottom right corner. One down, hundreds to go, he thought. It would be a long night.

Lilah left the office with a welcome sense of relief. The conference in Maryland was just weeks away, and the thought of putting some distance between her and the pyromaniac buoyed her spirits as she strode toward Wooden Center, leaning into the searing gusts that had carried on into November.

Kauffman was working out on one of the Nautilus machines when she arrived, snapping her towel at his butt as she passed. The kid lurched to a stop in the middle of a repetition and grinned. "I knew it was you."

"Well, tomorrow's the big day," she said.

He looked a little puzzled as he climbed off the chrome-plated apparatus. "Veteran's Day?"

"No, your OX-A probe hatches."

"Oh," he said warily.

"You mean, you're not dying to find out if your weird sexual impulses are due to a mutant gene?"

"Weird sexual impulses?" he wondered, managing to keep a straight face.

"Hey, it wasn't my idea to rub fuzzies on a room-service cart."

A smug grin tugged at the corners of Kauffman's mouth. "The ride of your life, huh?"

"Ranks right up there. Sure you don't want to know if you're negative or positive?"

TOUCHED BY FIRE

"Nope, I figure it's all perfectly normal behavior for a horny, twenty-three-year-old med student."

Lilah laughed, then spent the next half hour on a rowing machine, trying to disprove the Erma Bombeck adage that women over forty shouldn't wave to friends at the beach. Kauffman had already left for his study group by the time she'd finished. She was walking back to the hotel when it struck her that she hadn't heard from Merrick. She knew nothing of the theory he'd hatched after talking to her mother yesterday, nor that on leaving, he had driven straight to ATF headquarters.

"We're going to run this lady nine ways to Sunday," Merrick said to Fletcher when he arrived. His theory was so off the wall, he wanted to find some bit of evidence, some incident in the past, some connection to Lilah, that would support it, before confronting her.

They searched data bases and archives for the schools, colleges, and camps Lilah had attended; and the places where she'd lived and worked in the Boston, Berkeley, and L.A. areas; then ran the data through the WAR, APP, and UAI files. Like APP, the Unsolved Arson Index had national scope and generated a volume of data. They'd been analyzing it for hours when Fletcher left to make some phone calls.

"Just got off the horn with the CHP," he reported a short time later. "The night the mail room went boom? Eagleton spent it in their lockup. Busted in Trancas for vagrancy. Only call he made was to that legal eagle in tennis shorts."

"Shit," Merrick grunted.

"Yeah, we may be up against a pyro with a ponytail, but it ain't him. Now for the good news." He put a sheet of paper on the desk. "Fiona Schaefer's calls from Santa Barbara? None made even close to the time of detonation."

Merrick pumped a fist. " 'Cause she made it from down here. She's lying. I knew it."

"Easy now," Fletcher warned, putting another sheet on the desk. "Jack Palmquist's calls from Stockholm."

Merrick gasped. "He called L.A. that night?"

"Both nights—lots of nights."

"The times match?"

Fletcher waggled a hand. "First, there's a daylight savings thing we need to check; then we need to find out if the number is assigned to a beeper; and then—"

"No we don't," Merrick interrupted brightly. He took the list of Palmquist's calls, left Fletcher to continue analyzing the data they'd gathered on Lilah, and headed for the Computer Imaging lab. Pam Dyer was staring at a monitor where numbers were sequencing.

"What's doing, Tattoo?" Merrick boomed as he entered. "Come up with that cap-code thing yet?"

"Nope. Still a chance, though."

"Good, it has to be registered to whoever sent the fire bombs. Soon as you get it, run the number against these." Merrick gave her the list of Palmquist's calls, then looked to another monitor where an unidentifiable image was slowly morphing. The photos of the suspects she'd requested were tacked across the partition above it. "That ponytail still doesn't have a face, huh?"

"Don't know if it ever will."

Merrick frowned, then pointed to Eagleton's photo. "For what it's worth, he's history."

"Tell me about it. Computer kicked him out first thing. These went next." Pam indicated the three photos next to Eagleton's. "Their faces have the least points of coincidence with the video. *Those* are running neck and neck for the most." She pointed to the last two photos in the row—the faces of Fiona Schaefer and Jack Palmquist—which shared angular Nordic features.

"It's one of them?" Merrick prompted.

"No, it *could* be one of them."

Merrick pointed at Fiona's. "My money's on her."

"Still won't prove she sent the fire bombs."

"It *would* prove she's lying about being out of town; and, as every smart cop knows, Tattoo, if she *did* send them . . ." he paused, suggesting Pam finish it.

"The best way to break her is catch her in a lie," Pam responded smartly. "Of course, if she didn't, it still could be any of them, right?"

"Except him," Merrick growled, removing Eagleton's photo from the partition. "We keep hitting the wall on this one. It's really starting to piss me off."

"Well, as somebody once said, 'It helps to get away from it for a while.' Tomorrow's a holiday. Stay in bed till noon. Play with your sleep toys."

"I'm going to play with my kid," Merrick said, brightening. "I'm gonna help him with his—"

The phone rang, interrupting him.

Pam scooped it up. "Agent Dyer . . . Hey, I hear you're getting your wife a guitar for Christmas," she said with a sarcastic cackle. "Yeah, he is . . . Sure, no problem." She hung up and swiveled back to Merrick. "That was your sidekick."

"The horny married one . . ."

"Uh-huh. He said to tell you he came up with something on Dr. Graham."

CHAPTER THIRTY-FOUR

Lilah sauntered into the Westwood Marquis in her workout gear and got into an elevator without noticing Merrick slouched in a corner of the lobby. He gave her a few minutes to get upstairs, then followed. She was putting up her hair before showering when he knocked.

"Doc? Doc, it's me. It's Merrick."

Lilah crossed the room, pulling on a bathrobe, and opened the door. "Lieutenant . . ." she intoned, doing the waist tie as she led the way inside. "Why do I have the feeling you were supposed to call me?"

"I had to check a few things out first."

Lilah made the obvious assumption and brightened. "My father came up with something?"

"No," Merrick replied sharply. "Your mother did."

"My mother?"

Merrick stared at her. "You lied to me, Doc."

"Pardon me?"

"The name Laura ring a bell?"

Lilah looked as if she'd been punched in the solar plexus. "Yes it does," she replied, lighting a cigarette. "A very painful one. What's she have to do with this?"

"The cemetery. *Woodlawn* Cemetery. Your sister's buried there, dammit. You should've told me."

Lilah looked genuinely baffled. "She is?"

"Come on, Doc, don't play games."

"I'm not. I hadn't given the place a thought until you told me about the return address."

Merrick snorted skeptically. "Your mother said she can't get you to go with her. So don't try to—"

"Right," Lilah interrupted. "She says, 'Come with me to see your sister.' Not, 'Let's go to the cemetery,' let alone *Woodlawn* Cemetery."

"You really expect me to believe that?"

"Look, we're talking thirty-five years ago. I was seven. You're the guy who said, 'It's amazing what people forget.' Well, I *do* remember a whole lot of confusion and pain." Her eyes saddened in reflection, then came alive with an idea. "Are your parents living?"

"My mom is."

"You know where your father's buried?"

"Yeah," Merrick replied defensively. "Escondido. They retired down there."

"What's the name of the cemetery?"

"Holy . . . Holy something or other. Holy Family? Holy Moses? Holy Cow? Hell, I don't know."

Lilah smiled in vindication. "You have any idea what it's like to lose a sibling? An identical twin? I mean, we were like these little mirror images of each other. I was afraid that what happened to Laura would happen to me. I couldn't eat, couldn't sleep. I guess I figured I couldn't die if I was awake." Lilah put her hands together in prayer. "'If I die before I wake, I pray the Lord my soul to take.' Remember that?"

"Uh-huh. I always thought it had to be a cruel son of a bitch who dreamed it up."

"My mother said it with us every night; and after Laura

died, she said it with *me*." Lilah paused, toying with her cigarette, then drew the comforting warmth down into her chest. "As I said, that was over thirty-five years ago. The memories are still painful."

Merrick held her eyes for a long moment. There was nothing evasive in them, he thought, and her reaction to being challenged seemed genuine and spontaneous. But Fletcher's diligence had turned up something that gave credence to Merrick's theory, and he had to test her. "Let's talk *twenty*-five years ago."

"Twenty-five?" Lilah wondered. "Let's see, I . . . I was a freshman at Berkeley."

"Saturday, October twenty-eighth, nineteen seventy-three. You remember that night?"

"Not especially."

"There was a fire in your dorm."

Lilah nodded matter-of-factly. "Dorm fires were weekly events at Berkeley in those days. I don't see the connection."

"Well, according to the investigator's report . . ." Merrick let it trail off and made a ritual of lighting a cigarette, waiting for signs of anxiety to surface; but impatience born of curiosity was all he detected. "As I was saying, according to the A.I.'s report, the fire started in the mail room."

"It did?" Lilah blurted, astonished. "Are you saying, the first time this nut came at me was twenty-five years ago?"

Her incisive question stopped Merrick cold. He'd been so taken by his audacious theory that he'd failed to consider any others, even one as obvious as Lilah's. "I don't know," he replied, shaken by the lapse. "All the evidence was destroyed by the fire. It was arson, but we don't know if it was a fire-bomb-in-a-box or not."

"How'd you find out? My father say something?"

"Your father?"

"Uh-huh. He was there. Parents weekend. I begged them not to come, but they insisted. I was mortified. When I was at Berkeley, nobody, I mean nobody, wanted their parents around. No sex, drugs, or rock 'n' roll for an entire weekend?" She broke into laughter, expecting Merrick would do the same.

He dragged hard on the Marlboro and arched an accusing brow instead. "You didn't have any trouble remembering *that*, did you, Doc?"

"No, I didn't," she replied indignantly. "Someone has made two attempts on my life, and—and—" Her voice faltered and her eyes brimmed with emotion that turned them a rich indigo. "And you're treating me like a suspect." Her jaw dropped as the implication of what she'd just said dawned on her. "My God, you—you actually came up here thinking I sent these things—these—these fire bombs—to myself?"

Merrick cocked his head challengingly. "Did you?"

"Why?" she demanded in a plaintive wail. "Why would I do something like that? How could you think that I'd—" She began sobbing and let it trail off.

Good question, Merrick thought, filling the space between them with smoke. He hadn't been able to come up with a motive and hoped confronting her would force one to surface, but even through the tears, her eyes still engaged his forthrightly. She seemed upset rather than threatened, and genuinely offended that he could think such a thing of her. "Sorry, Doc. When you've been at this as long as I have, you learn to consider anything, no matter how crazy. As I said, *everybody's* a suspect till it's over."

"You could've been more up front with me about it."

"Occupational hazard," Merrick explained. "We're trained to be devious."

"You're also trained to see the obvious, aren't you?" She whirled to the table, opened her briefcase and removed some papers with her handwriting on them. "Does this look like bold angry printing to you?"

"I 'saw' that, Doc. I also 'saw' that whoever it is could be disguising their handwriting."

Lilah pulled a sleeve over her teary eyes and settled on the sofa, taking a moment to collect herself. "I think you were right the first time. This pyromaniac is a real sicko; and the sick joke is, I'm going to join my sister in the cemetery."

"No you're not," Merrick said in a heroic tone that surprised him. "I mean, just because we eliminated one suspect"—he paused and smiled sheepishly at what he'd said—"doesn't mean the others are off the hook."

"But the pyro has to be someone who knows Laura is buried in Woodlawn Cemetery, right?"

Merrick nodded.

"Well, whoever it is, I didn't tell them. So how'd they find out?"

"You didn't have to tell your mother, did you?" Merrick responded, a little too sharply.

"Come on, I told you, we have our moments, but I can't believe that—"

"And as I told you, 'Everybody's a—'"

"No need to repeat it, Lieutenant."

"Good. Far as the rest goes, maybe one of them knows a friend of the family, or the doctor who cared for your sister, or they came across an old obituary."

"Yeah," Lilah said, her tone sharpening. "Someone like Fiona Sutton-Schaefer."

"Yeah, I'm still looking real hard at her. But we just found out your pal Jack-be-nimble in Sweden has a thing for calling L.A.—especially on certain nights."

"Really?"

"Uh-huh. How a guy in Stockholm comes up with a thirty-five-year-old obit puzzles me a little, but—"

"Try the Internet, the World Wide Web . . ."

"Damn . . ."

"Sounds like we're right back where we started, doesn't it?"

Merrick shrugged with resignation.

"Not the first time, Lieutenant," Lilah teased with a demure smile. She was tucked into the corner of the sofa in her loosely tied robe, eyeing him with that combination of childlike vulnerability and mature sexuality that she always seemed to exude.

"Maybe . . ." Merrick said, his eyes sweeping over her desirously. "Maybe we should do something to change our luck."

"What do you have in mind?" Lilah wondered in a sexy whisper that sent a current surging through him. She had just finished putting up her hair when Merrick arrived, and now she arched back sensuously, running her hands up behind her neck, and began taking it down. Her slender fingers moved with practiced grace until the flame-red waves spilled wantonly onto her shoulders and across the front of her bathrobe and breasts.

This was the moment. They'd both felt the rush. They'd both acknowledged it with their eyes. The bed was plush, inviting, and just steps away; they knew that in a few seconds, seconds during which the pent-up sexual tension would explode in a passionate frenzy, they would be naked and writhing beneath the sheets. But despite their past flirtations, despite all the entendres—now, at the very moment of truth—they both froze like members of a religious order faced with breaking their vows of celibacy.

Merrick had suddenly found he was as baffled and confused about Lilah as he was about women in general, starting with his ex-wife. He'd thought he understood her, only to be informed after twelve years that he had completely missed the mark in every category; and he had no reason to think he might not be missing it where Lilah was concerned. She was complicated, neurotic, and promiscuous, not to mention marked for death by a pyromaniac. The more he learned about her, the less he knew; though he had no doubt she was dangerous, which, along with the scent of her perfume, made her all the more tempting and all the more forbidding.

Lilah quickly sensed Merrick's ambivalence along with her own. From the moment she first saw him she wanted to have sex with him. She'd fantasized about what it would be like, and resented his indifference; and now, with a reassuring glance at the mirror, she was on the verge of doing something more to seduce him, something like letting her robe slip open to reveal a bit of thigh or a glimpse of a breast that she knew men found more stimulating than blatant nudity. But she found herself securing the tie and clutching the collar instead. She wasn't sure why. Maybe what she saw in Merrick's eyes wasn't uncertainty, but pity. Maybe he wasn't safe like the others, wasn't someone she could control. Or maybe she just couldn't bring herself to have sex with a fireman, with someone who had the burnt scent and fiery temperament of her father; then again, maybe it was just her turn to reject him.

Merrick sensed her coolness and sighed, pondering her

question. What did he have in mind? "Algebra," he replied with a grin. "Can you do it tomorrow?"

Lilah looked blank, then made the connection. "Oh yeah, sure. In the morning. My afternoon is jammed."

"Manhattan Beach Coffee Shop. About ten?"

"I'll be there."

A short time later, Merrick was driving home in the Blazer, his mind racing much faster than the rush hour traffic. One of the suspects had found out about Lilah's sister and about Woodlawn; but which one? The medical community is a relatively small, interconnected group, he thought. It's more than possible for Fiona to have gotten to know the doctor who cared for Laura all those years ago. He could've been one of her professors in med school, or be running a department at UCLA now. Maybe she came across some records, or a case study somewhere. Then again, maybe she just found it on the Internet. Maybe Jack Palmquist did.

Merrick was finally approaching his exit when, despite Lilah's earlier admonitions, Marge Graham came powerfully to mind. She knows about Laura and Woodlawn, he thought, and also carries a beeper, probably the same model used to detonate the incendiary devices—but so do thousands of other Angelenos. Furthermore, how could a woman who couldn't light a barbecue turn a beeper into a remote detonator? And why would she send fire bombs to her daughter?

On the other hand, it was obvious there was no love lost between them; and if whoever cooked up that prayer was cruel, what was a mother who forced a seven-year-old who'd just lost a sibling to say it every night? Maybe *she* was into getting her rocks off? Her hair wasn't long enough for a ponytail, but she did show up at the condo the night the mail room blew; she did follow them from the crime scene to the hotel; and she certainly could've been lying about the reason.

It would take a deeply rooted pathology like insane jealousy over Lilah's relationship with her father, or an extreme hatred for Lilah, because she was alive and Laura wasn't, to motivate her. But why now? Merrick asked himself. Why thirty-five years after the event?

He bounced a fist off the steering wheel in frustration. The more he tried to assemble the pieces, the more confused the picture became. He was cruising down Rosecrans when it occurred to him that maybe Tattoo was right. Maybe he should get away from it for a while, loosen up, have some fun. The Sandpiper wasn't his kind of place, but Orville & Wilbur's was. The surf and turf joint, just off the beach on Rosecrans, had served as the local pickup joint since the early seventies. He'd been a regular during its heyday, and his. Many a night he had tied one on with the guys; and, on rare occasion, he'd actually gotten lucky with the girls, though picking up women in bars wasn't his forte then, and certainly wasn't now. He started turning into his street, then had a change of heart and continued toward the ocean.

The near miss with Merrick left Lilah feeling hollow and unsettled. She'd spent about an hour pacing the hotel room, and had paused at a window to admire Westwood's flickering lights when the bursts of violet, yellow, and white began exploding over the rooftops, and the neon-green tentacles came lashing at her out of the darkness. She stood her ground as the rising wave crested, threatening to drown her in churning terror; then, in an anxiety-driven frenzy, she threw on some clothes, stuffed the rest of her things into the overnight bag, and checked out of the hotel.

Lilah wandered Westwood's teeming streets still in the throes of the episode. By the time she came out of it, she had completely traversed the village and found herself walking up the hill toward her condo. Her eyes narrowed at the sight of the Jaguar, parked where she'd left it the night of the fire. She threw her briefcase and overnight bag inside, got behind the wheel and took a winding, high-speed drive along Sunset Boulevard to the ocean. The moon was almost full, and huge waves were breaking over the rocks, sending up plumes of spray. She left the car and walked to the bluff that overlooked the boiling surf. Putting her hair up in a ponytail, she sat there for a while, staring at the sea; then, stirred by its power and intensity, she returned to the car and headed home.

A short time later, the Jaguar came up the hill toward the Spanish-style complex, passed several parking spaces, and turned into the driveway that led to the underground parking. Lilah thumbed the remote on the visor. The door yawned open, and she drove straight into the garage beneath her condominium.

CHAPTER THIRTY-FIVE

The Manhattan Beach Coffee Shop was buzzing. On workdays the crush started about six-thirty and began tailing off a couple of hours later; but on holidays the regulars slept in, arriving mid-morning for a late breakfast or lunch. Jason slouched in a booth by the window, toying glumly with his Kings cap. An algebra workbook, spiral-bound pad, and pencil were on the table in front of him. Lilah sat opposite, sipping coffee and keeping an eye out for Merrick, who was late. "Come on, algebra's not that bad," she prompted, sensing Jason's mood.

"That's not it," he lamented. "My mom washed it."

Lilah looked confused. "Washed it?"

"My jersey," he replied glumly. "It's gone. All the Enforcer's blood is gone."

"Oh," Lilah intoned, as disturbed now by his dismay as she'd been at the game by his elation. "Why don't we get started, and take your mind off it?"

Jason shrugged. "I guess."

"Okay. For openers, do you understand the concept of balance? I mean, whatever you do to one side of the equation, you must do to the other, right?"

"Uh-huh. I got that. I mean, I was doing great till we got to negative and positive numbers."

"Ah, they do have a way of ruining your day."

"I mean, like I get the right answer, but I'm a total doofus when it comes to figuring out the sign."

"You mean whether it's negative or positive."

Jason nodded sheepishly.

"Well, there's a little trick that'll let you know what it should be even before you solve the equation."

"Really?" he exclaimed, his eyes brightening.

"Uh-huh. If the numbers in the equation are all the same sign, whether all plus or all minus, the answer is always positive."

"Always?"

"Every time. But if they're different, a mixture of plus and minus signs, the result is always . . . what?"

"Negative?" Jason ventured hopefully.

"Exactly. Same signs—plus. Different signs—minus. For example . . ." She had just begun writing out an equation, taking care to make her physician's scrawl legible, when a waiter appeared with an order pad.

"Sorry for the wait. We're short-handed today."

"So are we," Lilah said with a smile. "You think maybe we should wait for your father?"

Jason shrugged. "He probably forgot and went to work or something."

"Maybe he just overslept. Why don't we call him?"

"I'll be back," the waiter said, moving on to the next booth.

Lilah took the cellphone from her briefcase, then dialed as Jason supplied the number. The line was busy. She waited a few minutes and tried again. "Still busy," she reported with a shrug.

"He leaves it off the hook sometimes when he's really

zonked," Jason explained. "It's not far. I could bike over and get him."

"I've a better idea. How does he take his coffee?"

"Black, two sugars," the waiter piped up.

A short time later Lilah was following Jason's bicycle through the winding streets. The Blazer was in the carport when they got to Merrick's apartment. The boy leaned his bike against the wall and dashed up the stairs, the untied laces of his high-tops slapping at the treads. "Dad? Hey, Dad?" he called out, knocking on the door as Lilah, carrying the container of coffee, joined him on the landing. "It's me, Dad. It's Jason!"

A few seconds passed before the sound of someone stumbling about came from within. "Yeah, yeah, hold on. I'm coming," a raspy voice replied. Finally, the door opened, revealing a bleary-eyed Merrick in a T-shirt, fumbling with the zipper of a pair of jeans. He stood blinking at the brightness. "Sorry, Son," he groaned, distracted by sounds that came from inside the apartment. "I must've overslept."

Jason nodded knowingly and lowered his eyes, then noticed a manila envelope leaning against the stucco wall.

"You and me both," an equally disheveled and distraught woman chimed in as she came charging from the apartment like someone who was very late for work. Jason's eyes widened in recognition as Faye clambered down the stairs, clutching her waitress apron in one hand and working a hairbrush with the other.

Lilah tightened her grip on the container of coffee and glared at Merrick in stunned silence.

"You better wait inside, Son."

"But Dad—"

"Inside now, okay?" his father said more firmly.

"How could you do this?" Lilah demanded angrily the instant the door closed. "How could you accuse *me* of lying, and then pull a stunt like this? How could you be so deceitful? How could you leave me out there vulnerable and exposed like that?"

Merrick was stung and baffled by the onslaught. Deceitful? Vulnerable and exposed? he wondered, running a hand through his matted hair as he tried to make sense of it. "I think you're a little over the top here, Doc. Frankly, I'm not sure I know what you're talking about?"

"I'm talking about last night, Lieutenant."

"Last night? I left you at the hotel. You're secure there. No one's going to bother you."

"God," Lilah groaned in exasperation. "I meant *her*. If you had other plans, you should have said so, instead of playing a game with me."

Merrick grunted, realizing he'd misunderstood, though he still had no idea what she meant by leaving her vulnerable and exposed. "I didn't have plans, Doc. It just . . . happened. Come on, you know damn well I think you're pretty hot."

"You have a funny way of showing it."

"Hey, when it came time to get down to business, I didn't see you making any major moves either."

"I had my reasons."

"Makes two of us."

"I'm listening, Lieutenant."

Merrick shrugged matter-of-factly. "It's no big deal. You're the victim of a crime. I'm the guy stuck with solving it. I figured it'd be smart for us to keep it that way."

"That's a crock and you know it."

"You really want to know?" he challenged in a threatening tone.

"Sure," Lilah replied, thrusting her chin forward. "Go ahead, take your best shot."

"Okay. You're too much work. Too damn complicated. I've just been through weird and neurotic. I'm not up to it again. Right now, a simple slam-bam-thank-you-ma'am is all I can handle."

Lilah's eyes filled with tears. "You—you—you bastard!" She reared back and threw the coffee at him.

Merrick lunged sideways as it zipped past his head and hit the wall behind him. The impact blew the lid off the container and sent coffee splashing across the stucco wall.

Lilah whirled and ran down the stairs. By the time Merrick recovered and went after her, she was getting into the Jaguar. He'd just reached the bottom when the engine roared to life. Lilah smoked the tires, then made a screeching U-turn, narrowly missing Merrick, who sidestepped to safety. The car jumped the curb and clipped some garbage pails, sending them tumbling into the street.

Merrick got to his feet and watched in shock as the Jag fishtailed around a corner at high speed. She *was* dangerous, he thought; dangerous and troubled, and he was suddenly convinced that what he'd been thinking about her wasn't so unthinkable anymore.

Jason had heard the commotion and came running down the stairs, clutching the envelope he'd noticed earlier. "Dad? Dad, you okay?"

"Yeah," Merrick grunted, righting the trash pails and setting them on the sidewalk.

"She was really mad, huh?" Jason prompted, fetching one of the covers. "Kinda like Mom gets sometimes."

"Yeah, it seems I have a real knack for pissing women off."

TOUCHED BY FIRE

"Me too. I asked this girl in my class if she wanted to study with me and she gave me the finger."

"A girl did that?"

"Uh-huh. Girls sure are weird."

Merrick nodded at the irony, thinking if Lilah had sent the fire bombs to herself, he still didn't have any idea why—but a psychiatrist, one who knew her well, might. He was making a mental note to ask Paul Schaefer about it when he noticed the envelope in Jason's hand.

"What's that you got there?"

The youngster shrugged and handed it to him. "Found it up there by the door."

Written across the envelope in impromptu script was: "*Sounds* like you took my advice! Decided not to disturb you. Tattoo." Inside, Merrick found a color print taken from a frame of the surveillance video that Pam Dyer's computer had finally resolved. The ponytailed image was still grainy and deeply shadowed, but the face was unmistakably Fiona Schaefer's.

CHAPTER THIRTY-SIX

Paul Schaefer was at his desk, proofing transcripts of the prison interviews, when the TV suddenly came on. A moment later the CD player erupted with a thundering symphony. He got to his feet, then saw Merrick in the doorway, thumbing a remote control.

"Checking the range," Merrick said with a grin as the answering machine came to life. "Sorry I kept it so long." He gave it to Schaefer, who went about shutting everything off. "By the way, how's the missus doing?"

"Fiona's been a basket case all week."

"She oughta be," Merrick taunted. "Get on the horn and tell her to hustle on over here."

"Right now? I'm not sure that she's—"

"*Now*. Make the call."

Schaefer grumbled but complied, and minutes later Fiona strode into the office. "You got me out of an important meeting, Lieutenant," she said, bristling.

"You lied about being out of town that night, didn't you?" Merrick countered.

"Do we have to go through that again?" Fiona whined. "I told you I was at a seminar in Santa—"

"Not when this was taken!" Merrick interrupted, tossing the print from the video on the desk. He stabbed a finger at

TOUCHED BY FIRE 249

the date and time block. "See that? It proves you were on campus just before the fire bomb went off. You've been lying through your teeth."

Fiona squinted at her likeness and the condemning data, then recoiled and paled. "Yes," she whispered contritely, "I'm afraid I have."

"Fiona..." her husband said admonishingly.

"Actually, I *was* in Santa Barbara," Fiona went on, her voice strengthening. "But I came back to—"

"Kill your husband's lover!" Merrick charged.

"No, to get some data for the seminar," Fiona said evenly. "My J.R. was supposed to quantify it and fax me the results, but he had trouble running the program, so I left the workshop early, drove to Westwood, and ran it myself, then drove back. End of story."

Merrick grimaced, then mulled it over. "Your J.R. will back you on this?"

"Yes. So will the department's computer tech."

"Why the hell didn't you say this before?"

"Because I was frightened. As you said, I *do* have a powerful motive." Fiona paused and fired a withering look at her husband. "But I'm innocent—and I felt as if my reputation and career, even my life, were being threatened. We've all heard the horror stories of people wrongly accused. What would *you* have done?"

Merrick studied her, aware that she had maintained her composure and engaged his eyes throughout. "Probably lied through my teeth."

"Well," Schaefer intoned a little too cheerily. "It sounds like your prime suspect is in the clear."

"Not yet," Merrick retorted, eyeing Fiona's beeper, which looked a lot like Marge Graham's. "Not till my people run down a certain cap code for me."

Schaefer looked puzzled. "Cap code?"

"High-tech evidence," Merrick replied, purposely intensifying the mystique. "Like a fingerprint on a murder weapon—only better. In the meantime, there's another theory I've been toying with. Thought I'd run it past you." He turned to Fiona and said, "Weren't you in an important meeting, or something?"

Fiona got the message, forced a smile, and left.

Schaefer peered haughtily over his oval lenses. "I don't have time to toy with theories, Lieutenant."

"What if I said, I'm thinking—maybe your girl Lilah's been sending these things to herself?"

Schaefer looked astonished. "To herself? Why?"

"That's my problem. Most arsonists are introverted, impotent men with the IQ of a fire hydrant."

"Not exactly Lilah's profile," Schaefer said with a thin smile. "What makes you suspect her?"

"A little lie here, a little coincidence there, and some really off-the-wall stuff when she showed up at my apartment this morning."

"Off-the-wall stuff?" Schaefer intoned, taking exception to the slang. "Are you saying Lilah's behavior was inappropriate, or that it was—"

"Let's cut to the chase," Merrick interrupted. "She said you wanted her to see a shrink. Why?"

Schaefer frowned with disdain. "I have no intention of sharing my observations with you, Lieutenant."

"Why not? Patient confidentiality isn't an issue. It's either her or some nut who's trying to kill her. I have to know what you know."

Schaefer steepled his fingers, then sighed in concession. "First off, it probably won't surprise you to learn that Lilah . . . tends to be . . . promiscuous."

Merrick nodded impatiently. "Keep talking."

"We often see this in people who mistake sex for love and have problems with trust and meaningful relationships. In addition, Lilah is a risk taker, prone to impulsive extravagance and sudden mood swings, and can have difficulty modulating her anger."

"Okay, assuming she's your patient, what are you thinking? What's driving her?"

Schaefer shifted uncomfortably. "We're getting awfully close to crossing ethical boundaries here. I could end up before the state medical board."

Merrick's eyes flashed with anger. "You'll end up before a grand jury if some nut kills her."

Schaefer shuddered, then sighed resignedly. "Taken to the extreme, these traits are often seen in adults who were . . . were sexually abused as children."

Merrick winced and stared at him.

"*That's* why I suggested she seek help," Schaefer went on. "Though I never told her that." His eyes drifted to the mirror, which came alive with stirring images of Lilah: her head thrown back in ecstasy, flaming mane snapping wildly, passion-racked torso arched atop him—an idiosyncrasy to which he'd eagerly submitted and, now, attributed to psychosexual claustrophobia. "Of course, they don't prove Lilah was an abused child."

"If she was . . ." Merrick prompted softly. "Who?"

"Someone in a position of trust or authority—more than ninety percent of the time it's a parent. Incest is the most common and devastating form."

"Her folks seem decent enough. . . ."

"They always do."

Merrick nodded, then, testing him, casually added, "They've sure had their share of tragedy."

"Her father isn't dead yet, Lieutenant."

"Her *sister* is," Merrick fired back.

Schaefer looked genuinely shocked. "Lilah had a sister?"

"Died from leukemia. She never mentioned her?"

"Never."

"An identical twin."

Schaefer's eyes widened, then drifted to the mirror, which had taken on new meaning for him. "How old were they when her sister died?"

"Seven."

"Oh, that's a very powerful dynamic," Schaefer said authoritatively. "At that age she could easily assume her sister was being abused too, and conclude her death was punishment for telling. Pedophiles often make such threats. If so, the trauma could have forever blocked it from her mind."

"Sounds like you're talking about repressed memory," Merrick concluded. "Very controversial stuff, no?"

"Very," Schaefer replied, taking a book from a shelf. *"The Myth of Repressed Memory,* Dr. Elizabeth Loftus: 'There is no cogent evidence that memories can be deeply repressed and then reliably recovered.'" He closed it and fetched a binder of scientific articles. "Dr. Paul McHugh: 'Severe traumas are not blocked out by children but are remembered all too well.' On the other hand, my colleague Dick Metzner says: 'Memories of sexual abuse are . . . usually locked into secrecy by unspeakably frightening threats from the abuser.' And Dr. Judith Alpert: 'The sexual abuse of a child can be so painful . . . It's as if it happened to someone else. That memory can be locked away for decades.'"

"But how could she function? Perfect scores on the SATs, all those degrees, the research she's into..."

"You'd be amazed at how well the human psyche can compartmentalize. You remember Marilyn Van Derbur?"

"Rings a bell. Beauty queen, no?"

"A Phi Beta Kappa beauty queen," Schaefer corrected. "Not to mention Miss America, talented pianist, public speaker, and daughter of a prominent doctor. She was in her late twenties before she recalled being violated by her father from age five to eighteen."

Merrick shuddered visibly.

"Oddly enough," Schaefer went on, "her sister, whom he also abused, didn't repress any of it."

"Okay, for the sake of argument, *if* Lilah's father abused her—I mean, she swears he was the guy in *Father Knows Best*—why not send the incendiaries to him?"

"Because she'd have to accept the ugly truth and admit that he was her abuser."

Merrick was still puzzled. "So she sends them to herself instead?"

"Well, these children usually hate themselves for allowing it to happen. It may be symptomatic of that, or a way to get attention—your attention."

"You mean to get caught."

"Exactly. To finally get the ugly secret out." Schaefer smiled at a thought. "It's been boxed up all these years, and finally exploded."

Merrick nodded in tribute, then shrugged. "I don't know. I gave her the chance to spill her guts—turned the screws really hard—and she blew it. She's either the best liar I've ever seen, or there *is* a pyro out there trying to kill her."

Schaefer mused for a long moment. "There is a third possibility," he said enigmatically.

Merrick arched a brow.

"Still speculating—it's possible we're dealing with what we call dissociative identity disorder."

"Which is what?"

"A split personality. D.I.D. could explain not only why she doesn't remember the abuse, but also why she's sending fire bombs to herself."

"Then if it *is* Lilah, the one I'm dealing with really believes someone's out to get her."

"I'd have no doubt of it. Abused children often create this other person who deserves the abuse. Miss Van Derbur said she coped by splitting herself into a high-achieving day child and a terrified night child."

"So, this other person sort of hangs out, and then kicks in when 'Lilah' feels threatened?"

"Precisely. For example, assuming promiscuity is her way of keeping her abuser at bay, when she's *without* a man, the other personality would take action to keep him from reentering her life."

"That lets her father off the hook," Merrick said relieved. "Poor guy can barely get out of his chair."

"Yes, but we're not talking about rational fear. This would have been buried in Lilah's subconscious for decades."

"Try the cemetery. The one where her sister's buried was used as the return address on the fire bombs."

Schaefer looked stunned. "It was? That gives this theory impressive weight." His eyes suddenly darkened with a thought. "Her father was a fireman, wasn't he?"

Merrick nodded grimly. "I think I know where you're headed: She felt safe when he was on the job; but when he was home—violating her—she'd have fantasies about starting fires."

"Very good, Lieutenant. And this desire to be in two places at once could have split her personality."

Merrick nodded pensively. "Why now? Why not ten years ago? Or twenty? Or next year or the year after?"

"Because her father is dying *now*," Schaefer explained. "The pressure on Lilah to deal with her demons while he's still alive would be enormous."

Merrick's brows arched with understanding. He plucked a cigarette from the pack with his lips and left it unlit. Schaefer smoothed his mustache and stared into the galaxy of halogens overhead. They were both digesting their theory when a cellphone twittered.

Schaefer went for his attaché.

Merrick went for his belt. "Dan Merrick," he growled, brightening at the caller's voice. "Hey, Tattoo, what's doing?" His jaw slackened in astonishment at the reply. "What? No, no way ... Yeah, yeah ... Son of a bitch ... Uh-huh, uh-huh ... Yeah, thanks, I owe you one." He clicked off and stared at Schaefer, awestruck. "We were wrong."

"It's not Lilah?"

"Neither of them. It's her mother."

"Her mother?" Schaefer echoed incredulously.

Merrick nodded. "The pagers that were used as detonators are registered to Margaret Graham, her address, her zip code, her phone number."

"As I believe somebody famous once said," Schaefer quipped defensively, "anyone who goes to a psychiatrist ought to have his head examined."

Merrick nodded again, reflecting on the theory he had developed and then discarded while driving home last night. "She does have a mean streak, and there's a lot of friction between them, not to mention all this dead twin stuff."

Schaefer tilted his head, reconsidering his joke. "You know, actually, some of the broad stroke dynamics might still be germane."

"Good, because *four* pagers are registered to her. The one she uses daily, the two used in the fire bombs, and . . ." Merrick let it trail off forebodingly, and lit the cigarette. "You do the math."

"Oh my God," Schaefer exclaimed as it dawned on him.

"Yeah," Merrick said, watching the smoke rise in graceful curls. "Three down and one to go."

CHAPTER THIRTY-SEVEN

Lilah returned to the lab from her encounter with Merrick to find a sleep-deprived Cardenas and several hundred autorads waiting for her. She wasted no time turning her simmering rage into productive energy. For the last hour, she'd been hovering over a light table evaluating patterns of lanes and bands in search of the telltale shift—the threefold increase in base pairs—that would signal the presence of a defective MAOA gene. She handed another autorad to Serena, who was entering the data in the computer log, and pronounced it "Positive."

Serena glanced briefly at the pattern of gray oval smudges and nodded in confirmation, then drew the light pen across the bar code. The corresponding number immediately appeared on the monitor. She positioned the cursor next to the subject's name and broke into an insidious smile as she entered the result with a click of the mouse. "Well . . . who would have thought it?"

"Thought what?" Lilah prompted, taking the bait.

"That your latest boy-toy would be positive."

Kauffman? Kauffman has the MAOA mute? Lilah wondered with chagrin and amusement.

"My God, Lilah," Serena went on, pretending she was horrified. "He might be a sexual thrill killer!"

"Can you think of a better way to go?"

Serena grinned. "I imagine you've been conducting a relentless search for his environmental trigger."

"Relentless, in depth and exhaustive," Lilah replied with a girlish giggle, enjoying the exchange, which brightened her mood.

Cardenas poked a forefinger into his mouth in protest. "Give me the barf bag, man."

"Pardon me?" Serena challenged haughtily.

"No way," he said, feigning that he was offended. "This is sexual harassment. I mean, if a couple of guys said stuff like that, they'd be outta here in a minute."

"Don't be a sod, Ruben," Serena scolded. "We were paying you a compliment, weren't we, Lilah?"

"Right," Lilah replied. "We think of you as—just one of the girls."

The two women erupted with laughter.

"Can we get on with this?" Cardenas pleaded when it subsided, placing the next group of autorads on the light table.

They had gone through dozens of them when Serena drew her light pen across the bar code of yet another—one Lilah had pronounced negative—then smiled at the data. "Ah yes, the mysterious Mr. Blank . . ."

Lilah knew that one of the autorads in this group had been processed from her blood sample; and since OX-A—a men-only protocol—didn't screen for gender, she also knew a given autorad wouldn't reveal a subject's sex. However, because women have two X chromosomes, and men but one, a trained eye could detect subtle differences in their X bands. Lilah routinely spotted them, but between the banter and endless flow of autorads, this one had gotten past her.

"Mr. Blank," Lilah repeated. She seemed shaken, more crestfallen than threatened or angry. "May I see that again?" She took the autorad and scrutinized it as if a more intensive examination might change the outcome; but there was no telltale shift to be found, nothing to indicate a genetic defect. No, everything was right where it was supposed to be. She didn't have the mutant MAOA gene. She was undeniably negative.

Her vulnerability swiftly gave way to a visceral anger that rose from deep inside her, an anger she didn't fully understand. "Son of a bitch," Lilah exclaimed, tossing the autorad aside.

"What is it, boss?" Cardenas asked. "I screw up or something?"

Lilah ignored him, fetched her briefcase, and bolted from the lab with a petulant stride.

"What's her problem?" Cardenas wondered.

"Ten past. She's late for class."

Cardenas rolled his eyes. "You know, I thought I had this figured out. She's usually later in the month, isn't she? And you're usually more—"

"Don't say it, Ruben," Serena warned sharply.

"See?" he exclaimed, throwing up his hands. "Girls can be sexist, guys can't."

Serena forced a smile, then retrieved the autorad. Her upswept eyes flickered knowingly as they scanned the X band. "Perhaps it has something to do with Mr. Blank being transformed into *Mrs.* Blank."

"*Mrs.* Blank? You saying it's a woman's sample?"

Serena nodded, pursing her lips in thought. "I've a nasty feeling she tested herself."

"Why would she do that?" Cardenas challenged. "No women allowed in this protocol."

"I'd look to the most rudimentary precepts of our trade, if I were you, Ruben."

"Try speaking English once in a while, will you?"

"Oh, come on," Serena coaxed impatiently. "Who else can one screen by screening one's own blood?"

"*One's* parents," he replied, mimicking her.

"Precisely. The MAOA defect is found on the X chromosome, and women have two X chromos, don't they?"

"Last time I checked. One from Mom, one from Dad."

"Well, keeping in mind a negative result means neither harbors a mutant MAOA gene; and since, as you so astutely pointed out, we haven't included women in this protocol, an intelligent person might conclude . . . ?"

"She was testing her father."

"Quite incisive of you, Ruben," Serena said giving her sarcasm full rein.

"But why test her own blood when she's been taking his every month anyway?"

"He'd be required to sign a consent form, wouldn't he? Perhaps she wanted to protect him, or perhaps . . ." She let it trail off mysteriously. "Perhaps she preferred he not know what she was about."

"She didn't sign one either, Serena," Cardenas said pointedly.

"Ah, but what the boss, as you so fondly call her, does with her own blood, is her business, isn't it?"

"Yeah, but I still don't see what ticked her off. I mean, her father's negative, right?"

Serena nodded and thought about the inmates they'd tested, about their sexually abusive behavior, about the controversial, if unproven, implications of the OX-A study—implications that sex offenders who had the mutant gene had no choice but to engage in such lurid activity, while those who didn't have the mute engaged in it of their own free will. She concluded, "Maybe that's her problem."

Cardenas looked baffled. "You lost me."

"Well, as you Americans say, this may be a bit of a stretch, but I suspect it would be somewhat easier to forgive incestuous behavior in a parent who couldn't help himself, than in one who had made a conscious choice, wouldn't you?"

"If you're right," Cardenas said apprehensively, "I'd sure hate to be the guy she takes it out on."

CHAPTER THIRTY-EIGHT

"Sorry I'm late," Lilah said as she blew through the door of the lecture hall. She dropped her briefcase next to the podium and shot a glance in Kauffman's direction. "Where one ends up in medicine often has a lot to do with one's personality," she began, sending knots of chattering students to their seats. "And since personality is arguably related to genotype, I thought we'd spend some time talking about specialization."

The students yawned and settled in as she turned to the blackboard and, chalk clacking loudly, listed the areas of medicine in her barely legible scrawl.

"Okay," Lilah exclaimed, her lab smock billowing as she whirled to face them. "For openers, the action-oriented types with uncanny hand-eye coordination tend to slice and dice their way to fame and fortune by—"

"Becoming surgeons!" one of the students called out before she could finish.

"Obviously I should've included rude and impatient in that profile," Lilah said, circling the word *Surgery* on the board. "Next come the methodical, analytical types who most often calculate their way into . . . ?"

"Radiology," someone replied.

"And diagnostic procedures," Lilah added. "The aerobics freaks make a mad dash for the cardiopulmonary areas. The bedside manner folks talk their way into internal medicine, family practice, and pediatrics. The hopheads turn into drug pushers and gas passers. Those with an aptitude for plumbing tinker with gastro and gyneco; and last but not least, the neurotics seek refuge in neuro and psycho."

"I thought they went into research," Kauffman called out.

Lilah forced a smile and waited for the laughter to subside, then asked, "Anyone have a focus yet?" A number of hands went up. Kauffman's wasn't among them, but he'd been Lilah's target from the outset, and now her eyes locked on to his. "What about *you*, Mr. Kauffman? What areas do you think you might have a flair for?"

"I'm not sure," he replied. "That's why I didn't raise my hand."

"Proctology," one of the students called out.

"Cashectomy," another muttered behind her hand.

"Veterinary medicine," a third shouted.

"Okay, okay," Kauffman finally said, goaded into a reply. "The way things have been going lately"—he let it trail off and broke into a smug grin—"I think I've got a real flair for fornicology."

The classroom rocked with laughter.

Lilah's eyes narrowed to vengeful slits and locked on to Kauffman's. "You're all wondering what this is all about, aren't you?" she taunted. "Well, thanks to a study I've been conducting, I just happen to know that—"

Kauffman stiffened with apprehension. Her rhetorical question-and-answer combined with the deepening ugliness of her mood left no doubt his wisecracks had been a serious mistake. *He* knew what it was all about now, and his eyes held Lilah's, pleading with her to spare him.

Despite her chaotic state, she saw the terror in them and paused as a particle of empathy pierced the darkness. "I just—I just happen to know that . . . one of you . . . has a serious genetic defect," she resumed, unable to embarrass him as she'd planned, "and would do the rest of humanity a huge favor by staying the hell out of—" She whirled to the blackboard and circled *Gynecology* and *Pediatrics*.

The uneasy murmur that rose from the students drowned out Kauffman's sigh of relief.

"And you all thought you were perfect, didn't you?" Lilah taunted, her voice taking on a derisive growl as the thin fabric of her reality began tearing away. "No, no, no, no! There's a nasty little marker lurking in one of your genomes. A biological time bomb that could detonate at any moment, claiming innocent women and children as its victims."

The class squirmed in discomfort.

"Oh, come on," Lilah chastised, her lip curling with disdain, her eyes taking on a manic glaze as she continued to unravel. "Don't look so shocked. You know what I'm talking about. You all know those nasty little D words." She whirled to the board and began writing frantically, chalk clacking, lab smock rustling, voice breaking with emotion as the pressure rose and the safety valves failed and the last few threads snapped and she began shouting: "You know about—deviant—degenerate—despicable—demented—disgusting behavior, don't you?"

The students sat in stunned silence. Any hope that this would turn out to be some sort of practical joke had been destroyed by her tone and loss of control.

Lilah finished writing the last words and threw the piece of chalk with a ferocious snap of her wrist. It hit the floor and shattered, emitting a little puff of white dust, the broken pieces radiating from the point of impact like debris from a meteorite. "Deviant, degenerate, despicable, demented, disgusting behavior!" she shrieked, repeating it over and over in an angry rhythm as she bolted from the lecture hall: "Deviant, degenerate, despicable, demented, disgusting behavior!" The door slammed with surprising force, which sent a crack streaking across the glass.

The students were traumatized. Their fists clenched and lips sealed, all of them stared in disbelief at the door—all except Kauffman, who was staring, awestruck, at the blackboard.

Moments later Lilah came charging out the main entrance of the medical school and hurried across the pedestrian bridge toward the parking structure. The blistering winds were whistling through the concrete grillwork as she got in her car and drove off, smoking the Jaguar's tires in her haste and anger.

CHAPTER THIRTY-NINE

At about the same time Lilah stormed out of the lecture hall, Merrick exited the Neuropsychiatric Institute and started walking in the direction of Mac-Med. After his session with Schaefer, he'd spent some time on a conference call with Logan and an assistant district attorney who would secure the necessary search and arrest warrants. Confronting Marge Graham with several counts of arson and the attempted murder of her daughter wasn't something he relished, and he intended to notify Lilah in person and ask her to accompany him. He was approaching the broad staircase that led to the plaza when his cellphone started chirping. "Yeah, Merrick."

"Danny-boy, glad I got you," Gonzalez enthused. "You know a guy named Kauffman? Joel Kauffman?"

"Uh-huh. He's a med student at UCLA."

"That's him. This is going to sound real crazy; but he just called and said to tell you Dr. Graham sent those incendiaries to herself."

"That sounds real crazy, Gonzo," Merrick said with an exasperated sigh. "It was her mother."

"Her mother?"

"Yeah, I'm heading over there now."

"Hey, it's your call, Lieutenant," the dispatcher conceded. "But I pushed this guy pretty hard and he kept insisting he had proof."

"Like what?"

"Like he said he'd show you when you got there. Lecture hall twelve. He said he'd wait."

"Shit," Merrick grunted. It seemed every time he had the puzzle assembled, something came out of nowhere and scrambled the pieces. He holstered the phone, reversed direction, and hurried toward the medical school.

The lecture hall had emptied by the time Kauffman returned from making the call to Dispatch. He was slouched dispiritedly in the front row, toying with the latches on his backpack, when the door flew open.

"Okay, where is it?" Merrick challenged, skipping the preliminaries. "Where's the proof?"

Kauffman pointed to the blackboard. "That's how she always writes," he said, indicating the areas of medical specialization listed in Lilah's barely legible scrawl. "And today, right in the middle of class, she goes ballistic and starts writing like that." He pointed to the words—deviant, degenerate, despicable, demented, disgusting—that had been printed in the bold angry strokes he'd seen before. "It's the same writing that was on the box."

"The one you carried from the mail room to her car."

Kauffman nodded glumly.

Merrick's eyes shifted from one end of the board to the other and back. The Lilah Graham he knew was on one side, the Lilah Graham he'd never met—the one who had made and sent the incendiaries—was on the other. This was the last piece to the puzzle, the piece that tied her directly to the fire bombs, the keystone that could lock all the others into place. "You're positive?"

Kauffman nodded again.

"Don't bullshit me now," Merrick said, provoking him because he had to be certain.

The kid bolted from the seat. "Fuck you!" he snapped, still unnerved by Lilah's behavior. "I said it's the same, didn't I?"

Merrick nodded, bemused by his outburst.

"Well, it is!"

Merrick cocked his head with a thought: Marge Graham said the pager was Lilah's idea, but it had to be more than that. Lilah must have *bought* it for her too. As a matter of fact, she must have bought four pagers, registered them all in Marge Graham's name, then gave her one and kept the others. "You have any idea where she's at?"

"Nope. I mean, she blew out of here in the middle of class," Kauffman explained, his arms gesticulating wildly. "Really went bonkers. Weird. Like she was somebody else."

"She was," Merrick said, darkening with concern as he reached for his phone. He called the lab in search of her, then the hotel. The switchboard operator at the Westwood Marquis explained that Lilah had checked out last night, leaving instructions that callers be informed she could be reached at home.

A short time later the Spanish-style condominiums stood in silhouette against the fading light as Merrick parked the Blazer and hurried to Lilah's unit. He rang the buzzer, rang it again, waited a few moments, then bashed a heel into the latch. After several tries the wood splintered with a sharp crack, and he shouldered the door open, calling out, "Lilah? Doc? Dr. Graham? Lilah, you here?"

There was no reply as he charged in, no sign of her in the entry or main living area, no sound to suggest her presence.

He crossed the room and leaned into the kitchen with the same result, then made his way to the bedroom, calling out tentatively, "Doc? Lilah?"

He pushed through the door, took a few steps into the room, and froze at an astounding sight. It wasn't Lilah's face that he saw, nor was it dozens of his own. No, the room didn't come alive with startling images as it did the last time, and as he had expected this time. His every movement wasn't being reflected in perfect synchronization on every wall, surface, and shelf.

The ornate frames, gilded frames, carved wooden frames, frames of sleek chrome, colorful plastic, and stained glass, were still there, as were the frames hanging on walls, standing on dressers, and perched atop pedestals. No, none of Lilah's incredible collection had been removed; and the visual impact was still as powerful, if not even more so, because every mirror had been smashed.

CHAPTER FORTY

The green Jaguar came south on Fourteenth Street, passing the credit union where Marge Graham worked, then continued up the hill toward Pico and turned into Woodlawn Cemetery.

The modest abutments at the entrance and graceful rows of headstones beyond were awash in the amber light of an autumn sunset that sent long shadows across the neatly clipped grass and made the names that had been chiseled into the granite appear to glow from within.

The gravel roadway crunched softly as Lilah slowed, letting the car glide beneath the canopy of bare fruit trees. The tiny, Depression-era cemetery took up only a few square blocks, and moments later she found the grave she was after. She left the car and walked slowly toward it, then paused, staring solemnly at the words cut into the pale pink granite.

LAURA GRAHAM

AGE 7 YEARS

THE LORD GIVETH AND THE LORD TAKETH AWAY

"Hi, it's Lilah," she said softly, as if Laura could hear her. Her eyes drifted to the spray of flowers her mother had left earlier, then they filled with tears that went rolling down her cheeks. Each time she blinked, the drops that glistened on her lashes caught the sun's rays, setting off tiny bursts of light; and with chain-reaction speed and intensity, they began refracting into the all too familiar purple, yellow, and white flashes of her nightmare.

Soon her naked body was soaring through infinite blackness, ringed by the glowing tentacles that were lashing out at her like a jungle of neon whips. They were within an eye blink of ensnaring her when something happened that had never happened before. The long, flaming red hair that swept in waves across her breasts and pelvis suddenly parted, revealing not the mature voluptuous form of a woman, but the pristine angular body of a child, a child who hadn't experienced even the initial stirrings of adolescence let alone the flowering of womanhood. And just as she was about to crash headlong into the explosions of colored light, something else happened that had never happened before: her journey ended not in the terrifying uncertainty of the netherworld but in the blissful community of Santa Monica by the sea, where—dressed in the white blouse and plaid skirt of her grade school uniform—Lilah Elizabeth Graham was running across her lawn toward her father's outstretched arms.

Doug Graham worked three days on, three days off then, during those wretched, gloomy days when Laura was taken ill and died; and whenever he was off duty, he'd be waiting outside for Lilah when she came bounding off the school bus. He'd always smile and say, "Give us a hug, princess," picking her up as she ran into his embrace and gave him a big kiss on the cheek. Then, wrapping her arms around his neck and her legs around his waist in the innocent way children do, she'd cling to him as he stood and carried her inside, heading straight into the kitchen for an after-school snack. It was their little routine, their own special time together on his days off; and Lilah looked forward to it with the excitement daughters reserve for these moments with their fathers; moments that made her feel loved and secure; moments that she especially enjoyed because, like all little girls going through that stage where they're secretly planning to dispose of Mommy and marry Daddy, Lilah didn't have to compete with her mother for his attention and affection.

This time, as she clung to her father and he carried her inside, he spoke in a tender whisper and said, "You're my girl, Lilah. The only one I have left now; and I'm going to do something that will show you just how much I love you, okay?"

Lilah nodded excitedly, listening with curiosity and delight as he explained it would be their special secret and that she shouldn't tell Mommy or anyone else about it. Then, instead of taking her into the kitchen so she could get the cookies while he fetched the milk, he went into the den and sat in his new recliner, still hugging her to him, hugging her tightly, hugging her, she thought, as if afraid he was going to lose her or never see her again.

"Take your hair down, Lilah," her father said in a soft, trembling voice.

Lilah settled in his lap, then reached up behind the nape of her neck and did as he asked, letting the carrot-red waves cascade over her shoulders and across the front of her uniform; then she leaned her head against his chest, savoring the faint scent of fire that seemed to linger on him despite the harsh soaps and numerous showers. Her eyes were peering over his shoulder at the lounger's colorful fabric, her heart racing with anticipation, as she wondered just what this supreme expression of her father's love might be, when she felt the movement beneath her skirt, felt his cool, trembling hands caressing her thighs, felt the tip of his finger slipping inside her panties and gently stroking her in a place he had never touched her before. Her eyes widened in surprise and confusion, her adrenaline-charged pulse surged uncontrollably, and her mouth opened in curiosity and protest, but no sound came out.

That was more than thirty years ago, and Doug Graham continued to show his daughter how much he loved her with increasing regularity and intensity until she went away to college, a goal that Lilah set early on, a goal that drove her to excel as a student, a goal she subconsciously knew was her salvation.

Now, as dusk fell, enhancing the cemetery's air of solemnity, Lilah had no trouble emitting an anguished scream. The long-pent-up wail shattered the silence and brought the terrifying flood of memories to a sudden end. She was on her knees when she came out of it, though she had no memory of kneeling, and remained perfectly still for a long moment until she was certain she had regained her equilibrium; then she brushed the tears from her eyes and reached out to the headstone. Her hand was surprisingly steady as it touched the sun-warmed granite, her fingertips gliding across it, tracing the graceful letters of her sister's name.

She felt surprisingly secure and in control as the terrifying sense of uncertainty that always gripped her after an episode gave way to a clear sense of purpose and unwavering resolve. "Don't worry, Laura," she said with eerie calmness. "Everything's going to be okay now."

CHAPTER
FORTY-ONE

The tableau of smashed mirrors had stopped Merrick cold. He took a few moments to gather his wits, then backtracked through the condo to the kitchen and located a door that he had noticed was slightly ajar.

It opened onto a flight of stairs that led beneath the condo. He threw the light switch and started down cautiously, calling Lilah's name; then, detecting the faint scent of napthalene, he took the remaining steps two at a time, and found himself in the garage.

Lilah wasn't there either, but he found an impressive variety of tools, along with surgical gloves, spools of wire, shipping cartons, packing tape, and a workbench covered with evidence. The latter included chunks of crumbled fireplace logs, cans of charcoal lighter, disassembled lightbulbs, and empty mothball and fertilizer boxes.

Merrick picked through the clutter, coming across a crumpled supermarket receipt and several pieces of recently delivered mail from which the postal stickers, X-RAYED CLEARED FOR DELIVERY, had been removed. He took a moment to search the rest of the garage, found nothing else of interest, and charged up the stairs, intending to leave. The flashing indicator light on the answering machine caught his eye. He pressed Play and waited with growing impatience as the message tape rewound.

"Hi, guess who?" Marge Graham's voice finally chirped. "Your office said you were in class, so I waited and tried you at the hotel. I'm sure glad you're out of there. Wasting all that money and everything. You really should try to be more frugal, Lilah. Anyway, a package came for you today. You think by now people would know enough not to send you things here. Don't worry, it has those stickers on it. You know the ones. Come by and pick it up whenever you want. No rush as far as I'm concerned, but—" There was a pause, filled by a mischievous giggle. "—your father says you can't have it until he gets his next checkup. So I suggest you . . ."

Merrick was on the move the instant he heard the word *package*. Marge's voice was still droning on when he went out the door and ran to the Blazer in the falling darkness. He got the four-by rolling, then dialed the Grahams' number on his cellphone. The line was busy. He pressed Redial, then pressed it again and again.

CHAPTER FORTY-TWO

Moments before Merrick left the condo, Marge Graham was in the kitchen of the modest bungalow in Santa Monica. She had just begun preparing dinner when the phone rang. The last time she checked, her husband was dozing in his recliner, and she picked up the wall phone on the first ring, hoping it wouldn't wake him.

"Hi, Mom, it's me."

"Oh hi, you get my message?"

"I went to see Laura," Lilah said beatifically, oblivious to her mother's question.

"Laura?" Marge echoed incredulously. "You mean, you went to the cemetery?"

"Uh-huh. I'm with her right now."

"It's about time," Marge grumbled. "After all these years I can't imagine—I mean, what could have possibly prompted you to go today?"

"Is Daddy there?" Lilah asked in a tiny, childlike voice.

"Of course he is," Marge replied dismissively, as perplexed by the question as ever. "Oh, before I forget, a package came for you this afternoon. That's why I called." As Marge spoke she drifted into the doorway and glanced down the entry hall to the den. She could see the box on the floor just inside the archway, where she'd had the

276

courier leave it. Her eyes swept across the CLEARED FOR DELIVERY stickers, the ones that had assured her it wasn't an incendiary. "Oh, and don't worry," she went on blithely, "it's been cleared and all. I mean the package. Any idea when you might be able to come by? . . . Lilah?"

Lilah smiled strangely and didn't reply.

"Lilah? Lilah, you there?"

Lilah pressed a key on the cellphone, ending the call, and pressed another, one of three she'd assigned to the pagers when prestoring their numbers, then pressed Send. The cellphone immediately autodialed the number, transmitting a page to the third, and last, of the Motorola personal pagers that she had transformed into remote detonators.

Seconds later the pager inside the box in Marge Graham's entry hall received the signal, and the appropriate microcircuit closed, but the pager didn't vibrate to indicate the presence of a message. Instead it acted like a switch, connecting the wire that came from the lantern battery to the wire that went to the lightbulb filament inside the matchbook. The delicate curlicue came to white-hot life. The matches ignited with a soft whoosh. And the surrounding excelsior, which had been sprinkled with charcoal lighter, filling the box with volatile fumes, burst into flame.

Marge had given up on Lilah and was at the sink washing lettuce when the phone rang again. The constant busy signal had prompted Merrick to dial an operator and use his authority to initiate an emergency intercept; but by the time it had been arranged, the line was clear and the phone rang normally.

Marge dried her hands and was crossing the kitchen to answer it when the heat and pressure within the box reached explosive force and burst the taped seams with a deafening crack. The shock wave rocked the house, propelled bits of burning cardboard in every direction, and sent flaming sludge from the incendiary-filled Ziploc splashing against the walls and rolling across the floor.

Marge Graham's ears popped about the same time the items in the kitchen cabinets started tinkling. She thought it was an earthquake at first, but the pungent smell and crackling roar that followed left no doubt what had happened. She ignored the phone and dashed from the kitchen into the entry hall. Shafts of fire were already racing up the walls and bending across the ceiling. She screamed and screamed again, then ran toward the den where her husband slept, shouting his name. A towering wall of flame blocked her way, and the phone was still ringing when the eye-stinging smoke and intense heat sent her running outside into the darkness in search of help.

Moments later columns of smoke were twisting skyward above the house. Most of the windows had been left open, in hopes an ocean breeze might come up and take the edge off the sweltering heat, and the fire was consuming oxygen so fast that air was rushing through them at gale force velocity. Fanned and fed by the infinite supply of oxygen, the blaze literally spread like wildfire.

Paint was blistering and panes of glass were popping from their frames when the Jaguar came down the hill toward the golf course. Lilah saw the smoke and orange glow against the sky, punched the gas and made a looping turn into the driveway, screeching to a stop behind Marge Graham's sedan. She found her mother stumbling about the front lawn in the darkness. Her hair was singed, her face blackened, her mouth trembling with fright, muttering her husband's name.

"Mom? Mom, where is he?" Lilah shouted, trying to snap her out of it. "Where's Daddy?"

Marge whimpered helplessly, nodding at the house.

"Daddy's still inside?" Lilah exclaimed, running the words together into a mournful screech as she ran toward the house.

Her mother pursued and tried to stop her. "No! Lilah, no!" she shouted, getting hold of her arm. Lilah pulled free and dashed up the walkway to the entrance, plunging straight into the inferno in search of her father.

The interior of the tiny structure was alive with the death rattle of burning wood, which snapped and popped with the crisp retort of gunshots. Panels of drapery were going up like sheets of flash paper. The plaster was buckling from the intense heat and popping off the walls in massive sheets. Immediately upon exposure, the sixty-year-old desert-dry framing and lath beneath ignited like kindling. The floors were rolling seas of blue-orange flame.

By the time Merrick arrived, Marge Graham had progressed from shock to hysteria and had been joined by several frantic neighbors. One woman had fetched a garden hose and was aiming the stream of water into a flaming window. "Lieutenant! Lieutenant!" Marge wailed, running toward the Blazer as it screeched to a stop. "They're in there! They're in there! Doug and Lilah! They're in there!"

Merrick pulled his fire coat from the rear of the four-by, hooked an arm through the strap of his air tank, and ran toward the house, commandeering the garden hose en route. He wet down the entrance, then dropped to his knees and went in below the smoke. Dragging the air tank alongside him, sucking heavily on the mask, spraying the griddle-hot floor in front of him with water, he began crawling down the entry hall between the columns of flame and swirling smoke toward the den. The gauntlet of fire led to an archway that framed the raging blaze beyond like the mouth of a massive oven.

In the distance Merrick saw the pale silhouette of a body sprawled on the floor. His eyes were burning and tearing heavily and he could barely keep them open, let alone determine whether it was Lilah's body or her father's. The hose was literally melting in his hands as he wet down the flaming debris in his path, inching forward on his belly, feeling his way until his hand found Lilah's. It was limp and lifeless.

Merrick quickly wet her down, then discarded the hose, slipped off his fire coat, and threw it over her head and torso, protecting them from the tongues of flame that lashed out from every surface. He gulped several frantic breaths from the air tank, burrowed beneath her until his shoulders were squarely under her midsection, and lunged to his feet. Bent beneath Lilah's weight, blinded by eye-stinging pain, he lumbered back down the flaming gauntlet and through the blizzard of orange cinders as fast as he could.

Marge emitted a euphoric scream as Merrick burst through the blazing rectangle that had been the front door and stumbled across the lawn with Lilah. He dropped to his knees and, with the help of several neighbors, laid Lilah flat on her back.

With swift, practiced hands he opened her mouth, put his lips to hers and forced his breath deep into her lungs. He did it several times in rapid succession, then locked his hands together, placed the palms on her chest and began rocking back and forth rhythmically, counting to himself as he pumped the oxygen-rich blood to Lilah's brain. He repeated the procedure several times and had his lips pressed to hers again when she finally stirred and began coughing.

Seconds later her eyes fluttered to life, blinking in confusion at the hazy image that gradually came into focus. "Merrick?" Lilah wondered weakly, squinting at him with a totally baffled expression.

"Yeah, easy now, take it easy," Merrick said reassuringly. "You're going to be okay."

A faint, dopey smile broke across Lilah's face. She'd been waiting more than thirty years to be rescued, and it had finally happened. "Thanks," she said, in a dry-throated rasp.

Merrick nodded and smiled thinly. "You're some piece of work, Doc."

Lilah was aglow with relief, then her brow furrowed at a thought and her watery eyes snapped open in panic-stricken awareness of what had happened. "My father!" she rasped. "My father! Did you get him out?"

Merrick glanced at the roaring inferno behind them, and shook his head no, sadly.

The sound of a wounded animal came from deep inside Lilah. She lurched into a sitting position and started to get to her feet.

"Nothing you can do, Doc," Merrick said, holding her back. "He's gone."

"Let me go, dammit!" Lilah shouted plaintively. "Let me go!" She struggled to break free of his grasp and pummeled him feebly with her fists, her reddened eyes staring forlornly at the house that was now totally consumed by fire. "Daddy! Daddy! Daddy!"

She kept shouting it over and over until she heard the

rising scream of sirens, felt the throbbing rumble of fire trucks, and saw the multicolored flashers sweeping the darkness; then, amid the screech of brakes, the pounding of thick-soled boots, and the chatter of hose against pavement, Lilah crumbled beneath the weight of overwhelming exhaustion and grief, collapsing into Merrick's arms, sobbing uncontrollably.

CHAPTER FORTY-THREE

Early the next morning, wisps of gray smoke were still spiraling upward from the burned-out bungalow. The stucco was blackened and cracked. Whole sections of the tile roof had collapsed. And almost every window had been blown out. Merrick's Blazer was at the curb along with a fire truck, Logan's ATF van, and a coroner's wagon. Several firemen were patrolling the grounds with extinguishers, knocking down hot spots.

Marge and Lilah Graham were standing on the lawn amid the scorched and charred items the firemen had removed from the house. Lilah had spent the night in a local hospital, where she was treated for minor burns and smoke inhalation. Her mother had spent it with neighbors after being treated at the scene. They were staring at the aftermath in stunned silence when a gurney with Doug Graham's sheet-wrapped body was rolled from the house. Marge recoiled at the sight; then, tears streaming down her face, she pulled Lilah into a crushing embrace as two women in blue jumpsuits wheeled the gurney down the walkway and into the rear of a black van.

"You okay?" Marge asked as she disengaged.

Lilah nodded stiffly.

"Well, as I always say . . ." She saw the look in her

daughter's eyes and let it trail off. "I guess the good Lord decided to take him sooner than later."

Lilah nodded again.

"And you won't be calling and asking, 'Is Daddy there?' anymore, will you?" Marge prompted, her voice trembling with emotion.

"No, and . . . and I won't be parking behind your car anymore, either," Lilah said with a trace of bitterness.

Her mother responded with a soft, puzzled smile. "I'm glad to hear it, Lilah, but what does that have to do with this?"

"Come on, Mom."

"Come on, Mom, what?"

"You really expect me to believe you don't know?"

Marge shrugged and splayed her hands.

"It was because I didn't want you to leave, Mom. Because I was afraid to be alone with him."

"Afraid?" Marge wondered, clearly baffled. "Afraid of your father? Why? He never laid a hand on you. Never struck you. Your father loved you, Lilah."

"I loved him too."

"Of course, everyone did. He was a fine, decent man. Respected by his coworkers, his friends, his fellow churchgoers. There wasn't a person who didn't have something good to say about Daddy. Why, just the other day in the market when I was buying flowers—"

"Forget it, Mom," Lilah interrupted. "That's not going to work anymore."

"What's not going to work? You're always making these . . . these ambiguous remarks. How am I supposed to know what you're talking about if you don't—"

"Mom? *Mom!*" Lilah interrupted. "For once in your life, just shut up and listen, will you? I'm talking about your mindless chatter. Your—your endless prattling. The way you—"

"Mindless chatter?"

"Yes, it's a defense. It's how you keep people from saying things you don't want to hear."

"You have something to say to me, Lilah, say it."

Lilah's eyes hardened like gemstones and locked on to her mother's. Then, in a steady, unemotional tone that belied her anger, she replied, "He raped me."

Marge Graham shuddered as if struck by lightning and emitted a feeble cry. Thirty years of denial had been stripped away in less than thirty seconds. The wound was raw. The pain excruciating.

"He touched me," Lilah went on evenly. "And he made me touch him, and—and taste him. He forced me to have sex with him over and over. Whenever he was home and you weren't. Every chance he got until I went away to college."

The first blow had caught Marge Graham off guard. Her reaction was genuine and deeply felt, but decades of conditioning had trained and toughened her; and she quickly recovered, steeling herself to the onslaught that followed.

By the time Lilah finished, Marge's eyes had taken on the blank, emotionally deadened stare of a corpse. "I have to go now," she said, as if they'd been talking about shopping. "I'm expected back at the Whites' for coffee. I don't suppose you want to come along." It was a statement, not a question, and she began walking toward a neighbor's home before Lilah could reply.

Inside the burned-out bungalow, Merrick was munching some Tums and washing them down with coffee while sorting through the debris scattered around the remains of

Doug Graham's recliner. The old fellow had lived in it, violated his daughter in it, and died in it. Last night he'd heard the fire bomb explode, heard his wife's screams, and, upon awakening to blinding smoke and raging fire, tried to get out of the recliner; but his lungs filled with the deadly fumes and, in his frail and weakened condition, he passed out before he could get to his feet.

Logan began taking photographs of the blackened chair at Merrick's direction. The flash of the strobe, always startling in the sooty darkness of a fire scene, got Fletcher's attention immediately.

The young A.I. was in the entry hall where the fire bomb had erupted, digging through the debris. He paused briefly, wondering why they were photographing the recliner, then resumed his excavating. Nothing of the corrugated box or its deadly contents remained, but beneath the chunks of charred framing and plaster strewn across the floor, Fletcher unearthed a craggy rectangular depression. It had burned completely through the fused synthetic carpeting and "crocodiled" the hardwood below. "We have us a flash point here," he called out.

Merrick drifted over and took a few moments to examine it. "Flash point? How do you figure that?"

"The burn pattern," Fletcher replied, plucking a roll of crime scene tape from his field kit. "It's just like the other two. Same size. Same shape. Same explosive distribution of accelerant."

"Possible," Merrick mused, seemingly unmoved. "On the other hand, it could've been made by some piece of highly flammable debris."

"Like what?"

"Like a plastic picture frame," Merrick replied. "That wall was covered with 'em. One could've easily blown off and landed here. Those ethylene-based polymers burn real hot."

"Get serious," Fletcher said, tying the yellow tape to a piece of charred framing. "We're talking a fire bomb in a box, Dan. You know why I'm so sure? Because I've got the best damned teacher in the business. He taught me to call 'em as I see 'em, and that's what I'm doing."

"He'd be pretty pissed off if you didn't," Merrick countered smartly. "But he also taught you that things aren't always what they seem, right off."

Fletcher's face twisted with confusion. "I don't get it," he said, toying with the roll of crime scene tape. "You saying this wasn't an arson fire?"

"I'm saying to consider the possibility."

"Why? We found the flash point. It's the same M.O. as the other two. And we know it was the doc."

Merrick stared at the young A.I. for a long moment, then nodded. "One of her."

Fletcher looked at Merrick like he was crazy.

"She's two people, Billy," Merrick explained in a confidential tone. "Thanks to this"—he gestured to the burned-out recliner shell—"the one who sent the incendiaries is gone. The one out there is a victim."

"A victim . . ." Fletcher echoed sardonically.

Merrick nodded. "You *are* the guy who lectured me about standing up for them, aren't you? Well, that's what a victim who's been through hell looks like."

"Bullshit," Fletcher erupted. "The pile of burned flesh they put on that gurney is what a—"

Merrick's lips tightened into a thin, angry line. "Bastard had it coming," he interrupted. "He abused her, Billy. He sexually abused her."

Fletcher cringed and turned pale. "Aw, for God's sakes," he finally moaned. "Makes you want to throw up."

"Makes you want to give the lady a break."

"The abuse excuse?" Fletcher prompted, referring to his mentor's hard-line stance. "We're still talking homicide here, Dan. It's not our job to be judge and jury. I don't have to tell you that."

"Then don't," Merrick retorted sharply. "I need you to work with me on this, Billy. It's important to *me*. Really important."

"Important enough to put our careers on the line?"

"I'm not asking you to do that. I'm the senior A.I. here. I sign the report. I take the rap if it goes wrong."

Fletcher looked puzzled. "Why? Why take the chance? I mean, even if you did, how do we account for those goodies in her garage?"

"You mean the fertilizer, mothballs, charcoal lighter—that stuff?"

Fletcher nodded.

"Nothing that other people don't have in theirs."

"And the beepers?"

"Most commonly used model in L.A. All registered to her mother. And we know it wasn't her."

"There's still the printing on the blackboard."

"Probably been erased by now."

"But that med student saw it. You can't erase the memory of a witness."

"I can blur it a little. I mean, soon as he hears about her old man, he's going to swear there's no way he could testify it was the same printing as the box."

Fletcher sighed, wrestling with the dilemma. "A man died here, Dan. There's no getting around that. What do we put in the report?"

"He fell asleep smoking. More domestic fires start that way than all others combined, right?" Merrick pointed to the charred recliner without waiting for a reply. "Put an evidence tag on that and take it downtown."

"I don't know," Fletcher said. "I'm still—"

"*I* do, dammit!" Logan interrupted, his voice ringing with impatience and authority. Arms folded across his chest, the old-timer had stood quietly aside throughout, like a wise parent, letting scrapping siblings go at it for a while before stepping in. "You two finished?"

Merrick and Fletcher were taken aback by his outburst, and nodded curiously.

"Good," Logan growled. "Now that you got that out of your systems, I'm going to tell you what's really going to happen with this lady."

"Be wasting your breath, Pete," Merrick said.

"Maybe, but it's my right and I'm older than you."

"Shoot," Fletcher said, anticipating support.

Merrick cocked his head challengingly, then nodded.

A short time later Lilah was standing alone amid the burned and blackened items on the lawn when Fletcher and Logan emerged with the recliner and set it down next to her. Lilah shuddered at the sight of it.

The wooden frame had been turned into a charred skeleton, and most of the slipcover and upholstery had been incinerated, exposing the blackened springs—all except the areas that had been beneath Doug Graham's body and were still intact. The loose pieces of the slipcover had fused to his warm-up suit and went with him onto the gurney. Lilah was staring at what was left of the original fabric, the fabric in which she buried her face as a child when her father decided to show her how much he loved her, the fabric she glimpsed the day her mother unzipped the slipcover, the fabric with the yellow, white, and purple flowers exploding against a jungle-green background of twisting foliage and vines—the fabric of her nightmare.

Logan backed the ATF van into the driveway. Merrick helped Fletcher load the recliner into the rear. He waited until his colleagues had driven off before crossing to Lilah. "Whenever you're ready, Doc."

Lilah watched the van and its unnerving cargo turn the corner, then nodded resignedly. "Could I have a few minutes to look around inside first?"

"Sure, take all the time you like."

"That's not funny, Lieutenant," Lilah said, twisting a length of hair around her finger. The flame-red waves had been severely singed by the fire and hung around her face lifelessly. "We both know what happened and what's going to happen next."

Merrick nodded grimly. "Yeah, me and the guys were just kicking that around. You know any good criminal defense attorneys?"

"No," Lilah sighed glumly, "but I'm sure I'll have no trouble finding one."

"Yeah, soon as you do, you'll be taken downtown and formally charged. That'll be followed by a bail hearing at which the arson investigator's report and recommendations are filed. Don't ask me why, but I got this weird feeling that you're going to be released on your own recognizance."

Lilah was awestruck. She tried to speak but could only mouth the word, *Released?*

Merrick nodded matter-of-factly and resumed. "Then, sometime in the next couple of weeks, you, and I, and your counsel are going to sit down with an assistant district attorney and a judge and go over the whole story. Chances are you'll end up pleading no contest to a mutually acceptable charge, and cut a deal for community service and maybe some sort of a fine."

Lilah stared at him in utter disbelief. It seemed as if an eternity passed before she heard herself saying, "I'm still not sure I understand."

"I think it has to do with whether or not a person does something by choice," Merrick explained. "You know, of their own free will?"

Lilah was stunned and delighted and afraid to accept what he was suggesting. "I thought you'd dismissed that theory out of hand?"

"Totally. I couldn't function if I played by those rules; but I know an exception when I see one."

"Does that mean you don't think I was responsible for what I did?"

"For what *who* did?" Merrick replied. "That's the question as I understand it."

"I'd say it's a very fine line in this case."

"Not according to your buddy, Schaefer."

"You talked to Paul about this?"

Merrick nodded uncomfortably. "He helped me figure out what was going on with you and . . . and your father."

Lilah looked away for a moment, and bit her lip. "You think *he* was responsible?"

"That's in your bailiwick, isn't it? You think he had a choice?"

Lilah nodded sadly. "Yes, I'm afraid he did."

"Well," Merrick said, suggesting she'd answered her own question, "it's over. Get on with your life."

Lilah stared at him for a long moment. "Why? Why are you doing this?"

Merrick shrugged in his shaggy way and broke into an affectionate smile. Lilah sensed the meaning—at least she thought she did, hoped to God she did—and returned it. They were standing there, looking into each other's eyes longingly, when his phone twittered. "Dammit," Merrick growled, knowing what it meant. "Yeah, Gonzo—yeah, just wrapping it up. What's doing?"

"For openers," Gonzalez replied, "a witness to the Laguna burn saw a dark green van in the area."

"No kidding? Sounds like we're talking the same pyro as Las Flores."

"It gets better. The crew sifting the flash point found a matchbook igniter and an empty cigarette pack."

"Way to go. Have 'em run it for prints and—"

"Already did," Gonzalez replied with a suspense-filled pause. "*Yours* are all over it."

Merrick's jaw slackened. He knew all staff prints were routinely computer-compared to those lifted from evidence to eliminate any that, despite precautions, might have been left by field crews or lab workers. He also knew he hadn't worked on the Laguna investigation. "Mine?" he exclaimed, clearly baffled.

"Uh-huh, your brand too. When was the last time you were up there?"

"Laguna Canyon? Gotta be years. I mean"—Merrick stopped as if thunderstruck, then blurted—"My brand?! Son of a bitch, it's Rene!"

"Who?"

"Homeless lady. Name's Rene . . . Rene *Rogers*. I gave her a pack of smokes. Run her DMV. I'll hold."

"Two out of two pyros of the female persuasion? Sure gonna skew the hell out of the stats, if you're right."

"Naw, we're way overdue. Besides, the doc doesn't count. Now, run me that DMV, pronto." Merrick sensed

Lilah's curiosity, and explained, "Looks like we came up with a prime in the wildfires—a lady."

"Got her," Gonzalez said when he came back on the line moments later. " 'Seventy-nine Econoline van, dark green. Registration hasn't been renewed since 'ninety-four—but that doesn't mean she hasn't been driving it."

"Yeah, and ten to one she's up there right now admiring her handiwork. Thanks, Gonzo, I'm rolling."

"You have to go?" Lilah asked, unable to hide her disappointment.

Merrick shrugged resignedly. "Take care, Doc. I'll be in touch."

"Lilah," she corrected gently, not wanting him to leave. "I'd really like it if you called me Lilah."

Merrick nodded and took a step back, but their eyes refused to disengage. She reached out and touched his fire-reddened face with endearing tenderness. He took her hand in his, then, drawing her closer, kissed her forehead, then her cheek, then brushed her lips with his. Suddenly all the pent-up tension and emotional barriers gave way at once and they lunged into each other's arms in a surging release of empathy and passion that Lilah hoped would never end.

"Lilah? Lilah, I've got to go," Merrick finally said as their lips parted. "I've got to."

"No, I won't let you," Lilah whispered hungrily as they stumbled toward the Blazer, clinging to each other, not wanting the moment to end. "I won't."

"I'll call you," he said.

"I'll be knocking on your door bright and early with coffee if you don't."

Merrick laughed and pulled open the door, then he paused—as if something of staggering importance had suddenly dawned on him. He slipped the phone from its sheath and thumbed a prestored number. "Gonzo . . . Yeah, it's me. Do me a favor. Fletcher and Logan are on their way in. Bring 'em up to speed on Rene Rogers, and have 'em search that damned canyon till they find her . . . No, I won't . . . 'cause I'm not finished with the doc, that's why . . . The rest of the day. Maybe tomorrow . . . Yeah, keep me posted." Merrick tossed the phone on the seat, then turned to Lilah and embraced her.

She melted in his arms, her eyes brimming with tears, her heart pounding with euphoria, and kissed him. It was as if her soul had been imprisoned all these years and suddenly released. For the first time in her life Lilah Elizabeth Graham could sense the glimmering dawn of emotional security. For the first time in her life, she wasn't afraid her abuser might reenter it. For the first time in her life she was in the arms of a man who cared for her, a man who didn't want something from her.

They were staring into each other's eyes, savoring the moment, when something especially poignant dawned on her. The Lord giveth and the Lord taketh away, she thought— and now, He taketh away and giveth. Lilah brushed a tear from her cheek, then hugged Merrick tightly and smiled at the irony.